Thanks Thunderfoot

Dan Bomkamp

Lovstad Publishing
Poynette, Wisconsin
Lovstadpublishing@live.com

ISBN: 0692490035
ISBN-13: 978-0692490037
(Previous ISBN: 0615751512)

Printed in the United States of America

Cover design by Lovstad Publishing
Cover photo by Dan Bomkamp
On the cover: Cody Meckley and Katie
as Thunderfoot and the dog.

DEDICATION

This book is dedicated to Jamie Buroker,
My Thunderfoot.

Foreword

Sometimes you make a good decision in your life, sometimes not. I was fortunate enough to make one of those good ones when I asked young Jamie if he wanted to go squirrel hunting with me one afternoon, many years ago. It was on that hunting trip that I nicknamed him Thunderfoot. That was the first of our many hunting and fishing trips—the first few hours of the thousands we would spend together over the next several years.

My own dad was taken from me on the last day of my eighth grade school year. An accident suddenly turned my safe, happy home into a nightmare. Later that same summer, both of my grandpas died, too. It was a bad summer for me.

But I was lucky in that I had spent so much time with my dad and grandpas, and that I had a lot of great memories of them. My dad was an outdoorsman and started taking me with him on his fishing and hunting trips when I was just past diapers. My grandpa and grandma would meet us after church every Sunday morning, and we would all go off fishing together as a family. My childhood was filled with wonderful memories.

And after my terrible summer, I found that I had a lot of good people around me who cared enough to give me a hand and to keep me from going astray. I had a good neighbor, Fred, who took me fishing all the time. I had friends and relatives who took me hunting. I had people who cared about me.

When I reached the age when I was on my own, I always had the feeling that I wanted to be there for someone else, to lend a hand, and to be a friend. That is probably what prompted me to ask Jamie to go hunting. I never dreamed that we'd become such good friends, or that we would have such a great time together.

Life is full of opportunities. Sometimes we step up and take the chance; sometimes we don't. I did with Jamie, and I've never regretted it. I look at him now, a fine young man with a wife and two kids, and I'm very proud of him. Would he have turned out like this if I hadn't taken him hunting? Probably. But I like to think that I had a little to do with him becoming such a good person. Sometimes we make a good decision, and I think this was one of those times.

There is no better way to ensure our future than to share your knowledge and talent with a young person. And, hey! You never know. You just might have a lot of fun doing it, too.

—*Dan Bomkamp*—

Thanks
Thunderfoot

Here We Go Again

The setting sun was a shimmering orange globe that was just about to sink into the silvery water on the western horizon. I was standing in the middle of the river, casting a small surface bait to an old bridge piling where I hoped to get a small mouth bass to strike. It was the middle of the summer and the water was bathtub warm, so I was barefoot and clad in some old cut offs and a tee shirt. I was carrying my rod and reel, and without getting them stuck in the fabric, an extra lure and a couple of jigs hung from the top of my shirt pocket. That allowed me to fish without having lots of stuff to carry. I could wade and cast to the rock piles, remnants of old bridge piers from long ago, lined up across the river just above the new bridge. I cast my little imitation crippled minnow just past the rocks and pilings and gave it a twitch. I let it rest a couple of seconds and then twitched it again. The water exploded before the rings from the motion of the second twitch had even begun to radiate across the water, and a nice small mouth bass jumped halfway out of the water as it engulfed my bait. I snapped the rod up and set the hook. The bass took off like a rocket for the deeper water. I held steady pressure on my rod, and suddenly the bass jumped out of the water, shaking its head, trying to throw the lure free. A hundred drops of water flashed against the red-orange sky and looked like little sapphires as they fell back into the river. I kept working the fish and it jumped a half-dozen more times, but finally gave up as it tired from exertion. The water came just to the bottom of my cut off shorts, so I led the fish close and carefully grabbed it by the lip and lifted it from the water. It was a typical river smallmouth; bronze sided with dark bars running from top to bottom. I took the hook from the fish's lip and bent over to hold it in the water – to let the current flow through its gills so it revived before I released it. After a short time in the current, the fish began to swim. I let go and watched it lazily sink away, back to the rock pile to fight another day.

I started to stand up straight, but I heard a ripping sound. I looked down to find that the extra lure I had hanging from my shirt pocket had caught on the bottom hem of my shorts, and I was hung up, bent over in the middle of the river. I tried to get the hook from the denim, but it was past the barb, and the more I struggled with it, the deeper it became imbedded. I tried to free the other end of the lure from my pocket, but that hook too, was past the barb. I needed two hands to get out of this mess, but there was no place to set my rod and reel down without dropping them into the river. I was trying to figure out how to get loose from the lure when I heard Thunderfoot snickering a few yards away. He was standing in the river just above the next piling.

"Got a little problem there, old fella?" he snickered.

"That's *Mr.* Old Fella to you!" I said.

He laughed and started wading toward me. "Jeez, this is just like taking someone from "The Home" out fishing. I should get college credit for my work with you."

I looked over at him from my upside down vantage point and I could see his grin and the sparkle in his eyes. He loved seeing me in unflattering situations; he was really enjoying this. When he got next to me, I handed him my rod and reel and began working the hook out of my shirt pocket – ripping a hole in the pocket, but at least I was finally able to stand up straight. Then I worked on the other hook in my shorts, and soon I was free of the lure.

"That was a real good idea to hook that extra bait on your shirt," Thunderfoot said.

"Yeah, I thought so, too," I said. "Why don't you go back over to your rock pile and fish and quit making wise-crack comments."

He looked distressed. "Ouch! Touchy! Here I came all the way over to rescue you… and that's the thanks I get?"

"Yup. That's it. Take it or leave it."

He grinned, punched me in the arm and began wading back to his rock pile. I watched him going slowly through the current and thought back to when I had met him over four years earlier. I owned a sporting goods store, and one day this new kid came through the front door with a younger kid tagging along. He introduced himself and his younger brother, and told me that his mom and dad had split up, and that they had just moved to town. He was hoping to find some new fishing spots, and he said that he had just passed Hunter Safety and was planning on going hunting the next season for the first time. About a week later, we took a day off and went squirrel hunting. He was just 13, tall and pretty skinny. I had lots of old hunting gear that I had outgrown over the years, and being one of those people who never throw anything away, I was able to outfit him with some hand-me-downs that worked quite well. His feet were as big as mine, so I lent him an extra pair of my hunting boots. As we walked along a ridge road up the first hill, he managed to step on every stick that was lying in the road. If he wasn't stepping on sticks, he was dislodging rocks that rattled down the hill, causing lots of noise and probably scaring away every living critter for a mile around. I slowed my pace and watched him from behind. He was walking bent at the waist, like he was sneaking up on someone, but never looked down to see where his feet were going.

"Hey, Thunderfoot! Why don't you look where you're putting your feet so you don't scare every squirrel away in three counties?"

"Thunderfoot?"

"Yeah. Your big feet make as much noise as thunder. Try sneaking a little."

Well, the nickname stuck, and we became best friends. Over the next weeks, he came around often, and before long he was helping me around the shop and watching things when I needed to run errands or take a little time off. Now, four years later, here we were, still enjoying the great outdoors together.

Although his real name was James – or Jamie, as his family called him – he was "Thunderfoot" to me. During the past four years, he had grown and matured to a fine young man. He wasn't much taller than when I first met him but he had filled out and had passed that gangly stage, and was now a handsome kid. He had a perpetual smile on his face and the brightest blue eyes I had ever seen. He loved the outdoors, and no matter how successful we were with our fishing or hunting – whether we caught a lot of fish or no fish, or got a lot of game or none at all – he always enjoyed himself. We just liked being there, and being together made it even more fun. Of course he was always ready to pull a fast one on me, and we enjoyed a lot of laughs from our pranks on each other.

He cast a small spinner to the rock pile he was fishing and after about three turns of the reel his rod bucked and the line took off for the current. "Whooie!" he beamed, as a nice smallie jumped and then made another hard run. He played the fish for a while, and then released it. He looked over at me and gave me one of his famous grins. "The Bass Master strikes again."

We fished for another fifteen minutes. The sun was almost gone when he suddenly yelled, "Holy cow, did you see that tail come up by the rocks?"

"What tail?"

"A fish tail. It was a foot across!"

"A foot across? Oh, come on. Are you sure the sun wasn't in your eyes and you just saw a ripple?"

"Ripple my eye! It was a fish tail and it came up out of the water and it... there, there, see?" he said, pointing to the rocks. There it was: a fish tail that was easily eleven or twelve inches across came up out of the water and then disappeared again.

"Wow! You weren't exaggerating," I said.

"What do you suppose it was?"

"Probably a shark," I said.

He just gave me a glare. "No. Really. What's in this river that's that big?"

"I don't know – maybe a big sturgeon or one of those paddle fish. It's a big one, that's for sure."

By now the sun had disappeared and twilight was settling in. I thought about a fish that was big enough to have a foot-wide tail, and it suddenly gave me a spooky feeling to be standing in the same water, only a few yards away from that monster. Thunderfoot must have gotten the same thought, because he began wading toward me as fast as he could go. "I don't know about you, but I'd feel safer on the bank," he said. I reeled up and we both headed for the sandbar a few yards from us. The closer we got to the sand, the faster we waded, until we were almost running through the water.

Once we were safely on the sand, I began to feel pretty foolish about getting spooked by a fish. "You know neither a sturgeon nor a paddle fish would hurt you. Neither one has any teeth. The sturgeon is a bottom feeder and the paddle fish is a filter feeder, so I don't think we were in any danger."

"I know. But it was just scary thinking of that big thing in there with us," he laughed.

Just then the tail appeared at just about the same spot where Thunderfoot had been, and it slapped the water like a cannon shot as it dove down. "Well, what do you think?" I asked. "Want to go back for some night fishing?"

"I believe I'll pass, thank you," he said. "But go right ahead if you want to. I'll just sit here on the sand and watch."

I decided that I wasn't that brave either.

We walked back to the pickup and drove back to town, stopped at the gas station for an ice cream and a pop, and then headed home to put our gear away. It was just another typical evening and another little adventure in the outdoors that can change a regular day into something special, where you just never know what will happen next. Of course, that's what makes each day in the outdoors fun. And boy, we sure have our share of that.

Thanks, Thunderfoot.

The Carperee

I peered out the window that overlooked the back yard. Thunderfoot was on his way over to my house with the local newspaper clutched in his hand. He was walking as fast as he could go without running, so I knew he was on a mission.

"Did you see this ad about the Carperee?" he said as he walked in the front door and handed me the paper. He had opened and folded it to the ad. I took the paper and began reading.

"Carperee," the headline said. "A fishing tournament for everyone. Two person teams will fish for rough fish only. No game fish allowed. Winning teams will split all of the entry money."

"Now there's something we can do good at," he said. "We always catch a lot of junk fish when we fish the river."

We looked the ad over some more. The contest was scheduled for the Saturday after next. We didn't have anything planned for that day, so we decided to enter and see if we could win some money. The entry fee was $25 per team, and the top three teams with highest weights of rough fish would split the pot: 60% to the first place team, 25% to second place, and 15% to the third place team. "If there are a lot of teams," Thunderfoot said, "we could win hundreds of dollars."

"Don't be counting the winnings just yet," I said. "We still have to catch some fish to win."

"Yeah, yeah, I know," he said. "But two experts like us should have no trouble winning a carp contest."

I wished that I was as sure as he was about it, but I thought it would be fun anyway, whether we won or not, so I wrote a check for the entry while Thunderfoot cut the entry form from the paper. We put the check in an envelope with the entry form and mailed it to the local fishing club that was sponsoring the event.

"We've got a lot of time to practice, so maybe we should put the boat in the river and go find some hotspots," Thunderfoot suggested.

"Practice? You think we need to practice fishing?"

"Yeah, sure. We need to find some places where there are lots of carp and stuff."

Well, I knew I wasn't going to talk him out of that idea, and it was a nice day to spend fishing, so we packed a lunch, picked up some night crawlers and headed to the river. We motored downstream to a likely looking spot. We set out the rear anchor and then tied the front end of the boat to a small tree that was hanging out over the riverbank. Then we let out some more anchor rope so the boat turned sideways, giving us each unobstructed fishing. We rigged our rods and reels with heavy sinkers and plain hooks, baited them with night crawlers, and tossed them out into the current. It didn't take long before Thunderfoot had a bite. He cautiously picked up his rod and concentrated on the tip, watching for the telltale sign of the fish eating the night crawler. The rod tip bumped again and he reared back to set the hook. "Got him! Hey ya!" he shouted as his rod doubled over and he began playing the fish. I grabbed the landing net and waited for him to bring it alongside the boat. Soon a good-sized carp was thrashing in the water below me. I scooped it up into the net.

"What do you think? About 4 pounds?" he said.

"Yeah, probably. Maybe a little more. That would be a good one to catch in the Carperee," I said.

He would have given himself a pat on the back if he could have reached it. We removed the hook from the fish and put it back into the river. Just as I laid the net down in the boat, one of my rods began bucking like mad and I grabbed it and set the hook into the fish. I fought a good-sized fish for several minutes and then led a sheepshead into the net. "Those count too," Thunderfoot said. "Any rough fish – carp, sheepshead, blue buffalo, suckers, gar – anything that isn't a game fish. Oh boy, oh boy! This is a good spot. We're gonna do good here."

We decided that we should move from the spot so we didn't "sore mouth" all of the fish in the area, and so none of our competitors would see us there and steal our spot. We pulled up the anchor and untied the front of the boat and motored down the river for a while, looking for more similar spots.

"That looks like a good drop off over there," Thunderfoot said, pointing to a sandbar just ahead. There was about a foot of water running over the sandbar and at the lower end you could see that there was a deep pool. We slowed down and I maneuvered the boat below the shallow bar. We anchored cross current again at the top of the drop off.

"This looks good. Deep water and good current," I observed.

We each baited up and cast out our lines. It didn't take very long for Thunderfoot to catch a big white sucker, and then I caught another just like it. "Both about two pounds – not huge but not bad either," he said. We both re-baited our hooks and cast out again.

It was a gorgeous morning. There were a few big cotton candy clouds scattered here and there across the sky, and the temperature was just about perfect mid-70s. There was a gentle breeze blowing across the water that was just enough to keep the bugs off us without bothering our fishing. We each had two rods and reels propped against the side of the boat, and after a while without a bite, I picked up a boat cushion and laid it against the up-river side of the boat. I slipped my shoes off and put my feet up on the other side and laid back to rest in the sunshine.

"You better not go to sleep," Thunderfoot said.

"Don't worry. I'm alert and ready for a bite." My eyes were getting kind of heavy when Thunderfoot whispered, "Your right pole." I looked. The tip of the right rod bounced once. I watched it for a few seconds and it bounced again. I took my feet down from the rail of the boat and began to sit up and slowly put my hand down to pick up the rod. Just when I was about 6 inches from it, the rod bounced three times really hard and shot out over the side of the boat like a javelin hurled by an Olympic champion. It all happened so fast that I didn't have time to think. The rod hit the water about five feet from the boat, and I hit the water right behind it. As I dove toward the bottom of the river, I opened my eyes and the first thing I saw was my sunglasses falling toward the bottom. I hadn't thought of taking them off when I dove into the water. I reached down to grab them and when I did, I also grabbed the line from my rod, completely by accident. A second later the rod came sliding up into my hand.

Now that I had my rod, I swam for the surface and came up about twenty feet downriver from the boat. I put the sunglasses into my mouth and began swimming on my side toward a sandbar downstream, holding my rod in my other hand. I looked back at the boat. Thunderfoot sat there with his mouth hanging open. "I'll swim over to that sandbar and walk back up," I shouted. He just sat there, his mouth agape, amazed.

I swam to the sandbar and waded onto the sand. The fish that had pulled my rod overboard was still hooked on, so I reeled and played him until I drug him up on the sand. "About a 10 pound carp," I shouted to Thunderfoot. He *still* was just sitting there looking stupidly at me.

I released the carp, walked back up on the sand bar and then across the shallow water. I stepped into the boat from the upper side. "Jeez. You could give a guy a little warning if you plan to go over the side," Thunderfoot said. "I thought you had a heart attack and died or something."

"I didn't have time to say anything," I told him. "If I had taken time to inform you of my plans, my rod would have been downriver and I'd have never caught it."

He just shook his head. "Well, it was a nice carp at least."

We spent the rest of the day fishing and found some pretty good places where we caught quite a few rough fish. That following week we went out two more times "practicing."

Friday evening we got our gear ready and made lunch for the Carperee the next day.

We arrived at the village park where the contest was to be held and got in line with lots of other teams to get our boat number and an official weigh-in bag. In about half an hour all the teams were ready and we got the rules and regulations and all took off for the river. There were boats going every which way and soon we were at our first hot spot. We tied up with the boat across current so we could cover the maximum amount of water and not be in each other's way. We laid the landing net on the seat between us so it would be ready when we needed it.

Thunderfoot got a bite in just a short while. He picked up his rod and waited for the fish to bite again. When it did he set the hook and fought it up to the boat.

"Oh nuts. It's a walleye," I said as it came to the surface.

"We don't want any walleyes today," Thunderfoot said, and took the fish off the hook and slipped it back into the river. I got the next bite and caught a real nice smallmouth bass.

Then Thunderfoot finally caught a catfish. "What happened to our carp spot?" he said.

"I don't know. But it's full of *good fish* now."

We fished for another hour and caught one sheepshead, three more walleyes and two bass.

"We'd better try another spot."

We went to the sandbar drop off where my rod had been pulled in and caught one small carp right away. Then walleyes, catfish, and bluegills plagued us. "I'm not believing this!" Thunderfoot said. We tried another spot, and another with the same luck, and then we tried one final spot and before we knew it the time was getting close for us to be back at the riverside park for the weigh-in. "Let's just go home," Thunderfoot said, "we don't have enough to even go back for the weigh-in."

"You never know. Maybe everyone had the same luck as we did." That brightened his spirits. We pulled the anchors and motored back to the park.

The fishing club had a dump truck backed up to the weigh-in station and had made arrangements with some farmer to spread the fish on one of his fields for fertilizer. There were many teams bringing their strings of junk fish to the scales. We had managed to catch three small carp, one fair buffalo, one gar and two sheepsheads. Our total weight was 16 and a half pounds. "That puts us in third place," Thunderfoot said. Our hopes were pretty high until we saw my next-door neighbor and his wife pull up in their boat.

"What do you think of this one?" his wife said as she held up a sheepshead that looked to weigh about 25 pounds.

"Jeez. They got one fish that's bigger than all of ours put together," Thunderfoot groaned.

When all was said and done, we ended up in 8th place. As teams kept coming in our weight got lower and lower on the chart. "Oh well," I said. "We had fun, anyway."

"Yeah, I guess so," Thunderfoot said. "I think we ought to enter some walleye or bass tournaments. We seem to catch more of them than anything."

"Yeah, but you know what would happen then," I said.

"Of course. We'd catch carps and suckers," he said grinning.

Well, anyway you look at it, catching any fish is fun, as long as they pull and give you a fight. And spending a day on the river fishing is way better than working.

Thanks, Thunderfoot.

Bank Poling

I was reading the morning paper when Thunderfoot came in through the front door. He was instantly mobbed by Katy and Kirby and spent a couple of minutes wrestling with them until they were properly assured that he had noticed them. He came into the kitchen, retrieved the cereal and a medium-size mixing bowl from the cupboard and sat down at the table to have his breakfast.

"Are you out of cereal at your house?" I asked.

"Nope. I just like yours better," he grinned. "What do you know about bank poling?"

"What do you mean? How to do it, or what it is?"

"Both. I heard some guys talking about it and I wondered if it was something we should be doing," he said.

"Well, it's not rocket science," I said. "You cut down some small trees, strip the branches off them, find a likely looking spot and shove them into the riverbank. Then you tie some 200# braided nylon line on each one with a big heavy sinker and about a 10/0 hook, and bait them with a bullhead. Each fisherman can have five poles, but he has to buy a license that gives him five metal tags to tie onto each pole. You set them in the evening, and then check them for fish in the morning."

Thunderfoot was sitting there poking cereal into his face and nodding his head up and down as I talked. When he'd finished the first bowl, he poured another.

"Why can't you bait them in the morning when you check them for fish?" he asked. "That would seem to be a lot less work."

"If you bait them in the morning, turtles and gar will eat your bait. They don't feed during the night. But that's when the big catfish are active, and they have a better chance of getting your bait then."

He nodded some more, thinking over all the information. "So, have you ever done it?"

"No, but I went with a friend a few times when he baited and raised his lines. It was fun, but I guess I just never got the bug to do it myself. When I was a kid, my dad's friend caught a catfish that was almost 5 feet long. It weighed over 60 pounds."

"Sixty pounds!" Thunderfoot's eyes were as big as his cereal bowl. "Holy cow! That's a big one! Why don't we try it?"

"Sixty pound fish are pretty rare. I haven't heard of one that big for years," I said. And there's a lot of work in this. You have to catch a lot of bullheads, and cut all the poles, and find spots to set them and then go to the river twice a day."

"Oh boy, that sounds like work," he replied with a little sarcasm thrown in. "Let's see… use a hatchet to chop some poles, fool around on the riverbank, catch bullheads, and then go out on the river two times a day? What a terrible thing to have to do."

"Ok, smart guy. I guess it's not so terrible. You want to try it?"

"I'm almost finished with my breakfast. Lets get started," he said, pouring his third bowl of cereal. I picked up the box and there was about a tablespoon of cereal left in the bottom. I poured it into his bowl and threw the box away.

"You better get more cereal. You're out," he said grinning.

Regular license stations didn't have Bank Pole licenses, so our first mission was to drive forty miles to the County Clerk's office for the license and tags. Then we took the ax and hatchet, drove down to the river bottoms and found some appropriately sized small willow trees that would make good poles. They were about 12 feet tall and about as big around as a baseball bat, and being willows, they were really tough and springy. Thunderfoot attacked the trees, cutting them off at the bottom. I trimmed all the branches off with a small hatchet, and cut them all off at about ten feet long. By the time we had ten of them, we were pretty tired out and went home for some lunch and a rest.

My eyes had gotten heavy right after lunch and I was snoring in my recliner when Thunderfoot shook me awake. "We've got no time for a nap now. We have to get the rest of the stuff and get our poles out."

"Jeez. Don't be in such a hurry. We have to catch bait yet. We won't have time to get them out today, so just be patient." Thunderfoot was not the patient type.

We tied braided twine on all the poles and rigged them with big, heavy sinkers and huge hooks. Then we wrapped the lines around the poles and stuck the hooks in the butt end. Our poles were ready. Now for the bait.

"A friend of mine has a pond on his farm that's full of nice sized bullheads," I said. "I'll call him and see if it's ok for us to catch some." I went in the house and placed the call. My friend told me to take all we wanted, so Thunderfoot and I grabbed a couple of rods and reels and some plastic buckets for the bullheads. Off we went to the bullhead pond. We arrived at the farm and drove through the pasture to the pond. It was about an acre of water and was a great place to fish because the cattle had kept the weeds and grass chewed down. It was almost like a little park. Besides the cows, there were several ducks and geese, and one huge tom turkey waddling around.

"Holy cow! Look at that big turkey," Thunderfoot said.

"That's a tame bird," I said. "He's way too big to be wild. He'd be quite a trophy if he was a wild one."

We baited our hooks and began fishing. In no time at all we began catching bullheads, and as we caught them, we put them in the pails. We had about ten bullheads in one pail, so Thunderfoot volunteered to haul it back to the truck. He carried the pail across the pasture and as he got near the turkey, he began talking to it and tried to reach out to pet it. Wanting no part of such activity, the turkey quickly ran away. Thunderfoot put the bucket in the truck and started back to the pond. As he got near the turkey again, he said something to it, and it puffed all up and began strutting. "Hey look," Thunderfoot said. "He thinks I'm a girl turkey and he's trying to impress me."

Thunderfoot sat down in the grass by the pond again and resumed fishing. Soon the turkey came waddling up to the pond and began strutting and drumming next to his new best friend. It would run at him all puffed up, and then spin around and make a spitting and drumming sound. "Pfffft, boooom!"

"You'd better watch out," I said to the boy. "He'll be trying to mate with you if you're not careful." I had no more than said that when the turkey rushed forward and jumped up on Thunderfoot's back. Thunderfoot jumped to his feet and almost fell into the pond.

"Hey, you big bugger. Get away from me!"

I was laughing my head off as Thunderfoot backed away from the bird and it kept coming at him, spitting and drumming and making itself look as big and beautiful as it could. "You're his choice of a mate," I said. "He thinks you're looking pretty foxy."

"Oh, ha ha. You're really funny," Thunderfoot said. The turkey chased him around the pond for a half-hour. When the bird finally got tired of his advances being ignored, he wandered off to pester the geese that were lying in the sun, enjoying the day.

"I wish you'd quit fooling around and help me catch these bullheads," I said. He just glared at me and baited his hook and cast out. He kept looking over his shoulder every few minutes to make sure his suitor wasn't coming back. In about another half-hour, we had enough bullheads for the time being. We loaded our poles and the fish into the back of the truck and drove home. It was too late in the day to try to set the poles, so we decided to set them out in the morning, and bait them the next evening.

The next morning we motored slowly up the river just after breakfast, looking for deep water along the bank – areas that looked like a place where a big catfish would live. We found a good-looking spot and tied the boat to a tree, and began trying to shove one of our poles into the bank. It wasn't an easy task.

When we tried to stick the pole into the ground, the boat slid away from the bank and we didn't make any progress. "One of us has to get out and work on the river bank," I said.

"I'll go," Thunderfoot said. "There might be a snake out there and I wouldn't want you to have a hissy fit."

I didn't argue with him.

We finally got the first pole into the bank, found the water depth, tied the line at the correct length, and then wrapped it up on the pole. "There, one down," I said. "Only nine more to go." It was a good thing we started early because it took us all day to get the poles all set. We worked straight through without lunch, and Thunderfoot was so weak from hunger that I had to get out on the bank, despite the threat of vipers, and shove the last three poles into the dirt.

"I'm feeling faint from lack of food," he said as he lay limply in the bottom of the boat.

"You poor baby. I feel so bad for you."

"If I loose consciousness, shove a hamburger or something in my mouth and move my jaw, and maybe I'll come back to life," he said as he tried to raise his head.

We loaded the boat and went home for some food. Thunderfoot fired up the grill and soon had a dozen hot dogs cremated. He stuffed them into his face as fast as he could lay them in a bun and squirt ketchup on them. "I think I may survive after all," he said as the 7th hot dog disappeared.

"I was worried about you for a while," I said, "but I knew how tough you are, so I knew you'd pull through." Big grin as hot dog number 8 began to disappear.

After we finished eating, Thunderfoot said, "Do you think we have time to bait the hooks yet?"

"It's getting pretty late. I don't know."

"Let's try. Otherwise we'll have to wait a whole day more."

Making sure there were ten bullheads in the pail, we took off for the river again. One by one, we baited the poles with a bullhead on each line. It was nearly dark when we got back to the boat landing and loaded up. It had been a long day.

The next morning I could hear cupboard doors slamming and the refrigerator open and close so I knew Thunderfoot was having his breakfast, and doing it as noisily as possible so I'd get up. "Can I pour you some cereal?" he said cheerily as I walked into the kitchen.

"Have the dogs been out yet?"

"Yup. I took them out half an hour ago."

"Again, I must ask: are you out of cereal at your house?"

"Of course not. I just enjoy your sunny smile every morning, so I come over here for breakfast," he said, with a grin from ear to ear.

I couldn't help myself from smiling, and cuffed him on the side of the head. "Pour me some cereal and give me the newspaper."

After we ate, we hopped into the truck and headed for the river. The boat was still hooked on the back of the truck from the evening before. We launched the boat and began motoring upriver to the first pole. As we got alongside the pole, Thunderfoot reached out and took hold of the line, lifting it carefully. The bullhead was gone. "Wow. We got robbed on this one."

"Hook it up on the pole and we'll check the next one."

The next two poles had live bullheads on them so we just left them in the water. As we approached the fourth pole Thunderfoot took the line and began lifting it up. He had raised it about a foot when his hand was jerked down into the water. "Holy cow! There's a fish on here!" he shouted.

"Pull him up!" I said.

He pulled and the line jerked down, and then he gained a little on it only to have it pulled back down again. "It's a big one," he said. Finally he began to gain on the fish as the water boiled beneath the line. I got the net out and prepared to net the fish. Suddenly a catfish that weighed about ten pounds came to the surface and I slid the net under it. "Whooie," Thunderfoot said. "Our first bank pole fish."

"Not bad."

"Jeez. If that one pulled that hard, how would you ever get a fifty pound one up?"

"Very carefully," I said.

The next two poles were minus their bullheads, and the next one was snagged up on some roots or something next to the bottom. We pulled and pulled and finally had to cut the line. We decided to move the pole to a new spot. Pole number eight was just ahead, and as we came near, the pole began bucking like a bronco. There was a fish on it, and it had to be a big one – it was pulling the pole right down into the water. "Holy cow," Thunderfoot said. "I'm scared to grab it."

"Just go slow and steady," I said as I held onto an overhanging branch to steady the boat. He took hold of the line and began cautiously lifting it. It came up easily. He looked at me. "Maybe it got off."

"Doesn't look like there's anything on it now," I said. He shrugged and began hauling the line up hand over hand. Suddenly the sinkers appeared and then the head of a huge catfish appeared on the surface of the water.

"Holy smokes!" The fish's head was about a foot across with a mouth big enough to swallow your arm, clear up to the shoulder. The catfish dove for the bottom, ripping the line through Thunderfoot's fingers. He tried to stop it and almost got pulled over the side. "Come here and help me," he yelled. "It's gonna pull me in!"

I raced to the front of the boat and grabbed the line and together we fought the fish. It was a grand battle. We would gain a few feet of line and then the fish would drag it back through our hands and we'd have to work to get it all back. This went on for a long time, before the fish began to make shorter and shorter runs to the bottom.

"He's tiring out," I said.

"So am I," Thunderfoot panted.

Finally, the fish came to the top and lay on its side. There was no way it would fit into our net. "How we gonna get it in the boat?" Thunderfoot asked.

"Just a minute. Hold it." I stepped to the back of the boat and put on a pair of gloves I kept ub vgnbvcncnder the seat. Then I went back to the front and reached over the side, grabbed the fish by its lower jaw, lifted and drug and finally slid the monster into the boat.

We both fell back onto the floor of the boat panting. "Jeez!" Thunderfoot said. "That's the biggest catfish I've ever seen."

"It's a big one, for sure. The biggest I've ever caught."

The huge catfish was over three feet long and must have weighed 30 or 40 pounds. It lay there breathing air through its gills, wiggling from side to side every so often. We watched it for a couple of minutes and I think we both had the same idea at once. Thunderfoot looked at me. "Are you thinking what I'm thinking?"

"Let it go?"

"We think alike," he grinned. "A fish that's been in the river for as long as that one has deserves to go back and live for a while longer."

"Get the pliers and let's get the hook out and turn her loose," I said. We removed the hook and I took the fish's lower jaw and Thunderfoot lifted its tail, and we put it over the side. We held it in the current for about a minute, and then it began to struggle to be free. We let go and watched it swim into the depths of the river.

Thunderfoot slapped me on the back. "We did good."

"Yeah, we did," I said. We both were exhausted and sat down in the boat to rest. I was sitting there just catching my breath and began to notice that Thunderfoot had red welts on his arms and legs. "You look like you got into some poison ivy or something."

He looked at his arms and legs. "Wow! You're right, and you've got it too." I looked and sure enough, I had little red welts on my arms and legs, too.

"We probably got into it when we were jamming those poles into the bank yesterday," I said.

"Whatya think of this bank poling?" Thunderfoot asked.

"I think catching the bait was the best part, except for releasing that big fish."

"Me too. Let's pull up the poles and go back to regular fishing. This was fun, but I don't think I want to do it every day."

I didn't argue. We pulled up all the other poles on the way back to the landing, turned the rest of our bullheads loose and stacked the poles in back of the garden. "They'll be good for building duck blinds this fall," Thunderfoot said.

We cleaned the ten-pound fish and chunked it up so we could deep-fry it later that evening for supper. Then we went to the pharmacy and got a couple of bottles of Calamine lotion.

We probably looked a little funny as we sat on the patio with the deep fryer. We'd fry a batch of battered catfish chunks, then a batch of French fries, and then a batch of onion rings. We ate as we fried, and we kept it up until we were both stuffed.

We both were covered with pink spots where we had dabbed the Calamine to take the itch out of the poison ivy. "Well, that was quite an adventure," Thunderfoot said as he chewed on a piece of catfish. "We got to be lumber jacks; I got attacked by a lovesick turkey; and we caught Jaws. And now, here we sit looking like a couple of clowns with pink spots all over us."

I glanced over at him and smiled. "So, why is this much different from most of our adventures.?"

"I guess you're right," he laughed. "Nobody can say we aren't willing to try something new."

So true, so true.

Thanks, Thunderfoot.

You Should Be On TV

Thunderfoot and Katie were playing ball with an old half-flat soccer ball and Kirby was lying in the sun snoozing. I was puttering around in the greenhouse when the phone rang. I ran for the house to answer it, and as I went through the front door I noticed the peeling paint on the trim that had been in need of a coat of paint for a quite a while. But I had kept talking myself out of getting the painting job done for quite a while, too. As I hung up the phone I decided to go to my workshop, get the paint scraper, and begin the dreaded task. Finally, the trim would be repainted.

Well, the scraper made short work of the chipped trim, but then I noticed that the edge of the roof overhang was looking a little shabby, so I started scraping that, too. When that was done I saw a couple of places on the siding that needed a little touch-up, and soon I had a pretty large area all scraped and ready for painting.

Meanwhile, Thunderfoot had made it a point to ignore me. "You wanna help me paint this?" I asked.

"I knew you were making work for me when I saw you starting that," he said.

"Oh, come on. It won't kill you to paint a little."

He grudgingly sauntered to the porch. "Where's the paint?"

"I have some in the closet from a couple of years ago. I'll get it," I said. Well, of course, the paint in the can was as hard as a stone, so we hopped in the truck and went to the hardware store for some new paint.

"Might as well get a gallon, so we have enough," I said.

Thunderfoot gave me an apprehensive stare. "We're just gonna paint the door frame and stuff, right?"

"Of course."

We bought a handful of disposable foam paintbrushes and a piece of plastic sheeting to catch the drips, too, and soon we were back at the house painting the door frame, the fascia board, and the rest of the trim. "That looks good," I said. "But now the siding looks shabby. While we're at it, let's paint just this area by the door."

Thunderfoot shook his head – like he knew what was coming – and kept on painting.

As the siding on the wall we were painting was almost finished, I decided to move to the adjoining wall and spruce it up, too. While we worked, we heard the honking of a flock of geese. We both stopped and looked up. A flock of about thirty geese flew overhead. "There they are," Thunderfoot said, pointing up to the northwest. "Have you ever noticed that when geese fly in a V, one side of the V is longer than the other?" he asked.

"Well, yeah, I guess you're right. I never really thought about that before."

"You know why one side is longer?" he asked.

"Nope. Why?"

"Because there are more geese on that side!"

I just looked at him, trying to figure out if he was being smart, or if he was serious. Suddenly he burst out laughing. "Jeez. What a fish. You fell for that hook, line, and sinker."

I had to laugh, too. He got me on that one.

We continued painting, and Thunderfoot said, "Do you think one of those big military helicopters with a propeller on each end could lift your house?"

I stared at him. Another joke? "What?"

"Do you think one of those big helicopters could lift your house?"

"Are you serious?"

"Yeah. Of course."

"What is going on in your head? Where did you get that idea?"

"I don't know. It just came to me," he said grinning. "Do you think they could lift it?"

"I have no idea. And just for the record, you scare me," I said.

"How many people do you think are dead in the cemetery?"

I stopped painting again. "How many people are dead in the cemetery? Did you have a sharp blow to the brain recently?" I asked.

Thunderfoot looked at me as seriously as possible. "How many people are dead in the cemetery?"

"I don't know."

"All of them!" He doubled over with laughter. Score two for Thunderfoot.

We finished the adjoining wall, and then I was looking at the trim above the front window. Thunderfoot moaned. "I knew it. I just knew it. We're gonna end up painting the whole house before we're done."

"Oh, quit griping and paint."

"Know what the white part of bird poop is?" he asked.

"Are you trying to drive me crazy?" I said. "Because if you are, you're doing a good job of it."

"You majored in biology in college. I'm just thirsting for knowledge."

"Sorry," I said. "I thought you were being smart again."

Thunderfoot just shook his head.

"I'm not sure. I guess we never studied bird poop," I said.

"Well, I just happen to know what the white part of bird poop is," he said. "It's bird poop, too!" Again, he burst out laughing and slapped his knee. "Jeez, you're so easy."

A little while later he said, "Knock, knock."

"Ok. You win. Let's quit," I said. I began putting the lid on the paint can and gathering up the plastic tarp. Thunderfoot just stood there watching.

"You don't have to be mad. I was just trying to make a little joke."

"I'm not mad. We already painted three times as much as I

planned, and I don't like painting any more than you do. So let's quit."

We threw the disposable brushes away, woke up the dogs, and started into the house. I stopped by the front and looked at our paint job. "It looks a lot better, but you know, it really could use a second coat."

"Let's have some lunch, and then we'll do it," Thunderfoot said. "I've got lots more material to try on you."

Well, at least his jokes were better than his singing.

Thanks, Thunderfoot.

Just Call Me Oliver Twist

During the summer, my Sport Shop had an added sideline business. I had ten canoes and rented them to people to canoe the Wisconsin River. Part of the rental business included a shuttle service. I had an old van and a canoe trailer to haul the intrepid paddlers upriver to a drop-off point so they could start their journey, and then I picked them up at the time and place they wanted to leave the river.

Now that Thunderfoot was old enough to drive, he was my canoe hauler for the summer, which was just fine with him. I charged the renters for the service and gave Thunderfoot two-thirds of the charge for his time, and kept one-third for gas. It worked out to some real good money for him on some weekends, for not too much work, and he occasionally got a tip for his help unloading canoes and giving advice to the tourists on how to read the river and to be safe.

Usually, most of the canoe business was on the weekends, but occasionally some people would show up during the week wanting to take a canoe trip. It worked out really well for me to have Thunderfoot living so close, and he was usually home. And if he wasn't home, he was usually at my house, anyway.

Such was the occasion when a couple showed up one Wednesday and wanted to spend the day on the river. I called Thunderfoot's house and his mom answered. She told me that he was outside painting the picnic table and she'd send him right over. I took care of the rental forms and in a couple of minutes, Thunderfoot came trotting across the back yard, wearing an old pair of cut off jeans and a tee shirt that was torn and covered with dark red paint. "Jeez! Don't bother dressing up just for work," I said jokingly.

"I thought you wanted me right away. I didn't take time to clean up."

"Well, take these folks up to the Lone Rock landing, and then work out a time to pick them up," I instructed.

"Okie dokie," he said, and went out to load up the voyagers.

After about an hour he came back and parked the van. "I'll be back to go get them at about five," he said. "Oh, hey. By the way... I keep all tips that I get, don't I? Or do I have to share them with you?"

"Tips? Nope. You get all tips. Why? Did they give you a tip?"

"Yup," he said, pulling three dollars from his pocket and grinning like a cat with canary breath.

"They were probably entranced by your lovely wardrobe and quick wit," I said.

"Actually, I think it was because I looked like a pauper, and they felt sorry for me."

I didn't think much more about it, and later that day he picked up the people and put the canoe and other gear away. A couple of days later, two couples came to the store and wanted a couple of canoes, so I called Thunderfoot. He came right over and hauled them to the river. I noticed he was wearing the same old cut off jeans and another equally tattered tee shirt, but thought he was probably painting or working for his mom, and I didn't give it much attention.

That day, when he returned from picking up the tourists, he was strutting like a peacock as he came into the shop. "I did good again," he said, pulling five dollars from his pocket.

"Another tip?"

"Yup. This is getting to be a good racket. I think these people think I'm real poor and feel sorry for me." I just shook my head. What a con man.

The weekend came and we had three groups of canoe renters coming on Saturday morning, so I told Thunderfoot I'd call him when some of them arrived at the shop.

When the first group showed up, I called, and told him to get three canoes ready with paddles and life jackets. He was out back loading the gear when I took the people out to meet him. I couldn't believe my eyes. He was wearing some old dress pants that looked like the legs had been cut off with a chain saw, about 6 inches different in length, and had strings and pieces of cloth hanging from them. One sleeve was torn from his tee shirt, and the pocket was partly ripped off and hanging down. But the clincher was his feet – one tennis shoe and one beat up, old, brown dress shoe.

"I... uh... this is Thunderfoot. He'll take you up river," I said to the people.

They looked at him and I could see the pity in their eyes.

"Hello," Thunderfoot said, giving the tourists his most wonderful smile. He glanced and winked at me as he turned toward the van. I just wished the people a good trip and went back to the shop.

A while later, the second group came, and just as soon as Thunderfoot came back from dropping off the first group, he loaded up the next bunch and took them up river. The final group arrived, and again he took off for the river with them. It was nearly noon when he returned, and he came in to the shop for some lunch.

"Please sir. May I have some porridge?" he mugged.

"Jeez. You're unbelievable. What is that get-up you're wearing? Is it Halloween?"

He grinned from ear to ear. "I figured if they thought I was real poor, I might get some bigger tips."

Late in the afternoon, when the canoe renters began arriving at the boat landing, Thunderfoot picked them up and returned them to their cars. He was in the back putting the paddles away and hanging up the life jackets to dry when I walked out. "Everyone back safe and sound?"

"Yup. All accounted for," he said.

"And how did poor Oliver Twist make out?"

His grin was as wide as the river. "Well, the first group gave me five dollars, that group of three couples gave me a ten, and the last ones – with the lady who looked at me so sad? Well, they gave me ten dollars too." He reached in his pocket and pulled out two wadded up tens and a five. His share of the charges for the shuttle amounted to 46 dollars, so he had a pretty good day.

I handed him his share of the money and he sorted and turned all the bills facing the same way. "Hmm. Not bad," he said. "Seventy one dollars for about five hours' work."

"But don't you feel bad about making those people think you're so poor?" I asked.

"Oh, yea. I feel real bad... Not."

I had to laugh at him as he stood there grinning like the little miser he was.

"You know," he said in a pondering sort of way. "I wonder if I could get a cast on my hand or one of my feet? That would work pretty good, too, huh?"

I just walked away shaking my head. Next he'd be trying to sell someone a building site in the river bottoms.

Thanks, Thunderfoot.

Houseboating

I had been talking with my friend Lumpy about another trip to Canada, and we had looked into some new ideas for our annual upcoming vacation. The fly-in trip had been lots of fun and we caught plenty of fish, but we wanted to try something else this summer. We checked into renting a houseboat on Lake of the Woods. We thought it would make a great summer trip, so we booked it, and now we were going to tell the boys. Lumpy's son, Chris, had been with us the year before, and he and Thunderfoot got along well. Both were died-in-the-wool fishermen, so we got together on a Sunday afternoon to break the good news to them.

We were sitting in the back yard, grilling hamburgers and relaxing while the boys played with the dogs. "Hey, you guys. Come here," I called to them. "We're kicking around an idea, and we want to see what you think of it."

They came running and plopped down in lawn chairs, panting after the roughhousing with the dogs. "What's up?"

"Well, we've been thinking of a fishing trip this summer, and wanted to see if you guys thought it would be okay."

"Trip? What trip?"

"Well, we thought since last year we did a fly-in, we'd take a houseboat trip on Lake of the Woods this year."

Their mouths dropped open. They both looked as though they had been struck in the head by a blunt object. "Lake of the Woods! That's huge. It's like an ocean. A houseboat? Holy cow!" They were both just about ready to bust.

"Here's how it will work," I said. "We drive up to the houseboat place, and we take our own boats along. We can piggyback them on one trailer since Lumpy's boat is a little smaller than mine. Then, when we get there, we tie our boats behind and tow them with the houseboat out on the lake. The houseboat has a kitchen, shower, toilet, and bunks, and we just live on it, like in a cabin for the week. When we fish, we take our boats out and then come back to where we've tied up the houseboat – on an island or beach. And we can always move the houseboat closer if we find some good fishing spots. What do you think?"

Both of the boys were ready to jump up and leave for the north instantly. "Ohmygosh," Thunderfoot said, jumping to his feet. "I gotta get my stuff ready. When are we leaving?"

"Relax. We're not going for two weeks. I don't think you have to pack just yet," I said, laughing. We spent the rest of the evening talking about what to bring and made our grocery list, and after a while, we had our plans pretty well figured out.

We began checking our tackle and rods and reels, and readied the boat and trailer for the trip. The time passed quickly, and all of a sudden, there were only a couple of days left before we were going to leave.

Thunderfoot and I were in charge of grocery shopping. We went to the grocery store to get the things we needed for a week on the big lake. Having had the experience of getting pretty tired of fish on the last trip, we were taking enough meat and food for breakfast, and one other meal a day. We planned on eating a shore lunch each day, so we needed food for the other meals. Not that there's anything wrong with fresh fish, but after half a dozen meals of it in a row, we wanted something a little different.

We also had a list for snacks. On that list were chips, cheese, crackers and SITSPN. "What's SITSPN?" I asked.

"Hmm. Let's see," Thunderfoot said.

"You wrote the list, and you don't know what you wrote down?"

"I can't remember what that was suppose to mean."

"Well, let's keep shopping. Maybe it'll come to you," I said.

When we had about everything on the list gathered up, Thunderfoot still couldn't remember what SITSPN was supposed to represent. "Well, we'll have to just forget it if we can't remember what it is," I said.

"I hope it's not something important."

We took the groceries home and packed all the dry stuff in a box, and put the meat and everything that had to be kept cool in the refrigerator. We called it a day. Thunderfoot went home, still trying to remember what it was that we hadn't gotten. I watched TV a little while, and then went to bed. I was sleeping soundly when I could hear a bell sounding, and I tried to ignore it. It kept ringing and ringing, and suddenly I realized that it was the phone. I jumped up and looked at the clock. It was just after one o'clock in the morning. I raced for the phone, fearing the worst. After all, who calls at one in the morning if it's not bad news? "Hello?" I said, as I picked up the phone.

"Good. You're up."

"Of course I'm up. I had to answer the phone!"

It was Thunderfoot. "I know what SITSPN is!"

"What? You called me in the middle of the night to tell me that?"

"Uh... well... yeah, I guess it is a little late. But I remembered what it is."

I sat down in my recliner, my heart racing from the mad dash to the phone, with the expectation that I was going to hear someone had been in a car wreck... or worse. "Well, you have my attention now. What the heck is SITSPN?"

"It's Salted In The Shell Pea Nuts," he said calmly. "Boy, it's a good thing I remembered that. I'd hate to go on a trip like this without them."

"Well, now I can sleep soundly, knowing that we didn't forget our peanuts," I replied.

"Jeez... you don't have to be such a grouch," he said, sounding a little hurt.

"Sorry. I'm like that when I get woke up from a deep sleep to be told such earth shattering news."

"Well fine. Next time I'll just not call you."

I had to laugh a bit, and said, "Oh, never mind. I'm glad we figured it out. I'll talk to you tomorrow. And if you think of anything else we missed, just write it down and tell me in the morning. Okay?"

"Okie dokie. Nighty night," he said.

The big departure day finally arrived. We loaded up all of our gear in the boat and in the back of the van, and met Lumpy and Chris. We finished loading all of their stuff, and then we strapped down Lumpy's boat upside down on top of mine. It was quite a sight to see how much gear four people needed for a fishing trip. But soon we were off toward the great north woods.

The drive would take about eleven hours, so to avoid getting too tired, Lumpy and I took turns driving. Of course, the boys kept volunteering to drive, but neither Lumpy nor I were too keen on riding with someone their age and with their limited driving experience. We stopped for a late supper. After we finished and were walking back to the van, Thunderfoot said, "Why don't you let me drive for a while? You guys are tired, and I'm a perfectly good driver."

"Oh, that's okay. I'm not too tired," I said.

"You could barely keep your eyes open when we were eating," he said. "I drive the canoe trailer all the time and it's no different than the boat trailer."

Well, he did have a point. "Okay. You can drive and we'll take a little rest. But be careful."

Thunderfoot and Chris sat in the front seat and Lumpy and I crawled in the back. Off we went, again, into the darkness.

"You'd better get some gas pretty soon," I said. "The towns are a long way apart up here, and we don't want to run out."

"Okay. As soon as we come to a gas station, I'll stop," Thunderfoot said.

I was dozing a bit when I felt the van make a turn and saw that we were pulling into a gas station. We slowed down by the pumps and then sped up again and back out onto the highway. "What are you doing? Why didn't you stop for gas?"

"It was too expensive. It was about five cents a gallon higher priced than the gas at home," Thunderfoot said.

"Well, don't go too much farther, or we'll run out."

My eyes were heavy again, and soon I was asleep. The next thing I knew, I could feel us pulling off the road and stopping. I opened my eyes and there was no gas station; there was no town; there were no lights; there was nothing but darkness. "What's wrong?" I asked.

Thunderfoot and Chris were huddling in the front seat, looking at the map.

"What's going on?"

"Well," Thunderfoot said, "We're about half way between that town with the expensive gas and this town here," he said pointing to the map. "But we don't have enough gas to get to that town, so I think we gotta go back to the last town."

"What? Are you serious? How far have we gone past that town?"

"About fifty miles," he said so softly that I could barely hear him.

"Fifty miles! And how far to the next town?"

"Maybe seventy, give or take a few miles, and we're below an eighth of a tank, so we can't make it that far."

I was about to blow my top when I realized that Thunderfoot had just made a mistake, and it wasn't worth making a big fuss over. "Okay. Well, turn around and we'll go back."

Thunderfoot shot Chris a quick glance, and they put the map away. He turned our rig around and started back to the expensive gas station. I looked at Lumpy and he just grinned and shrugged his shoulders. "Oh well, what the heck?"

After another short nap, we were slowing down again. I sat up in the seat. We were at the expensive gas station, but it was closed. Of course. It was two o'clock in the morning, so that was no surprise.

"Uh oh. It's closed," Thunderfoot said.

"No foolin, Sherlock. What was your first clue?" We all got out of the van and were standing there trying to figure out what to do next, when a police car pulled into the station.

"You fellas got some trouble?"

"We're just about out of gas, and I don't think we can make it to the next town," I said.

"You should have filled up earlier in the evening," the policeman said.

"Yeah. No kidding," I said as I shot a scowl at Thunderfoot.

He shrugged his shoulders. "I was just trying to save you some money."

"Well, there's an all night station about twelve miles east of here. Can you make it that far?" the policeman asked.

"Well, I think so," I said. "If not, one of these young lads will be glad to jog down the road with a can to get enough gas to get us to the station." I looked right at Thunderfoot who nodded his head like an obedient puppy.

"Well, good luck then," the policeman said and drove off.

"Well, let's go and find this station," I said. We all got back into the van. I drove this time, and we must have been running on fumes as we finally saw the lights of the gas station up ahead.

"We made it!" Thunderfoot said from the back seat.

"Yeah. How nice. We only wasted two hours and sixty miles of driving the wrong way. And hey, look! It's three cents cheaper than the last place," I said.

"Jeez... you don't have to be so sarcastic," Thunderfoot whined.

We gassed up, got some pop and snacks and then headed back into the darkness. This time we were going north again, which was a big improvement.

We reached International Falls at about eight in the morning and decided to stop before we crossed the border. At a neat little trading post type Tourist Stop, we had our money changed to Canadian currency. The place displayed lots of souvenirs and funny tee shirts. Thunderfoot and Chris each bought a shirt that had a picture of a walleye on the front and said "Walleyes, eh?" Thunderfoot snuck around and bought something else that he wouldn't show us.

"What are you buying?" I asked.

"Just a little souvenir for mom," he replied.

With our new Canadian money, we headed for the border and then on up into the country toward Lake of the Woods.

We crossed the border with little trouble. The border guard looked under the boat on top of the trailer as best he could, and then waved us through. He probably thought we looked too bedraggled to be smugglers.

We pulled into the houseboat rental place at about eleven that morning. We were a pretty motley looking group, having driven all night. But we were all full of enthusiasm, ready to get our boats in the water and our gear on the houseboat. The man who rented the boats helped us stow our gear and food on the boat, and then took us out in the lake for a lesson on how to drive the houseboat. He showed us some good places on the map to tie up at night for a camp. We took him back to shore and he wished us a good trip. Then, off we went for our first day on the lake.

"Can I drive?" Thunderfoot asked as we pulled away from the dock. I glanced Lumpy's way. He shrugged his shoulders.

"I guess so, but keep it slow for a while till you get a feel for it. We'll put all the gear away and tidy things up. And remember – this doesn't have brakes like a car, so if you think you have to stop, start doing it ahead of time."

"Aye aye, captain." Thunderfoot grinned from ear to ear as he sat on the stool behind the steering wheel inside the cabin. We started out across the bay, and Lumpy and I studied the map to decide on a place to park the boat for the first day. The outfitter had marked several locations on the map with a little red x – good places to tie up. He had also given us some pointers about good places to try the fishing. We decided on a spot and showed it to Thunderfoot.

"Can you follow this map to that spot?"

He peered at the map a few seconds and said, "I guess so. It can't be that hard."

The rest of us got busy and put the food into the refrigerator and stored our clothes and other gear in the little bedroom at the back of the boat. Our two boats were trailing along in the wake of the houseboat, and seemed to be riding just fine, but we checked the knots holding them, anyway, just to make sure we wouldn't lose one on the way. It had taken about an hour to get everything ship-shape, and when I went back to the main cabin to check on Thunderfoot, I noticed he was reading the map upside down. "What are you doing? That map is upside down."

"Yeah, I know. I like it that way," he said.

"Why are you doing that?"

"What's the difference? Don't worry. I know right where I am."

By then we had gone past several islands and I had no idea where we were, so I had to rely on him being right. "You know, there's 14,000 islands in this lake. Don't get us lost."

He gave me one of those looks, and then a while later he said, "Right around that island should be where we want to go. That's Rabbit Island." Well, sure enough, just as we got to the other side of the island, there was a nice sandy beach that was shown on the map as a good place to tie up. Thunderfoot just gave me one of his famous "*see, I told you so*" looks. We pulled up on the sand beach and the boys hopped out. They tied the boat to two trees by long ropes that were attached to the back of the houseboat.

"Let's go fishing," Thunderfoot and Chris said.

"That's what we came for," I said, and I began putting gear and our poles into the boats. Soon we were off, and we decided to all go to the same place to fish, since the day was almost shot and not a lot of time left to explore. We found a little bay that had a small stream running into it from one end, and we started casting walleye jigs up into the moving water. In no time at all we had enough fish for supper. We decided to call it a day.

The houseboat was just like a large motor home, but with pontoons instead of wheels. The kitchen was small, but it had everything we needed. There was a stove, oven, small refrigerator, and an eating area that could be converted into a bed. There was another sitting area that could be folded down to form another bed, if needed. The bathroom was just a little larger than a phone booth with a small sink, toilet and shower, all of which were supplied with water that was pumped from the lake, and heated by a small, concealed water heater. Wastewater was collected in a tank under the boat and would be pumped out when we returned.

The bedroom was in the back of the boat, and it wasn't what you'd call roomy. There was a set of bunk beds on each side of the room, with a narrow walkway between them. Against the back wall was a closet for storing clothes and gear. Outside the bedroom was a small deck with a rail around it to keep any sleepwalker from taking a drink, and a ladder that led to the roof, where one could soak up the sun. And there was a gas grill bolted to the floor on the roomy front deck. So, overall, it was a pretty nice little self-contained home on the water.

The boys cleaned the fish while Lumpy and I peeled some potatoes and opened a couple of cans of beans. Soon the smell of frying fish and potatoes filled the kitchen.

While the food was cooking, I decided that I'd try the shower. I found a towel, clean clothes, and my bathroom kit in the bedroom, and squeezed into the phone booth bathroom. After I shaved, I decided to see how the shower worked. I turned the water on, adjusted it to just the right temperature, and then squeezed in. It was a tight fit. I managed to wash my hair, and as I began to soap up my body, of course I dropped the bar of soap trying to reach my back. I tried to bend over to pick it up, but there wasn't room in the shower to bend, at least not for me. I had to open the curtain and step out into the bathroom to be able to bend far enough to pick up the soap, and then hit my butt on the sink while doing it. This was definitely not the bathroom for a full sized guy like me. I finally managed to get clean and rinsed off, and by the time I was dry and dressed, the supper was ready.

"How'd the shower work?" Thunderfoot asked.

"Not bad. The water was nice and hot, and it came out pretty good, but it's a little cramped for me."

"Maybe you could just rub soap on the walls and then spin around," he said, laughing.

That didn't sound like a bad idea.

It didn't take long for us all to start yawning and stretching after supper, and as soon as we had the kitchen cleaned up we all began preparing for bed. The bedroom wasn't big enough for four people to get undressed at once, so we took turns until we all were in bed. I was the last in line, and I turned out the light.

"G'night Lumpy."

"G'night Thunderfoot."

"G'night Chris."

"G'night Dan."

The quiet settled in.

Then Thunderfoot said, "G'night Mary Ellen. G'night John Boy." The whole boat was shaking from our laughter. Then it was quiet again and I began to dose off. Then someone farted. We were all laughing again like we were on drugs or drunk. Then it was quiet for a while.

"G'night Grandpa."

"G'night Mary Ellen." We all laughed again. Quiet again.

"Burrrrrrrp!" Raucous laughter filled the bedroom again. This went on for the next several minutes until exhaustion finally took us all off to dreamland.

Sunlight poured into the bedroom through the glass door, rousing our sleepy bunch the next morning that came much too quickly. It wasn't long until we all began yawning and scratching. Thunderfoot was the first out of bed and heading for the bathroom. "I'm gonna get in there before it gets all fouled up," he said. The rest of us arose and dressed, and soon Lumpy and I were busy in the kitchen making breakfast. In about an hour, all of us had gotten our bathroom duties out of the way, filled our bellies with hash browns, bacon, and eggs, and were ready for a day of fishing.

Off we went again, in both our boats, in search of the elusive walleye and northern pike. It was a grand day with little wind, and we found a spot about four miles from the houseboat that was just full of fish. "I'll go back and move the houseboat to that bay over there," Lumpy announced. He and Chris left to bring our house closer to the good fishing while Thunderfoot and I stayed and fished. That evening we had fresh walleyes with fried potatoes and beans on the side. We ate until we all just about exploded. Then we played a few games of cards, and at bedtime, the same old routine was replayed as we all "G'nighted." until we were nearly sick with laughter.

I was sleeping soundly when I thought I felt the boat moving a little, but it didn't wake up enough to cause me to worry about it. I was just dozing off again when I heard a loud bang outside the back door of the bedroom. That woke me up completely, so I sat up and swung my legs over the side of the bed. Lumpy and Chris seemed to still be asleep on the two bunks across from me, so I stood up to see if Thunderfoot was still in his bunk above me, but his bed was empty. I walked to the front of the boat and checked the bathroom to see if he was there, but he was nowhere to be found. Then I remembered the bang I had heard at the back of the boat. I walked back to the bedroom and out onto the deck. There was Thunderfoot, sitting on the deck in his underwear.

"What are you doing out here?" I asked.

He stared up at me with a dumbfounded look on his face.

"What are you doing?" I asked again.

"I... uh... I came out here to pee, but somehow I ended up on my back on the deck," he said. There was enough moonlight to see his footprints on the dew-covered deck, and the skid marks where his feet slid out from under him.

"You must have slipped on the wet deck," I said.

"Jeez... it's a good thing I didn't fall in the water," he said.

"It's a good thing your head is so hard, or you might have hurt yourself."

"Oh, funny," he said. I gave him my hand and helped him up. He was all wet on his backside, but he seemed okay otherwise.

"Why didn't you go in the bathroom?" I asked.

"I didn't want to wake you guys up."

"Well, you succeeded partly on that. Lumpy and Chris are still asleep," I said.

"No we're not," Lumpy called out from the bedroom. "Mr. Graceful woke us up, too, when he banged his head against the deck."

"Well, I had good intentions," Thunderfoot whined.

He dried off his back and changed into some dry underwear. He climbed back into his bunk and we all settled down for the rest of the night.

The next two days were spent fishing, eating and just having a grand time. The weather was perfect, the fishing was great, and the companionship was the best. On the morning of the fourth day, we decided to split up and explore more of the lake. So Lumpy and Chris headed north, and Thunderfoot and I headed west. We had our map and were looking for a river that ran into a huge bay a few miles west of our camp. We had been having some good luck fishing near creeks, so it seemed that a river must be even better.

At about mid-day we found the river and began fishing, catching some really nice northern pike. But then, the wind began to pick up. The surrounding timber sheltered the bay, so it wasn't too windy to fish, but I kept looking out past the point, and the big lake was getting pretty rough. "I think we'd better get back a little closer to home," I said.

Thunderfoot looked out toward the lake. "I think you're right. Those waves are getting pretty big."

We reeled up, put everything away, and decided it would be a good idea to put on our rain gear before we tackled the big waves coming at us across the lake. When we came out from the sheltered cove, we realized that the waves were much larger than we had thought. Many of them were three or four feet tall, and it was a long way across the lake. "Oh boy. Hang on!" I told Thunderfoot.

We started out slowly – going to fast just meant smashing the boat into the bone jarring waves. As it was, the cold water driven by the wind came splashing over the sides of the boat, and we were soon soaked even though we wore rain gear. And worse yet, it was impossible to see the other side of the lake, so we weren't sure where we were going.

"Once we get to the other side, we'll have to find our way between the islands to our houseboat," I yelled to Thunderfoot. He nodded in agreement. On we went... slowly.

After a few minutes, Thunderfoot turned quickly toward me and pointed to another boat, splashing and cutting through the waves, and coming in our direction. I steered toward the boat that carried just a lone person. As we neared, I recognized the old Indian guide who we had met back at the houseboat rental place. He looked to be about 70 years old and was barely over five feet tall. His face was brown and weathered, and now, in this weather, it looked like a wet catcher's mitt. He slowed down his boat and we pulled along side. "Yutta Hey! A bit bumpy out here, eh?" he said as he grinned at us with his three teeth that he had left, and the water dripping from his chin.

"Yeah, just a bit," I said. "Do you know which way it is to Deer Island?"

"Sure," he beamed. "Straight that way – two, maybe three miles." He pointed in the direction he had come from.

"Okay. Thanks," I said.

"Have fun, boys!" he said. He revved up his motor and headed out across the lake, seeming not to have a care in the world.

"Jeez... he's brave being out here all by himself," Thunderfoot said.

"He's probably been doing this his whole life," I replied.

"Well, two maybe three miles and we're home," Thunderfoot said just as a big wave slammed into the boat.

We pounded on ahead, and after about a half hour of being tossed among the surf and drenched with wind-driven spray, we reached the sheltered shoreline of the lake. We followed a cut between two islands, and eventually arrived at the houseboat. Glad to see that Lumpy and Chris were already home safe and sound, we noticed that the gas grill was sending out clouds of the most delicious smelling smoke. "Yutta hey!" Thunderfoot yelled as we drew near.

"Where you guys been?" Lumpy asked.

"Yutta hey. Two, maybe three miles yonder," Thunderfoot said, mocking the old Indian guide.

I knew we wouldn't hear the last of that for a while.

We tied up our boat, stowed away our gear, and changed into dry clothes. Lumpy had fired up the grill a few hours earlier, and as we walked to the front deck of the houseboat, he opened the grill lid, revealing the most beautiful golden brown turkey that I had ever seen.

"Holy cow! That's beautiful, Lump," Thunderfoot exclaimed.

"I think it's ready," Lumpy said. "And the rest of the meal is ready in the galley, so let's eat!" We sat down and ate like famished pagans, and in a half-hour or so, all that remained of the turkey was a skeleton, and Thunderfoot was gnawing on that like a hyena.

"That was the best turkey I've ever had," he said, wiping the grease from his chin. "Burrrrrp."

I don't know if it was the sleep inducing affect that turkey has on people, or just the wind and waves, but in a short while after the meal we were all rather tired. One by one we drifted off to the bedroom, and soon we were all fast asleep.

The map that had been left with the houseboat had markings on it from other groups of fishermen who had found good angling spots. "Look here. There's a place where they marked a crappie spot. I didn't know there were crappies in Canada."

I studied the map. "That's quite a ways from here. Do you think it's worth the boat ride?"

"It says fourteen-inch crappies. I think that would be a lot of fun," Thunderfoot said. "But if you guys don't want to go, Chris and I can go and check it out."

I wasn't absolutely sure that I trusted Thunderfoot and Chris on the lake by themselves, but Lumpy thought it would be okay, so I gave my approval, too. The two boys jumped in Lumpy's boat and took off out across the lake. Lumpy and I went searching for a bay that had the promise of holding some toothy northern pike.

We found the bay, and after a few hours we had caught a lot of pike. About mid-afternoon, we decided to go back to the houseboat for some lunch. As we came around the island to the bay where the houseboat should have been parked, we both were quite shocked to see that it wasn't there. "What the heck?"

"This is the right bay, isn't it?" I asked.

"I'm sure it is," Lumpy groaned. "Go closer and we can see if there are tracks in the sand."

I drove up closer to the beach, and sure enough, there was a groove in the sand where the houseboat had been beached, and footprints in the sand where we had walked to tie it up.

"Where do you suppose the boat is," I asked.

Lumpy just shook his head.

We sat there trying to figure out what to do next when I noticed a piece of paper pinned to a tree branch with a clothespin. "Look, there's a note," I said, pointing to the tree. I moved the boat close to the beach. Lumpy jumped out, retrieved the note and read: "Moved the house to the crappie hole. They're huge and millions of them."

“The boys moved the boat,” Lumpy said. He jumped aboard and handed me the note.

“Did you happen to look at the map to see where that crappie hole is?” I asked.

He shook his head.

“Oh, that’s nice,” I said. “They moved and we don’t know where they moved it to.”

Here we were on Lake of the Woods, with over 65,000 miles of shoreline and 14,000 islands, and our house had moved without us. “Well, I know that they took off to the north,” I said. “I guess we’d better get to looking for them before it gets dark.”

We fired up the motor and started up the lake toward where we had last seen the boys. It was like looking for a needle in a haystack. We drove for about two miles and then started looking around each island that we came to. If the boys had parked the boat on the backside of an island, we could easily miss seeing it. We looked at dozens of islands, and finally we came around the bend of one, and there was the houseboat pulled up on a beach. Thunderfoot and Chris were out on the deck with the fish cleaning board on a table, cleaning crappies. They waved enthusiastically at us as we drove up.

“Hey, look at these huge slab crappies.” Thunderfoot held up a couple of them, grinning like madman.

“Those are real nice,” I said calmly.

“Well, don’t go overboard to compliment us,” he said, his ego obviously bruised.

“Do you know where Lumpy and I have been for the last three hours?”

Thunderfoot glanced at Chris. “Fishing, I suppose. What else would you be doing?”

“We were searching for you two,” I said. “Trying to find the houseboat.”

“But we’ve been here for a long time, and we thought you knew where we were going.”

“How would we know that?” I asked.

"Well, because we told you we were going to the crappie hole."

"Yeah, but we didn't know where that was."

It was then that he and Chris instantly realized that we had had no idea where they were going. A grin came to Thunderfoot's face. "Oops. We didn't think of that. We thought we were doing good to move the houseboat close to the crappies."

Lumpy and I just shook our heads. "Well, we're here now, so let's see those crappies."

We tied up our boat and inspected the huge crappies the boys were cleaning. "They'll be pretty tasty tonight for supper," Thunderfoot said rubbing his stomach.

"We'll get some potatoes ready. You guys finish cleaning the fish."

That evening, the boys told us about the bay just around the corner where they had caught all the crappies, and we declared the next day would be a crappie-fishing day. The next morning, Thunderfoot and Chris thought they would go in the same boat again, and they were off before we had even untied my boat from its mooring. We followed them to the crappie bay, where we set the boats to drift, trailing a bobber with two crappie jigs suspended underneath. It didn't take long until we began catching huge crappies, one after another. We would drift across the bay and then fire up the motor and go back to the other side and drift again.

Thunderfoot and Chris had just completed their drift and were motoring past us. As they went by, Thunderfoot, in the front of the boat, stuck his feet up on the side of the boat and yelled, "Yutta hey! Two, maybe three miles." On his feet were two big, brown, pillow-like slippers that looked like bear feet, with little beige claws and spots like the pads on a bear's foot. He was grinning like a madman. "Yutta hey!" Now we knew what he had bought in the gift shop at the border. Lumpy and I laughed until our stomachs ached.

The next day Thunderfoot was with me again, and we were a few miles from the houseboat, fishing for walleyes. The sky darkened and the wind came up.

"Looks like a storm coming," I said.

"Did you see that trappers cabin back there?" Thunderfoot said. "Let's see if we can go in it until the storm is over."

We motored back down the lake and beached the boat on an island where there was an old cabin. The door was unlocked.

"I don't think they ever lock these, so people who need shelter can use them," I said.

"Well, we need shelter, 'cause here comes the rain."

We watched the storm rage from inside the cabin. The wind riled up the lake into huge whitecaps, and the rain pounded on the tin roof of the cabin that had a few leaks, but nothing too serious. In the corner was a pile of dry firewood, so Thunderfoot decided to make a fire in the potbelly stove. In just a short while, a fire crackled and the cabin was getting nice and cozy.

"Now if we only had some food, we'd be in good shape," Thunderfoot suggested.

"I planned on going back to the houseboat for lunch, so I didn't bring anything to eat," I said.

"Well, I'm getting faminished," he said rubbing his belly.

There was a little lull in the storm, and suddenly Thunderfoot bolted out the front door. "Be right back." He ran down to the lake and grabbed the stringer with three walleyes that was tied to the oarlock. He came running back to the cabin. "We can have fish for lunch," he said as he bounded through the door.

"How are we going to cook them," I asked.

"Just you wait and learn," he said. He picked up an old weathered board that had once been driftwood and placed it on the table. Then he got out his knife and filleted the walleyes. He ran down to the lake again with the fillets and rinsed them off. When he returned to the cabin, he put the fillets on the table, ran out to a bush near the cabin and cut a couple of branches.

Then he came back in and whittled the branches so they each had a fork on the end. Next, he cut a piece of fillet and skewered it onto the fork of one stick, opened the potbelly stove door and held the fillet over the coals. He turned to me, grinning. "Fish on a stick."

I watched as he carefully cooked the fish, and then slid if off onto the bare table. He picked it up and took a careful bite. "Mmm, not bad. Could use a little salt and pepper, but not bad."

I just shook my head. He never ceased to amaze me.

We ate all the fillets, and by the time we were done, the storm had passed, so we went back out on the lake and fished the rest of the day.

We had to return the houseboat back to the dock by eleven o'clock the next morning, so we started packing that night. Next morning we made a good breakfast before we started down the lake. Thunderfoot insisted on driving, and as surprised as I might be, he managed to find his way right back to the dock.

We loaded up the boats and gear, and much too soon we were heading south, toward home. The trip was uneventful, and many hours later we pulled up to Lumpy's house and unloaded his stuff. We bid Lumpy and Chris farewell and drove the last few miles home. As we pulled into town, Thunderfoot said, "Looks the same as when we left."

"Yeah. What did you expect to change?"

"Oh, I guess nothing," he said. "It seems funny that when you're on such an adventure, that the rest of the world just goes on the same."

We pulled into my driveway and the dogs came running out slobbering and jumping all over us. My dog sitter had done a good job of taking care of them, but they were glad to see their Dad and Thunderfoot. "Let's just leave the stuff and put it all away tomorrow," I said.

"Yeah. Good idea. I think I'd better go home and let mom know I'm still alive." Thunderfoot put his arms around my shoulders and gave me a bear hug. "Thanks for taking me."

"You're welcome," I said. That was all we needed to say about the subject, and he went walking across the lawn toward home.

Part way across, he stopped and put his hand up over his forehead, like he was looking for something. "Yutta hey! Three, maybe four miles," he said.

Yutta hey, Thunderfoot.

Do It Yourself

Shortly after we returned from our Canada excursion, a friend of mine offered me a roll of heavy-duty cyclone fencing. It had been a dog kennel, but his old dog had died and he wouldn't need it anymore. Of course, I couldn't turn down such a good offer, so I drove over to his house and picked it up. When I came home, I called Thunderfoot to tell him that I had a project for him.

"What ya gonna do?" he asked as he trotted into the back yard.

"I got this fencing for free, and I thought we could make a kennel for Katy and Kirby. Then, if we go someplace that they can't go along, they can lounge in the nice weather instead of being cooped up in the house."

"Cool. What you got in mind?" Thunderfoot asked.

"Well, I thought we'd mark out a rectangle here next to the garden shed and have someone come and pour a cement pad. Then we'll build a frame and put the wire on it, and if we cut a hole in the side of the shed, the dogs could go inside if it rained, or if they just wanted a nap."

"Why hire somebody to make the cement pad? *We* can do it. My grandpa has a cement mixer, and we can just frame it up and mix our own cement."

"Oh, I don't know," I said. "That sounds like more than we're capable of doing."

"What do you mean? You take sand and cement and water and roll it around in the mixer and it becomes concrete. How hard is that? Besides, just think of the money you'll save if we do it ourselves."

Well, I agreed to think about it. While I was pondering the idea, we rolled out the wire and measured it, to determine the size of the kennel. There was 28 feet of wire. We allowed space for a gate, and then measured out the size of the cement pad.

"That doesn't look so bad," Thunderfoot said. The area didn't seem that big, and after all – how hard could it be to mix cement? I agreed to give it a try.

The next day, Thunderfoot's grandpa drove into the driveway with a cement mixer in the back of his pickup truck. Thunderfoot and I drug the thing to the back yard, and then we went to the lumberyard for some two-by-fours for the form, and some sand and bags of concrete mix. The guy at the lumberyard helped us figure out how much of each ingredient we needed. We loaded it all in the pickup and headed for home.

The ground was kind of uneven where we wanted to build the kennel, so we had to shovel some of the dirt out to get it level.

"Where are we gonna put this extra dirt?" Thunderfoot asked.

I was standing there thinking about where to dispose of the dirt when he suddenly appeared quite enlightened. "Hey! Let's put it over there in the back of the yard and make a little hill, so the water can run down like a little waterfall into the pond."

"What pond?" I asked. (He had been pestering me for years to dig a pond in the back yard so we could put some bluegills in it during the summer.)

"Lake Thunderfoot," he said with a big, foolish grin.

"Oh, I don't know. This is gonna become a bigger job than we want – real fast."

"Oh, come on. It'll be fun." I knew he'd never let up, so I agreed.

We dug down so the kennel would be level, and dumped the extra dirt in a pile in the corner of the yard with a wheelbarrow. Then we built the form for the concrete pad. By the time all of this was done, it was time for lunch, and a nap for me, I hoped. Thunderfoot would not hear of it though, and kept hounding me until I agreed to pour the cement right away. "The sooner we get the kennel done, the sooner we can put in the pond."

We moved the mixer next to the form, began shoveling sand and concrete mix into the agitator and then added water until it became a soupy concoction that looked like cement. Once it was all mixed, we dumped it into the form.

"Holy cow! It's gonna take a lot of batches to fill this," Thunderfoot groaned as we surveyed the little puddle of cement. I just shook my head. I knew this was going to be one of those jobs that *seemed* easy at first, and then turned into a nightmare.

About fifteen batches of cement later, we finally had the form filled. We leveled it off with a two-by-four, and did our best to smooth it out with trowels when it started to harden. It wasn't exactly professional, but it did turn out pretty good.

"Well, are you ready to admit you were wrong?" Thunderfoot asked.

"We're not done yet. Let's wait until this is all finished, and then maybe I'll consider it."

We left the job for the day, while the cement dried, and the next morning, Thunderfoot was here bright and early for breakfast. When we removed the forms, the cement pad looked pretty darn good.

"Not bad for a couple of rookies," Thunderfoot said as we admired our handiwork.

We got out the saw, hammers and nails, and built the frame for the kennel, and fastened the wire to the frame. It fit like a glove. Then, with an old wire panel that I had saved for some reason, we built a frame and made a very nice gate for the kennel.

Thunderfoot stepped back and admired our work. "Very nice. All it needs now is a swimming pool, and the dogs will have their own spa."

I had to agree, but I wasn't too sure about the swimming pool.

"Well... let's go get the liner for the pond, and finish that up, too," he added.

"You still insist that we make a pond?"

"What? Did you think I'd forget?"

We went to the hardware store and looked over the choices for pond liners. Of course, Thunderfoot wanted to get one that was twenty feet by thirty feet – so we could have a *for real* pond. I was looking more at the little pre-formed ones that held a couple hundred gallons of water.

"Oh come on," he prodded me. "That thing is just a puny little puddle. We need a *real* pond."

"Well, I'm *not* going to turn the entire back yard into a lake," I advised. So we finally agreed on a compromise, and I bought it, along with a filter, hose and pump to keep the water circulating. We took it home and set it on the ground where we decided it would look best. We drew an outline in the dirt around it, and started digging. The dirt went up onto the ever-growing pile that we had started the day before. When the pond finally fit the hole and was level, I informed Thunderfoot that I had had enough for one day. "I'm pooped."

"Okay," he agreed. "But let's start early tomorrow so we can get the pond finished... and get some bluegills in it."

The next morning Thunderfoot was in the back yard bright and early backfilling around the pond and smoothing out the little hill we had created with all the extra dirt.

"You know," he said, "we should get some rocks and cover the dirt with them, and then maybe put in some plants and stuff so it looks nicer."

That sounded like a good idea, so I called a friend who had a quarry on his land and asked if we could get some rocks from him. He told me to take all we needed. In fact, he told me that he had an old trailer built from a pickup box hooked on the back of his truck, and that I should just use that to haul the rocks, so my pickup wouldn't get all scratched up. This was looking better all the time.

Thunderfoot and I drove out into the country to my friend's farm, got his pickup and trailer, and backed into the quarry. The stones were flat and of many different sizes – just what we wanted. The trailer was looking pretty squat after we had loaded up a lot of stones, so we decided to take what we had to the house and see if they would do the job. Thunderfoot drove my pickup back to town in case we needed it for another errand.

After we had backed the trailer into the yard and were ready to start unloading, we decided it would be a good idea to cover the dirt pile first with some of that porous cloth for gardening, so the weeds wouldn't grow up through the rocks. We got it all covered and began piling the rocks on the little hill and around the pond, to hide the liner.

"Wow!" Thunderfoot said. "We're gonna need a lot more rocks."

"No kidding. This isn't going to make a drop in the bucket. Aren't you glad we made the little hill so large now?"

"Oh, gripe, gripe, gripe," Thunderfoot said, grinning.

It took two more trips with the trailer to get enough rocks to cover the hill. While we were unloading the last load, my friend and his wife pulled into the driveway, and said that he needed his pickup, and that I should just pull the trailer back to the farm with mine. I thanked him for everything. We unhooked the trailer and he left.

When the last rocks were unloaded, we stepped back to admire our work. "Boy, that does look good," I said.

"Umm, see? What did I tell you? Now in the evening, you can come out here with a book and a beverage and sit and listen to the water cascade down the rocks and splash into the pond."

"And swat mosquitoes until I'm exhausted."

His face brightened. "Maybe we should build a little screened in house out here."

"I think we've done all the building we're going to do for a long while."

I had lifted enough rocks to last a lifetime. My back was sore, my hands were bruised and scraped, and my old body needed a shower and a rest. I insisted that we quit for the day.

The next morning, I heard water running and I went out to the garden to see Thunderfoot with the hose, filling the pond.

"We'll get it full, and then see how the pump works," he said with one of his big grins. We had hidden a length of hose under the rocks from the submerged pump to the top of our little hill, and placed three large, flat rocks as steps for the water from the pump to flow over, back into the pond, like a little waterfall.

Soon Thunderfoot was pestering me back inside the house to come and look. He had the pond filled and the pump turned on, and it was working like a charm.

"Not bad if I say so myself," he said proudly.

I had to admit – it was nice. We buried the electrical wire from the house to the pump and tidied up the rest of the area.

"Well, let's take the trailer and the cement mixer back and then get some bluegills for the pond," Thunderfoot said. "I'll drive the truck around and hook up."

A few minutes later he was honking the horn and I went around back to help him take the trailer back to my friend's farm. I decided to drive, since I wasn't real comfortable with him pulling the trailer. We had only gone two blocks, when we came to an intersection with a little dip in it. As we went through the dip, I suddenly heard a horrible screeching sound. I slammed on the brakes and looked in the side mirror. The trailer had come off the ball hitch and was passing us on the left side, streaking down the street all by itself. The tongue had dropped to the road and was making the screeching noise as it slid along. It passed us, then veered off to the left, plowed a furrow into my neighbor's yard, continued across the yard, and slammed into the side of his garage.

"Holy smokes!" Thunderfoot yelled. "It came off!"

By then I had the truck stopped and was surveying the mess we had made in the neighbor's yard.

"Didn't you hook it down?" I asked.

"Yeah. I had it real tight."

My neighbor had come out of his house and was walking

toward the trailer. "It's a good thing my garage was here, or you might have lost your trailer," he said.

"Jeez, I'm so sorry. I thought it was fastened down," I said.

"Don't worry about it," he said. "Nothing that a little paint and a couple of pieces of siding won't fix."

Well, at least he wasn't nasty about it. We pushed the trailer back to the road and set the hitch on the ball of the truck. Then I realized what the problem was: my truck had a one and seven-eighths inch ball, and the trailer had a two-inch coupler. "Didn't you see that this was the wrong size?"

"I didn't think an eighth of an inch would matter."

We rigged the hitch with a chain wrapped around the whole thing to keep it from popping off again, and then continued on to the farm… very slowly. We dropped off the trailer and thanked my friend for it and the rocks, and then drove back home.

I backed up my truck to the cement mixer. We put down the tailgate, laid some planks on it, and then slid the mixer up into the box of the truck.

"I think we should lay it down on its side," I said. "Your grandpa brought it here laying down."

"It's real sturdy," Thunderfoot assured. "I don't think it'll tip. Grandpa is just an old, cautious guy."

I was too tired to argue, so we slid it up to the front and started off to Grandpa's.

I drove slowly across the grass. At the edge of the driveway there was a little bump where my yard and the pavement met. As I drove onto the pavement, I looked in the rear view mirror to see how the cement mixer was riding, and just at that very moment, it tipped over and came crashing through the back window of the truck. In one second – BANG! – the rear window turned from one clear pane of glass to about ten thousand little chunks.

"Holy cow!" Thunderfoot cried as he put his hands over his head and ducked. The inside of the cab was covered with bits of glass that looked like thousands of ice chips.

I stopped and stared at my astonished passenger. "Grandpa's just a cautious old guy."

"He is!"

"Do you suppose he was cautious because he thought it might tip over?"

"Well, possibly."

I shook my head.

He picked up a handful of glass chips and let them trickle from his hand. "Well, you know, you've been talking about getting one those sliding glass windows for a long time. I guess now is the time."

We both started to chuckle.

"I knew we made it through this project too easy," I said.

"Yeah," he said laughing. "*Something* had to happen."

We brushed the glass off the seat onto the floor and took off down the street. "By the time I buy paint, siding for the neighbor's garage, and a new window, I think we could have hired somebody to do this and had a lot of money left over."

He nodded. "You're probably right, but just think of the bonding we've done with this. And besides, that cool breeze feels pretty nice coming through the hole in the back of the truck. Someday we'll think back and laugh about this." I glanced over at him and we both cracked up laughing. No time like the present.

Thanks, Thunderfoot.

Little Shop of Horrors

During the summer, the river became low enough that taking a boat and motor on it for fishing was more trouble than it was worth. The Wisconsin has dozens of hydroelectric dams along its length and they all hold back water to generate power. The last dam is many miles above our town, so in the summer when thousands of air conditioners are running, there isn't much water being allowed to flow down to the lower parts of the river. Consequently, sandbars begin to show and soon there is as much surface area that is sand as there is water surface. No matter how small your boat, you spend as much time pushing it across sandbars and shallow water as you do actually driving it or fishing from it.

So when the river gets low, the fishing gets more difficult because it's so hard to get to the good places to fish, but while it's hard to get around, the shallow water concentrates the fish, so when you find a fish, he usually has many friends with him.

These were the conditions that we faced as Thunderfoot and I set out with one of the canoes to spend a day fishing for small mouth bass. The canoe would still float over pretty shallow water, and was much easier to push if we did come to some places that were too shallow to paddle. The only problem with a canoe was the size of the thing. We usually took enough tackle and poles to outfit a small hardware store, but we had to scale back our selection because there just wasn't enough room to put a lot of gear. And, of course, a canoe is a tippy craft, and we had, a time or two, dumped the whole thing over into the river, and we didn't want hundreds of dollars worth of tackle to end up on the bottom.

When the water was warm, as it was at this time of year, the bass would congregate along steep banks with trees hanging over the water, and where there were brush piles and log jams. We often found bass and walleyes congregated below sandbars, feeding on minnows in the deeper water.

In the summer, Thunderfoot and I always looked forward to a day of canoeing and fishing for bass with fly rods, and today was the day. We left Thunderfoot's mom's car at the boat landing at home, and then hauled the canoe, two fly rods, and a couple dozen poppers and streamers upriver about fifteen miles. Of course, we had lunch, pop and cold water along so we could spend the whole day on the river.

"Look down there. See that island?" Thunderfoot said, pointing at an island a short ways ahead. "Lots of trees hanging over… should be a bass paradise."

We paddled toward the island and positioned the canoe just out far enough that an easy cast with our fly rods would place our poppers right next to the trees. My popper had hardly gotten wet when the water exploded and a nice small mouth engulfed it and bulldogged toward the treetops. "Whoa! Come back here!" I yelled. Just then Thunderfoot had a smashing hit on his popper, and he was fighting the twin of my fish.

"Jeez, I wonder what the poor people are doing today?" he said as he turned and grinned at me while stripping in his line. His fish jumped and threw the hook. "Dang. Got away." He made a false cast and then settled his popper back amongst the treetops. He had another fish on the hook before I had gotten mine to the boat.

"This is the day," I said.

"No kidding. Three casts, three fish on," he said with a huge grin.

It surely was the day. We fished our way down the river and caught bass after bass. We stopped at a few good sandbars and caught more bass and some real nice walleyes, too, using streamers that looked like minnows. "This is the way fishing is suppose to be," Thunderfoot beamed.

It was truly a great day of fishing, but costly. When you're drifting with the current, you have little time to cast, so your cast must be perfect. If you're off just a little, you usually don't have time to get your popper back from the treetops before the canoe has gone past and your popper is a goner. The current is swift, so paddling back upriver to retrieve the popper is almost impossible. The consequences are that you go through a lot of poppers in one day.

We had lost a couple dozen of them and were down to the last few as we brought the canoe in at the boat landing. "Whew. I thought we were gonna be out of baits before we got home," Thunderfoot said.

"It was close," I replied.

We took his mom's car back upriver, retrieved the truck, came back to the landing, loaded up the canoe and went home.

"You know, I think I could make some poppers for us to use," he said.

"They're not that expensive," I reminded him.

"Yeah, I know. But it'd be fun to make something that we could catch fish on." Well, that did sound okay. But I didn't think he'd pursue it, so I just forgot about it.

The next day, Thunderfoot came over to the shop and asked if he could take a box of hooks home and try making some poppers with them. "I have a fly tying kit that I got for my birthday a few years ago, and I think I can make us some good poppers."

"Go ahead. Take what you need," I told him.

The subject didn't come up for a while, and about a week later he called me. "Hey, come over and see what I've got ready for the bass." I walked over to his house and his mom said he was in the basement. "Go on down," she said. "He's in the closet."

"The closet?"

She just shook her head.

I went down the stairs and walked across the basement to the door of a little closet that was against the back wall, next to the laundry room. The door was closed, so I tapped on it.

The door opened and there sat Thunderfoot on a little stool.

It looked like the workroom of a voodoo witch doctor. Squirrel tails, chicken skins, pheasant tails, rabbit fur, and the skins and feathers of other critters that I didn't want to know about were tacked to the back of the door and the walls. Thunderfoot sat at a little workbench that he had built against the wall, with a fly tying vise mounted on it and a bare light bulb suspended above the work area. He was tying a popper. "Hey, come on in," he said cheerfully.

"Come in? Where would I come in? There's no room in there."

"Oh, yea. Well, what do you think of my little fly making shop?"

"Where did you get all these dead animals?"

"Oh, around. I just keep an eye out for stuff that looks like it would make a good popper. I found this pheasant run over out near the bridge, and this was off a chicken that my grandpa butchered. This is a squirrel tail that I found on the street – he must have been out practicing dodging cars and didn't dodge when he should have. And this..."

"Never mind. I get the picture," I said. "Why are you sitting in this closet?"

"Mom is acting like a girl about all this stuff, so I had to put it in here where she couldn't see it."

I could understand that.

He showed me the poppers that he had made, and some of them were pretty impressive. "Boy, this one looks great," I said, peering at one that was a good imitation of a small frog.

"That's my favorite," he said. "I'm trying to find something to make an imitation of those silver minnows in the river. I'd like to make one that looks like it's crippled and flipping around on the top of the water, but I haven't found the right stuff yet."

"That would be a good bait. There's lots of them on the river, and the bass love 'em."

I scanned over his creations a while longer, and then left him to his little room and went home. The next day, I had to meet the guy who prepared my taxes, so I called Thunderfoot and had him watch the shop for a while. When I returned, he was in a big hurry to get back to his popper business, and took off for home. That evening, I was getting the dog's supper ready when I noticed that the long silver hairs on Kirby's tail looked different. His tail usually had long, whitish hairs mixed with the blonde of his golden retriever hair, but most of the white hairs were gone. "Kirby, are you shedding already?" I asked. Kirby looked at me, without a clue as to what I was saying, but he wagged his less hairy tail enthusiastically anyway.

"I got enough poppers for another fishing trip," Thunderfoot said as he walked through the door later that evening.

"How about tomorrow," I said. It didn't take much coaxing to get me on the river when the fish were biting.

The next day we went through the same procedure with his mom's car, and soon we were coming up along the first island where we were going to fish. "Flip your line up here," he said from the front of the canoe, "and I'll tie on a popper for you." I did, and he tied on a popper just as we came up to the island. I didn't even look at the bait, but as he dropped it over the side of the canoe, I took up the slack, flipped it back and forth a couple of times, and then dropped it between two trees next to the island. Just like it was planned, a small mouth bass slammed the popper and the fight was on.

"Hey! That popper works great," I said. Thunderfoot just beamed. He cast his popper and soon we were both battling fish. I worked my fish in next to the canoe and lipped it. I took the hook out and slid the fish back into the water. Then I took a good look at the popper. It was a pretty nice bait. He had carved a piece of cork to make the dished face of the popper and then fit it on the long shank of the hook. Then he had tied some short white feathers – probably from grandpa's chicken – and then some long white hairs behind the feathers made it look like a small minnow. The head was painted white with big red eyes. "Looks like a professional job," I said.

He was proud as could be. "See? You made fun of my fly

shop, but I did pretty good, huh?"

"Yeah, you did," I said.

We began fishing again, and then something occurred to me. I reeled in my popper and studied it some more. "Where did you get this long white hair?"

He glanced over his shoulder and grinned. "Recognize it?"

"Kirby?"

He grinned again. "Yup, and do you know what I named this popper?"

"What?"

"The Kirbinator."

Thanks, Thunderfoot.

A Foot at a Time

"Wait a second. I'm gonna throw my shoes in the truck first," I said to Thunderfoot. We were getting ready to carry my johnboat down over the bank to one of our favorite lakes to fish for bass and northern pike. Thunderfoot was already barefoot and waiting by the back of the truck.

"You'd better roll up the windows a little, too," he said. "It looks like it might rain."

I took off my tennis shoes, threw them in on the truck seat, and rolled up the driver's side window. I walked around to the other side and rolled up Thunderfoot's window, too.

He pulled on the boat, sliding it out of the pickup box, and stopped just before the boat was free of the truck. I grabbed the other end and we started for the lake. It was a short carry – just down over the bank on a path that was plenty wide for the boat.

Our river bottoms craft was a fourteen foot johnboat, that was pretty light, and easy to carry. I had acquired it a few years earlier, when I happened onto a boat rental place that was going out of business. They were selling several of these narrow, lightweight johnboats real cheap, just to get rid of them. They had been rented to campers over the years, and had a lot of holes from being dragged over a blacktop parking lot to the lake. This one was one of the last to sell, and it had almost as much fiberglass patchwork as it had aluminum. "I'll let you have it for $35," the man had said. How could I pass up a deal like that? So I bought it and took it home.

The fiberglass patches worked loose every once in a while, so every few weeks, Thunderfoot and I would put it out in the yard upside down on a pair of sawhorses, and he would crawl under and look for light coming through a hole in the bottom. I'd stay on top and patch the holes with fiberglass until we had them all filled. After a few weeks of fishing, it would be leaking pretty badly again, and it would be time to repeat the process. It seemed that we never got *all* the leaks stopped, so we usually just went barefoot when we used the boat, and kept a coffee can in it to bail out the water. It wasn't much of a boat, but it was light, easy to carry... and cheap. There was no doubt that I had surely gotten my money's worth in return.

We put the boat into the lake and began fishing. It was an overcast day, and a storm was brewing in the west. It was just the best kind of day for catching northern pike and bass – hot, humid and ready to storm.

"We should have some great luck today," Thunderfoot said as he tossed a spinner bait next to the weeds. I didn't even have time to reply when he reared back and set the hook into a nice northern. He turned and grinned. "First cast!"

We cast the area, and then moved the boat down the lake a short ways and began working over another spot. I had a moss boss on one of my poles. I threw it into some heavy lily pads and began crawling it across the top, trying to make a bass think it was a frog or mouse working its way across the top of the vegetation. A moss boss is a lure that is shaped like a hard boiled egg that has been cut in half lengthwise and hollowed out. It has one big hook on the larger end, and because of its shape, it always falls with the hook up when it lands on the water or grass. Then you can move it slowly across the top of the grass, where you hope a big bass is hiding.

I moved the bait a little and let it rest. Then I twitched it again and saw some lily pads move about three feet away from my lure. "Uh, oh. Somebody's interested," I said. Thunderfoot turned to look just as the lilies exploded and a huge largemouth bass devoured my moss boss. I set the hook when I felt him pull the bait as he burrowed into the weeds, and I began trying to get him up and on top of the vegetation. The fish was much too heavy to slide up onto the weeds, and he fought for the bottom like a bulldog.

"Paddle us over there!" I said to Thunderfoot. I kept the pole up and the line tight as he moved us closer. When we were next to the mess of tangled weeds and lilies, I raised the rod as much as I dared, and I could see the fish in the middle of a big gob of weeds. I reached over the side and felt around for his jaw, found it, and lifted the bass and about twenty pounds of grass into the boat.

"Holy cow! That's a monster," Thunderfoot said.

I pulled the grass and lily pads off the line and threw them back over the side. I still had the bass by the jaw, and it truly was a trophy. "Wow! He must be eight or nine pounds," I said. It was huge – probably the largest bass I'd ever caught.

"I don't suppose we have a ruler or a scale," I said.

Thunderfoot shrugged his shoulders. "Nope, just our waterproof tackle box and a few lures."

Our waterproof tackle box was a plastic ice cream bucket, and it contained a pair of pliers, five or six spinner baits, a couple of moss bosses, a plastic frog, and a couple of daredevil spoons. We traveled light when we used the johnboat, and because it leaked, we just used the bucket instead of a real tackle box.

I laid the bass on the canoe paddle that was in my end of the boat and removed the hook from its mouth. Then I smoothed the fish out and made a scratch in the paddle handle with the point of the hook where the fish's tail ended. "We can measure the length when we get home, at least." Then I lifted the fish over the side of the boat, held it's mouth open and slid it back and forth in the water to get some oxygen into its blood stream, and when it began to struggle, I let it go and watched it slide down into the weeds. "That old girl has been here for a long time," I said. "I'm not going to be the one to end her life."

Thunderfoot nodded his approval.

We went back to the middle of the area we were fishing and began casting again. I cleaned up all the weeds and bits of lily pad that had littered my end of the boat, and then tossed my moss boss out into another tangle of weeds. I began crawling it along and almost instantly there was another huge explosion next to it, and a second huge bass pounced on it. "Jeez! I got another one!" I yelled.

Thunderfoot turned toward me. "Cripes. That's being a little piggish, isn't it?"

I fought the fish while Thunderfoot moved us over to it. I landed a bass that was a twin to the other, if not a little bigger. Again, I laid it on the paddle and measured. It was about two inches longer than the first one. "I'll bet this one is near ten pounds," I said.

"You got more luck than sense," Thunderfoot grumbled. I released the fish and cleaned up the boat again, and noticed that Thunderfoot was digging in the lure bucket.

"Switching to a moss boss?"

"Switching to a moss boss?" he mocked. "Yes, I'm switching to a moss boss, not that it's any of your business."

"Jeez. Touchy. Just because I'm the champeene bass master here, you don't have to get surly."

He looked up and grinned. "We're not done yet."

We moved the boat again and started casting. Thunderfoot was working his moss boss through a lily pad bed and I had switched to a spoon. Suddenly Thunderfoot whispered, "Look! The pads are moving. Here he comes."

I turned to look and I could see that a huge fish was swimming under the pads right toward his moss boss. He twitched the bait across a couple of lilies and just as the bait came to a little opening in the vegetation, the water boiled, and a beaver popped up through the hole in the weeds, with Thunderfoot's moss boss resting on top of its head. "Holy smokes! Look at that!" he said.

"Jeez! Don't set the hook into that thing!"

Thunderfoot didn't move a muscle while the beaver just looked around a little, and then like a ghost, he slipped below the water again, and the moss boss just slid off its head onto a lily. Thunderfoot turned and stared at me. "If I'da caught that thing, you would have had to take it off for me." We had a good laugh over that one.

We fished a couple more hours, paddled back to the shore, carried the boat up and slid it into the back of the pickup. When we opened the doors, the truck cab was like an oven, and it smelled like something in there was dead.

"Holy cow! What stinks in here?" Thunderfoot picked up my old tennies. "Cripes. These things are like toxic waste."

"Oh, come on. They're not that bad," I said.

"Oh no? Take a whiff."

Well, I had to admit that the shoes were a little aromatic, but not as bad as toxic waste.

"How long have you had these old things?"

"I don't know... seven or eight years, I guess."

"Jeez. Don't you think it's time to get some new ones? Look at them. They're full of holes, dirty like crazy, and they smell like last week's fish cleaning leftovers."

"But, they're comfortable," I said.

He shook his head. "You need new ones... *real soon.*"

All the way home he kept at me about the shoes. "Why don't you get some like mine?"

"Those fancy things? No way. They're too fancy for me, and besides, they probably cost a fortune."

"Well, next time we go shopping, I think we should look at shoes."

A few days later, we happened to be passing by a clothing store that sold shoes, too. "Let's stop and get you some new shoes, and then take those old stinky ones out and bury them."

I relented, and we stopped at the store. Thunderfoot started right in showing me all kinds of shoes with air pockets – so I could jump higher – and lights that flashed when you walked, and a lot of other ridiculous novelties. I found a pair that was a little more conservative… that I liked.

"Those are too plain," Thunderfoot said.

"Plain is just fine for me, and the price is about one forth of those things you've got." I tried one on, and it felt good, so I bought them.

The following weekend, there was a sport show a few towns away that we decided to attend. It was one of those places where vendors from lots of stores and companies try to convince you to buy their products. We strolled around, and took in all the new and wonderful things that were offered.

"Boy. These new shoes sure aren't as comfortable as my old ones," I complained.

"They gotta be broken in," Thunderfoot said. "Just wear them a while, and you'll see."

We browsed a while longer but I finally had to quit. My right foot was hurting so badly from the new shoes that I could hardly walk any more. "Man. The left one is fine, but the right one is killing me," I said.

We left the show, stopped for some lunch, and then went home. I was glad to get the shoes off and let my poor right foot rest for a while.

The next day, the weather was rainy and stormy, so we decided to go see a movie we had been waiting to see instead of fishing.

When I picked up Thunderfoot, he came from the house playing with a yoyo. "Where'd you get that thing?" I asked.

"I've had it a while… I just found it under my bed. I can do some pretty good tricks with it, too."

We arrived at the movie theater and I figured everyone else must have had the same idea. The parking lot was packed, and we had to park at the far end. "Jeez. A full house," I commented.

While we walked across the lot toward the theater, Thunderfoot was showing me some of his tricks. "This is rock the baby," he said as he made a triangle with the string around his fingers and then rocked the wooden yoyo back and forth.

Then he dropped it and let it spin at the end of the string, and then he gave a little twitch it and it climbed up the string again. He had a couple more tricks to show me as we walked. "This is 'Around the World,' he said, and I turned to look when a dull thump sounded in my inner ear and the top of my head felt like I had been hit with a ball bat. I saw stars, but I managed to stagger to the retaining wall of a planter that was filled with geraniums and sat down on the edge. I still didn't know what had happened, but I thought that maybe I'd had a stroke.

Thunderfoot was standing there with his mouth hanging open. "Are you okay?" he asked.

I shook my head. "I don't know what's wrong with me."

He kind of grimaced. "I think my yoyo hit you on top of the head when I did 'Around the World'."

I reached up and felt the top of my head. There was a knot about the size of a hickory nut right on the top. "Youch. I guess you're right."

"Boy, I'm real sorry," he apologized.

"Okay. I know you didn't do it on purpose, but if you've got any more tricks, let me get a little farther away."

He grinned. "It's a good thing you got such a hard head."

We went into the theater, and about half way through the movie, my right foot was hurting so badly that I had to take off the shoe. "I can't believe how that thing hurts," I whispered to Thunderfoot.

"Are you sure you got two shoes the same size?" he whispered back.

"Hmm, I never thought of that. I'll check when the movie's over."

I put the shoe back on as the movie finished and limped out into the parking lot. I sat down, took off the right shoe, and Thunderfoot looked at the number printed on the inside of the tongue. "Yeah, it's the same size," he said. He was just about to hand the shoe to me when he stopped and began laughing. "What an idiot!" he cried, and laughed some more.

"What?"

He was laughing like crazy as he stuck his hand into the shoe and pulled a wad of tissue paper out. "You didn't take the paper out of the toe. Holy cow! All that griping and you didn't take the paper out."

I stared at the wad of paper. "Well, there wasn't any paper in the other shoe. How come there was in this one?"

"The guy at the store took it out before you tried it on. Didn't you see that?"

Well, no, I guess I had missed that. And why do they need tissue paper in the shoes anyway? What a waste. I put the shoe back on and it felt great.

"How's it feel now?" Thunderfoot laughed.

"Lot's better."

He cackled all the way home about the tissue paper until I dropped him off at his house. "Well, thanks for the fun time. And if you need any help to get dressed or to get your shoes on, just call. I'll run right over."

I just didn't have any smart answer. I guess I had learned a lesson, but if these shoes lasted as long as the old ones, I'd forget about it by the time I bought a new pair anyway.

Thanks, Thunderfoot.

The Things We'll Do for a Duck

The days were growing shorter and cooler – the early duck season was only a couple of weeks away.

"You know, we'd better get working on the duck blinds," Thunderfoot suggested.

"Yeah, I guess so. It'll be Duck Eve sooner than we think," I said. Duck Eve was a big day for us. The season opened at noon, and it was our tradition to go the day before to set up camp on the high bank above the duck marsh, and then spend the evening camping while we waited for the opening hour. It was great fun for us, and for Katy, my golden retriever.

We had two blinds built on the marsh. Each year we went to the river bottoms and cut saw grass, wove it into mats, and then fastened them to the chicken wire around the outside of the blinds. The blinds made us invisible to the ducks – or, at least close enough for them to be lured to our decoys so we could shoot at them.

We usually spent one evening cutting a pickup load of grass, and then another two or three evenings weaving it into three mats – one for each blind, and one for the boat house that hid the canoe in the tall grass below the big blind. It was a lot of work, but when we were finished, we had some dandy blinds that would last all season.

"Well, let's go cut grass this evening and then we can work on the mats as we have time," I said.

Thunderfoot agreed, and late that afternoon we drove down to the river bottoms, and wearing our hip boots, we cut bundles of tall grass with big pruning shears, stacking them in the back of the truck. One of us would gather up a big double handful of grass, and the other would cut it off just above the waterline. When we had a good pile made, the holder would pick it all up and carry it to the truck. We'd take turns cutting and bundling. That gave one of us a little rest between trips to the truck.

"This is some good grass," Thunderfoot said.

"Yeah, it's nice and thick this year... and tall. This'll make a good blind," I replied.

Just then Thunderfoot gazed over my shoulder toward the pond. "Look, a loner! Two of them!"

I turned to see two wood ducks as they glided down and lit on the water. I bent over to cut the grass Thunderfoot was holding, and then the thought hit me, and I laughed. "Two loners?"

Thunderfoot started laughing, too. "Two loners. Yeah. That's sort of like a pair, I guess." We cackled about that for a while.

When the sun had set, we decided that we had enough grass, so we packed up and headed for home.

We parked the pickup in the back yard and left it for the night. During the next three days, we wove three large mats, and rolled them up so they looked like big green corn shocks.

"We can haul them down tomorrow evening, do a little repair and get at least one blind finished," I said, "and then do the other one the next night."

"Sounds good to me."

The next evening we loaded a couple of hammers, a saw, a few pieces of scrap lumber, and the grass mats into the pickup and drove down to the marsh. While we were getting ready, Katy, my golden retriever, was galloping around, begging to go along.

"Kate wants to go. Can we take her?" Thunderfoot asked.

"I guess so," I said. "She knows it's getting close to duck season and she probably thinks we're gonna hunt. She loves exploring the marsh, so load her up."

"How about Kirby?"

"Well, the part of him that's golden retriever isn't much into hunting," I said. "And I think the collie part of him likes napping better than hunting." I called to the dog, "Kirby! D'ya wanna go?" Kirby just looked up from his shady spot, rolled over and closed his eyes.

"I think he'd rather nap," Thunderfoot said.

So, off we went to the marsh, with Katy sitting in the front seat between us, panting and slobbering like a fountain. When I had parked by the marsh, we decided to take the tools, lumber and one roll of grass out to the blind. We could come back for the others.

I hefted the roll up onto my shoulder, and Thunderfoot hauled the rest of the stuff through the marsh to the blind. The first trips out each year were hard going. The grass was almost head high, and there weren't any paths to follow, so the lead person had to forge a new trail. I was, of course, that lead person. By the time we had gone the hundred yards from the high bank to the blind, I was pooped.

"Holy cow. I think I'm gonna have the big one," I panted. Thunderfoot was huffing and puffing, too, and we both stood there a few minutes to catch our breath. "Let's see how many repairs we have to make before we haul all the grass out," I said.

With the lumber and tools we walked out onto the narrow bridge we had built from the hard ground to the blind. We stopped to nail down a few loose boards, and proceeded the rest of the way.

The blind was merely an open box on posts, with the plywood floor about a foot higher than the water. The sides were just chicken wire stretched over a frame. There was a small hole for Katy in front so she could see the pond, and where the ducks fell when we shot them. We had built a little ramp for her to get out of the blind and into the pond.

On the bridge side of the blind, a little landing was just above our boat hide. We had driven three posts into the marsh about four feet apart in a straight line, and attached a three-foot by twelve-foot cattle panel to the tops of the posts. The result was a hinged trap door covered with wire. We could pull the canoe right up to the landing on the blind, climb out onto the landing, and then lay down the trap door covered with one of the grass mats to camouflage the canoe. It was a slick set up.

I had run across an old bus seat at a garage sale several years earlier. It was just the right height and quite comfortable to sit on while waiting for ducks. So when we built the blind, we included the bus seat.

"I'm gonna rest for a minute," I said. I opened the door of the blind and sat down on the bus seat. Thunderfoot was busy driving nails into loose boards, and Katy was exploring the marsh. It felt good to sit for a few minutes. The duck blind was one of my favorite places in the whole world. I had probably sat there for hundreds of hours, and enjoyed every minute of it, whether it had been during the hot, early season when we took off our boots and sat barefoot and in tee shirts, or during the late season when we wore so many clothes we could hardly move. It was just a special place for me.

I was sitting there enjoying myself when I heard a far off hum. I listened for a few moments and was trying to determine what was making the noise. It sounded like a far away chain saw, or it was possibly one of those three-wheeled trail bikes. "What's that noise?" I said to Thunderfoot.

Thunderfoot stopped his hammering and listened. "I don't know for sure... it sounds like it's getting louder... Holy Cow! It's bees!"

Just when he said that, I saw the first bee land on my arm. Then there was another, and then about ten more, and suddenly the air was full of bees. I jumped up and ran for the door. Thunderfoot cleared the end of the bridge and disappeared into the tall grass just as I started across the bridge. I was heading for the hard ground, but the bees caught up to me – hundreds of them, swarming around me and landing on me and stinging me. I tried to swat them away as I ran down the narrow bridge, but I had only gone a few feet when I accidentally stepped off the edge and fell into the marsh. It didn't take long for the bees to find me again, as I went slogging through the mud and water as fast as I could go, heading for the tall grass.

I made it onto the hard ground and ran as fast as I could for the high bank. The bees followed me for a ways, and then left and went back to their nest, which was most likely under the bus seat in the blind. Finally, I could stop, and I nearly collapsed from exhaustion.

"Are they gone?"

I looked around for Thunderfoot, but I couldn't see him. "Where are you?"

"Down here."

I saw his hand come up from the grass a few feet away. "Yeah, they're gone. You can come out now," I said.

He slowly rose up from the grass and looked out over the marsh. "Jeez! That was a lot of angry bees. Did you get stung?"

"Yeah, I got stung," I growled. "What did you think they'd do? Just escort me to land?"

He started to laugh. "I'm sorry. It was pretty funny though. Wow! You've got a bunch of red welts on your face and arms."

"Yeah, I was lucky," I said. "I fell in the water. That probably saved me from a lot more stings."

He laughed again. "For once, being clumsy paid off." We both had a good laugh over that.

"Well, we're gonna leave this blind until it cools off... so those bees are a little slower."

"Yeah," Thunderfoot said, "and we can spray them, but I think I'll do the spraying. I can run just a little faster than you can."

I certainly wasn't going to argue with that.

"Hey, where's Kate?" he asked.

"Katy?"

"Katy?" She didn't seem to be anywhere around.

"Let's go back to the truck and blow the horn. She'll hear that and come," I said. I figured she was exploring the marsh and had just wandered off. We walked our new path back to the truck and there was Katy, sitting in the seat. She had apparently decided to make a hasty retreat when the bees came after me, and must have jumped in through the open window.

"And who says a dog is a dumb animal," Thunderfoot remarked. Then he turned to me and said, "Well, you better sit in the back of the truck. You're all covered with mud." That was nothing new to me. I'd ridden home in the back many times. In fact, I was getting pretty used to it.

When we got home, Thunderfoot took delight in making a careful count of all seventeen bee stings, and then helped me put some ointment on the stings that was supposed to make them feel better. "Well, that was fun," I said.

"Yeah," he laughed. "Oh, by the way... when we go to the other blind tomorrow, I'll go first."

"I was just about to suggest the exact same thing." I said.

Thanks, Thunderfoot.

Robin Hood I'm Not

"Why don't you camouflage that old bow of yours and go hunting with me this fall." Thunderfoot said.

"Oh, I don't know. I like shooting the bow but I guess I've never thought much about hunting with it. For one thing, you have to go up in trees, and that's not one of my most favorite things to do."

"You don't have to hunt from a tree. You can just stand on the ground if you want to. Or, we can make you a nice tree blind and even put a ladder up for you. Come on. Why don't you give it a try? It's lots of fun."

"Well, I guess I *might* try it... if we have a nice, safe place for me to hunt from. But I'm not climbing up on some tree spikes. I want a *real* ladder!"

"Yes, oh mighty hunter. We'll make you a ladder, all nice and safe," he said grinning like a fool.

The season wouldn't open for another two weeks, so I dusted off my old bow, fixed up some arrows, and we practiced every evening after the sun was low in the sky and the temperature a little more comfortable. Thunderfoot was a real good shot with his bow, and after a week or so of practicing, I was beginning to catch up with him. I could put my arrows into a spot about the size of the bottom of a pop can almost every time, so I thought I probably could hit a deer where I wanted to when the time came.

We went to our deer hunting spot, looking for signs and a place to build a tree house for me. We were following a well-worn trail when Thunderfoot stopped and pointed to the top of the hill. "Look at that big oak. We could build a whole house up there for you."

I liked what I saw. The oak was huge – probably six or seven feet around. The branches were wide and many of them stretched out from the main trunk at an almost horizontal plane.

The first big horizontal branches were about ten or twelve feet off the ground, so I wouldn't have to climb up real high, and to me, that was a good thing.

We went to the tree and looked it over. "This'll make a good spot," Thunderfoot said.

"Yeah, I like it," I replied. "I don't have to go up very far, and there's a lot of open pasture here for shooting. Plus it's right here by that good deer trail." I was starting to like this archery hunting more and more.

The next day we nailed cross pieces every foot and a half between a couple of ten-foot two-by-fours to make a good, sturdy ladder. Then we lugged the ladder and as many planks and two-bys as we could carry up to the hill to the big oak tree.

"I'll go up and do some measuring and you hand the stuff up to me," Thunderfoot said. He stood the ladder up against the tree and climbed up onto the first large horizontal branch. He measured over to the next branch and then gave me the measurement. I cut off a piece of two by four and handed it up to him. He already had a pocket full of nails and a hammer tucked into his belt, so he nailed it down in place between the two large branches. Then he gave me more measurements, and soon we had a real nice, sturdy platform in the tree for me to hunt from.

"Come on up and give it a try," Thunderfoot said.

"It looks fine," I said. "I'll try it Saturday when I come up to hunt. Let's go. The mosquitoes are getting terrible." It was just dusk and the mosquitoes were swarming around us.

"Okay, suit yourself," he said.

We left the ladder standing by the tree and went home. The next evening, we took Thunderfoot's tree stand up to his spot on the opposite hill. He had hunted from there the previous year and it was a place he liked, so he knew just where he wanted to go. His tree stand was one of those that you had to hang on the side of the tree. As he climbed up, he screwed S shaped climbing steps into the tree. Once he had all of his steps in place, he climbed up the tree again, this time carrying his tree stand on his back with a strap. Up in the tree, he screwed in another T shaped spike, and then hung his stand on it. Then he wrapped a strap around the tree and stepped onto the stand.

"Boy. You're braver than I am," I said.

"I'm lots lighter too," he said, grinning.

He stood there surveying his area, reached out and broke off a couple of branches that were in his way, and then climbed down. "There, we're all set."

I kept the shop open during the day Saturday, and we even had some late season people who wanted to canoe the river, so we couldn't go bow hunting until evening. We packed up our gear and drove to the woods. Thunderfoot walked up the valley with me a short ways, and then started up the hill to his stand.

"Remember… quitting time is at five minutes to seven," he said quietly.

"Yeah, I know. Good luck."

"You too."

I went a little farther and then worked my way up the hill on the opposite side of the valley. In a short while, I was on top of the hill and at my tree. At Thunderfoot's suggestion I had two pieces of light rope with me. One was for tying onto my bow so I could pull it up into the tree after I was in my stand. It was dangerous trying to climb with a bow in your hand, and I wanted to be as safe as possible. The other piece of rope was for my ladder. I intended to pull it up into the tree with me, so the deer wouldn't see it and wonder what it was doing there. I wasn't sure that this was necessary, but I wanted to be as inconspicuous as I could be.

I climbed the ladder and right away I wished that we had put the rungs a little closer together. It was a long step between them – almost too far – but I managed to get up into the tree. The platform that Thunderfoot had built was dandy. There was plenty of room for me to sit or stand, and it was quite sturdy. I pulled my bow up, laid it on the platform, and then pulled up the ladder and laid it across two branches on the backside of the tree where it was out of the way.

I nocked an arrow onto the bowstring and sat down to wait. It was nearly an hour and a half until shooting time was over, so I relaxed and leaned back against the tree. Suddenly I felt like I was falling, and I looked around. I had most likely dozed off, and when I began tipping, I thankfully caught myself before I fell out of the tree and broke my fool neck. "I'd better stand up," I said to myself.

I stood and looked around the pasture near the tree. It was obvious that many deer had passed here in the past few weeks, as there were trails all over the hill, and droppings everywhere.

I caught a movement in the corner of my eye as a doe and a couple of fawns stepped into the clearing from the woods. They stopped, and the doe looked over the hilltop, and then they began walking to the middle of the hill, right toward my stand.

My heart pumped faster as they closed in, but I didn't raise my bow. I had already decided that if I were to shoot a deer, it would be a buck. And, watching the little family below made that decision even easier. The doe and fawns were just too cute and pretty for me to drive an arrow into them. I guess I was getting soft in my old age, and the killer instinct in me was getting less each time I went hunting.

I watched the three deer for almost half an hour, and then they disappeared into the woods on the opposite side of the clearing. Then a possum ambled down the trail below me, and he fooled around by an old stump for a while, giving me another fifteen minutes of entertainment. Movement caught my eye again as a hen turkey and nine chicks crossed the pasture about twenty yards down the ridge from me. A few minutes after that, a small, fork horn buck appeared at the edge of the pasture. I considered trying for him, but he made up my mind for me by turning and trotting off in the opposite direction.

Dusk was closing in now, so I checked my watch and found it was time to quit. Even if I hadn't fired a single shot at a deer, I had seen lots of cool stuff. I removed the arrow from the string, put it back into the quiver, and then tied the rope onto the bow and lowered it to the ground. Then I lowered the ladder down with its rope. When the ladder reached the ground beside the tree, it tipped over. Luckily, I still had hold of the rope, so I righted it and tried to set it in a flatter spot. Again it tipped. Hmm. I tried again, and this time it seemed to be pretty stable.

There was a good, solid branch just above my head and right over the ladder, so I held onto the branch and reached my left toe down onto the top rung of the ladder. As I put my weight on it, the ladder tipped and then fell away. There I was, hanging from the branch about ten feet from the ground, and my ladder was lying at the bottom of the tree. I looked around foolishly, hoping someone would be near to help, but of course, I was alone on top of that hill... except for a huge, nine point buck standing about fifteen feet away staring at me.

"Oh, *this* is just peachy." I said. The buck just stood there and watched me like I was some sort of novelty act. There was no way I could get the ladder, and no way to get back up into the tree. My only alternative was to let go and drop to the ground. I gathered up all my courage and let go of my hold on the branch. I hit the ground, luckily missing the ladder and my bow. The buck turned and shot over the hill like a rocket.

I lay there on the ground for a couple of minutes to let my heart rate settle, and then I stood up. There didn't seem to be anything broken or bruised except my pride, so I gathered up my bow and started down the hill. It didn't take me long to decide that in the future I would be a *ground* bow hunter.

Thunderfoot thought it was hilarious when I told him about hanging from the tree. "Why didn't you yell over to me on the other side of the valley?" he said.

"I couldn't hang on that long."

"I'd have liked to see that... maybe gotten a picture," he cackled.

"Well, too bad for you," I said. "Did you see anything?"

"I saw a doe and a coyote," he said.

After I told him about the critters I'd seen, we made our way down the valley to the truck and home.

"Wanna go early in the morning?" Thunderfoot asked as we pulled into the driveway.

"I'm not going up in that tree again," I said.

"Well, then just find a good spot and hunt on the ground," Thunderfoot suggested.

"Okay. I'll pick you up about six?"

"See you then."

The next morning we split up again and I worked my way to the top of the hill. I found a place where there were lots of deer trails, and I just stood against a big tree and watched. As the morning light increased, I could see a couple of deer on the other side of the hilltop, but they were making their way away from me. Later, I saw another family of turkeys, and if I hadn't jumped, a squirrel that came down the tree I was leaning against, would have climbed right onto my head.

After an hour or so, I decided to walk slowly along the line fence at the top of the hill and scout a bit. The sun was still behind some morning fog, and it was quite nice and peaceful on top of that hill. As I walked, I realized that because I had gotten up about two hours earlier than usual, it was now the time I usually had my morning bathroom session. Apparently my system didn't know I was hunting, and it had already decided it was time for my daily constitutional.

I tried to think about something else, but with every step, I came closer to the time to stoop. Finally, I knew that I could put it off no longer, so I found a log that was lying across the line fence next to a big tree. I laid my bow down, lowered my camo bibs, and sat across the log. It was no work on my part, as there was sufficient pressure built up and in no time I was finished. I fished in the front pocket of my bibs for my ever-present traveling roll of toilet paper, and as I was finishing up, the sun came out from behind the clouds. I was sitting there feeling pretty good when I noticed the shadow of the tree that I was sitting by. For some reason it seemed that something was wrong with the shadow.

It went up straight like normal, and I could see the branches coming off here and there, but about two thirds of the way up, there was a big blob. It was too big to be a squirrel nest. It surely wouldn't be a turkey sitting in its roost so late. As much as I hated to, I slowly looked up into the tree above me.

There, standing on a portable tree stand was another hunter, looking down at me!

Oh, no! I couldn't tell who it was because he wore a camouflage facemask. He didn't say a word, just looked down at me. I stood up, pulled up my pants, and picked up my bow. I looked back up into the tree and nodded at him, and then walked off down the hill.

I went back to the truck and took a nap while I waited for Thunderfoot. A while later he woke me as he put his gear in the back of the truck and climbed into the cab. "How long have you been here?" he asked.

I looked at my watch. "Oh, about an hour," I said.

"Why'd ya quit so early?"

"Oh, I don't know. I don't think I'm cut out for this bow hunting stuff," I said.

"What did you do *this* time?"

"What do you mean? Do I have to do something wrong every time? I just don't think this is the sport for me."

We left it at that and nothing more was said. Two days later, Thunderfoot came over after school and laid my pocketknife on the table. "Where did you get that?" I asked.

"My friend, Jerry, gave it to me at school today. He said you left it below his bow hunting tree on Sunday morning."

Busted! "Oh, thanks. Tell him 'thanks' for giving it back."

Then Thunderfoot reached in his shirt pocket and laid a photograph on the table. "Jerry said you might like a copy of this, too." He was barely able to keep from busting out laughing.

The picture, of course, taken from the tree by the mystery hunter, was of me, squatting over a log with my chin on my hands, contentedly communing with nature. "Oh, boy. He had a camera?"

"He *always* takes one of those throw away cameras with him. They take pretty good pictures, don't they?"

"I suppose Jerry's got lots of these?"

"Yeah, he's got a bunch of 'em."

I guess Jerry was about to become my new best friend.

Thanks, Thunderfoot.

You Gotta Be Nuts

"Chello!" Thunderfoot said as he answered the phone on the first ring.

"Sometime you're gonna do that when somebody other than me calls and you'll look kinda stupid." I said.

"Oh, I can tell when it's you. I've got ESP," he said.

"Oh? Well what did I call about if you're so perceptive?"

"Hmm. Well, I'd say it was about duck hunting… probably on the Mississippi river because the diving ducks are there and we should go over to Gus' cabin and try to shoot some of them."

I stood there with the phone in my hand and my mouth gaping. "Jeez. That's just what I *was* calling about. How did you guess that?"

He laughed. "I saw Gus at the gas station after school, and he told me he had already talked to you. Sheesh, you're easy."

I should have known. "Well, we'll leave right after supper, so get your stuff ready… and don't forget your chest waders," I said.

"My stuff is on the porch already. And by the way… what's for supper?"

"Why? Is your refrigerator empty?"

"Always."

"Well, then come on over. We'll find something to fill you up." I put a couple of frozen pizzas in the oven, and after we ate, we gathered up my stuff.

We met Gus at his house and off we went into the night over the hills to the Mississippi. His cottage was right on the river just above Lynxville. The river is about three miles wide there, and a huge stump field for the first two miles of it on the Wisconsin side. The stumps were usually just under the water, which was only about three feet deep in normal river stages. Before the Corps of Engineers built the dams on the river, the area had been a forest that extended across the bottoms all the way to the river channel along the Iowa border. Much of this forest was logged before the valley was flooded by the dams, leaving hundreds of stumps, some as big as the top of a car, just under the water's surface. It made for some tense boating, especially in the dark. In cold weather, like it was now, the water was only about 45 degrees – way too cold for a dip if you managed to upset your boat by running up onto a stump.

"We'll take the boat up the shore a ways," Gus explained. "There are two willow blinds built in the bay up there. I'll let you two off in the blinds, and then go sit in the boat in the willows by the lower side of the bay. These are bluebills and ringbills... they're not real smart, and they come to decoys real easy. You guys shoot them when they come in, and I'll pick them up with the boat."

Well... that sounded like a good plan.

The next morning we loaded up our gear and took a short boat ride up along the shoreline to the bay where some willows stuck up out of the water about a hundred feet from the shore. Gus pulled up by one of the stands of willows and told Thunderfoot to get out. "It's only about waist deep," he said, "and there's a wooden pallet anchored to the bottom of the river so you have something solid to stand on. When the ducks come by, just stand still, and when they're close enough, let 'em have it."

Thunderfoot gave us a big grin and slid over the side of the boat. He reached back in for his gun and a box of shells, which he slid down into the pouch in the front of his chest waders. "Okie dokie," he said. "See ya later."

Gus took me to the next blind up the bay a short ways. I got out of the boat and waded to the blind. The pallet made it much nicer to stand than it would have been, had I stood in the mud, but it was still a bit awkward trying to hold my gun up so it didn't dip into the water. And it didn't take long for the cold water to chill my feet and legs.

Gus dropped off a half dozen decoys between Thunderfoot

and me, and then parked the boat in some thick willows with the back pointed out into the river. He sat down in the bottom of the boat. We were ready.

In only about ten minutes we saw ducks winging down the river. They were bluebills, as we call them, because of the bluish color of their beaks. Actually, they were Greater Scaup, only distinguished from Lesser Scaup by their size. They are diving ducks, meaning that they live on bigger water and dive for their food, rather than living in small ponds and tipping for their food like Mallards and Wood Ducks. We hardly ever saw a bluebill on our ponds, so this was going to be a treat for us. The diving ducks seemed to be less wary than puddle ducks, probably because they saw less of humans in their usual habitat on big water. Anyway, they were fun to shoot at, and easy to decoy.

About twenty-five ducks made up this flock, and as soon as they spotted our decoys, they veered right toward us from Thunderfoot's side of the bay, passing in front of him first. He let go with his three shots and one duck dropped to the water. They flew on toward me, and I missed with all three shots.

Gus pulled the starter cord on the motor, backed out of the willows and went after the duck on the water, which was now floating downriver on the current. He had just picked it up and returned to the willows when a low-flying flock of ring necked ducks, which we call ringbills, came buzzing by. I managed to drop one, and Thunderfoot hit two. Gus fired up the motor again and retrieved them.

This went on for the next couple of hours, and by then we had a pretty good bunch of ducks. But my feet and legs were getting so cold I could hardly stand it. My feet ached, and when I tried to move around to get some blood circulating into them, I nearly fell down from the stiffness in my knees.

A lone bluebill came past and Thunderfoot took a shot at it. The duck continued on toward the middle of the river and looked as if it were joining its friends somewhere out there, when suddenly its wings folded up and it crashed to the water.

It was a long way out in the river, and I wasn't sure if Gus had seen it fall.

"Hey Gus. Did you see that one?" I yelled to our retriever.

"He missed, didn't he?"

"No. It fell way out there." Thunderfoot said.

"I didn't see it. I'll come and pick you up, and you can guide me to it," he yelled back to Thunderfoot.

Gus backed the boat out of the willows and drove to Thunderfoot's blind. Thunderfoot waded to the side of the boat and pulled himself up into it. "We'll be back in a bit," he said, and they took off for the middle of the river.

I was about to yell to them to pick me up, too, so I could get out of the cold water, but the motor roared to life and it was too noisy. I just watched as they drove away. Thunderfoot was standing in the bow of the boat as they slowly went back and forth, looking for one lone duck floating on the dark water. They kept getting farther and farther away down river. It seemed like hours passed, and they were still getting farther away, and I was getting colder.

"Well, this sure is fun," I thought to myself, standing there in the middle of the Mississippi River like an idiot, freezing to death.

By now, I was so stiff I could hardly shuffle my feet, and I was so cold that shivering was beyond my control. Finally, I saw Thunderfoot and Gus heading back. They pulled into the bay and Thunderfoot held up the duck. "Great! Hey, let's take a break and thaw out," I yelled to them. "I'm about frozen to death."

"Ok. We'll come and get you."

I turned and stepped off the pallet onto the muddy river bottom. My legs were so stiff and my feet so cold that I could hardly get them to go one in front of the other. I took about two steps toward the boat when my feet snagged on some underwater root or sunken log. I was tipping forward – and I was going down! I hit the water face first and went all the way to the bottom. The cold was like getting slapped with one of those tasers used to subdue criminals. My whole body shook as I scrambled to my knees and then to my feet.

Thunderfoot and Gus looked pretty worried as I came to the surface like a breeching whale. Gus pulled the boat along side me and I tried to climb in. My waders, now, were not only holding me, but about twenty gallons of water, too, and there was no way I could get over the side of the boat. Gus and Thunderfoot each took an arm, grunted and pulled, but they couldn't haul me aboard. "Hang onto him," Gus said. "I'll drive us over to shallower water so we can get him in." He started the motor.

I must have looked like one of those big elephant seals as they drug me through the water toward shore. When the water was shallow enough for me to touch bottom, I sprang up and flopped into the boat. I lay in the bottom of the boat, shivering and shaking, and we headed off to the cabin.

At the cabin, I managed to crawl to my feet and out of the boat. I unhooked the straps and pulled down my waders, letting the extra water run out onto the ground. "Sit in that lawn chair," Thunderfoot said. "I'll pull your boots off."

I waddled over to the lawn chair and collapsed into it. Thunderfoot took hold of the boot part of the waders and pulled them off, taking my socks with them. My feet were red as beets and all shriveled. Then I slowly walked, stiff legged because my knees wouldn't bend, yet, to the cabin deck. I stripped off my outer clothes and left them in a wet pile on the deck, and stiffly went into the cabin. Gus had run ahead of us and had a fire going in the fireplace. "Go in and take a warm shower," he said. I'll get some hot soup cooking."

I just nodded.

I took a nice, hot shower and toweled off. I looked like a lobster – bright red from head to toe. I put on the warmest clothes I could find in the bedroom, and then settled in a chair about three feet from the roaring fireplace. After a couple of bowls of hot bean soup, I thought I might just live to hunt another day.

"Jeez! You sure disappeared fast," Thunderfoot said, laughing. "All I could see was the tip of your gun barrel sticking up out of the water."

"Oh! My gun!"

"Don't worry," Gus said. "I took it apart, dried it off and oiled it."

"And I've got your clothes hanging on the clothesline out back," Thunderfoot said, "and your boots are turned inside out and are drying on the deck."

"Thanks guys," I said. "Sorry for being such a party pooper."

"Don't worry about it. The extra work was worth seeing you come up out of the water. You looked like Moby Dick," Thunderfoot laughed.

I finally began to feel my toes again, and after some lunch we dressed the ducks and put them in the freezer. Then we settled in for a few games of three-handed cribbage. Soon after, we all had a nap.

"What have you got in mind for tomorrow?" I asked Gus.

"What?" Don't you like the willow blinds?" he asked.

"Well, if that's what you want to do, I'll be the dog," I said.

Gus laughed. "No, I thought tomorrow we'd go out by the channel and do some stump hunting. The main rafts of ducks are way out, and usually fly up and down the channel. So what we'll do is find a couple of nice high stumps – ones that are up out of the water – I'll let you guys out on them, and then we'll do the same as today, except we won't use decoys. We'll just take passing shots at ducks that are flying by."

"We won't have to stand in the water?" Thunderfoot asked.

"Nope. You just sit on a stump, nice and dry." Gus said.

Well, that sounded like a much better idea to me.

The next morning we got up early, ate breakfast and then headed out across the river to the channel on the other side. Thunderfoot and I had taken this route to the other side a few years earlier, ran up onto a stump and almost sank the boat, so both he and I were a little nervous. Gus seemed to know his way quite well, and except for a slight glancing blow off one stump, we managed to get to the channel intact.

We cruised up river a little ways and saw some stumps that were up out of the water, high enough that the hunter would not be wet. Gus pulled up to one of them. Thunderfoot stepped out onto the stump and sat down with his feet resting on the roots that were just at water level. "Piece of cake." he said, grinning.

About fifty feet away, I stepped out onto the next stump. Then Gus parked the boat against a little willow island a couple of hundred feet downriver.

In just a little while, ducks began flying by us quite regularly. Almost all were bluebills and ringbills, but we saw some buffleheads and golden eyes, too. Both were ducks that we rarely saw on our marsh at home. We had some great shooting, and we managed to get a few ducks.

As the morning went on, the wind switched from the west to the north. The temperature dropped, and nasty looking clouds began to build up in the northwest. Soon the wind was making some pretty significant waves that slapped at my stump, splashing on my gear and me. Just minutes later, a few flakes of snow drifted by.

I looked over at Thunderfoot. He was all hunched down inside his waders and his down jacket like a turtle. I could see his grin as he shrugged his shoulders.

Just then I heard a boat and I thought, "Good, here comes Gus."

But as I turned to look, I saw three late season walleye fishermen in a boat going up the channel. They waved at us as they went by, and we waved back.

When they were just past us, the one in the front leaned back toward his buddies and said, "Look at those idiots sitting there on those stumps. They must be nuts." Of course, he didn't realize that in talking loud enough to be heard by his friends, his voice carried across the water to us, too.

His buddies yucked and laughed as they motored away.

"Maybe I should fire a volley across their bow," Thunderfoot yelled to me.

"Why across it? Just shoot a hole in their boat," I yelled back.

We had a good laugh at that, and then I heard another boat. It was Gus. Thank God!

"I think it's gonna get pretty cold out here pretty soon," Gus said. "You guys had enough?"

"Plenty," I replied.

By the time I had stepped into the boat, Thunderfoot was on his feet and more than ready to be picked up.

"That was fun, but I think it's time to put away the shotguns and get out the ice fishing gear," he said.

We motored back to the cabin, dressed the ducks, cleaned up ourselves and went to town for dinner. When we arrived back at the cabin it was just about dark. Gus and I went inside, but Thunderfoot walked down to the riverbank.

I saw him down by the water, so I slipped my coat on and ventured down to the edge of the river in the cold evening air. As the light in the sky faded, one late flock of ducks was just landing out near the channel.

"Well," he said, "we got our money's worth out of this duck season."

"Yeah, no kidding. I don't think I've ever hunted so late in the season. This was kind of fun, but I still like our duck blind and our decoys and our mallards and wood ducks."

"Yeah, me too," Thunderfoot said. "The early season is more fun... and the water's not so cold, and our duck blind is lots more comfortable."

He sure had that right. "Up for a little cribbage?" I put my arm around his shoulder and we walked back to the cabin.

Thanks, Thunderfoot.

War Games

It was time to get the yard ready for winter. The garden was mostly harvested, and now was a good time to pull up weeds, the dead tomato vines, and the rest of the dead things before the really cold weather set in. I was just stuffing some dead plants into my wheelbarrow when I heard a pop, and a little explosion of yellow liquid appeared on the tire. I stopped and looked at it, thinking the tire had gone flat when another splat of yellow liquid appeared next to it.

"What the heck?" I put my finger in the yellow stuff and it seemed to be some kind of paint. Then I heard Thunderfoot chuckling from behind the greenhouse.

"What's wrong? Bad tire?" he said.

"Is this some of your work?"

He came out from his hiding place carrying something that looked like a space ray gun. He pointed it at my birdbath and pulled the trigger. A loud pop came from the gun and a small pellet hit with a splat as another yellow splotch appeared on the side of the birdbath.

"Hey! Watch it. You're getting that stuff all over everything," I said.

"Don't worry. It's washable... just food coloring. It won't hurt anything."

He strolled over to me and handed me the gun. "It's a paintball gun."

I examined it. It was shaped kind of like a machine gun, but it had a CO2 tank screwed onto the bottom of it, and a hopper on top that sounded like it was full of gumballs or marbles. I aimed it at a tree across the yard and pulled the trigger. Pop! A yellow ball flew out and smacked against the tree leaving a yellow spot. "Hey, that's pretty neat. Where did you get that?" I asked.

"Mom got Caleb and me each one, so we can have wars," he said.

"You shoot those at each other?"

"Yeah, but we've got goggles to protect our eyes and ears, and we wear heavy clothes. They sting a little, but not bad. A lot of my friends at school have them. They're lots of fun."

It was one of those times that I wished I were about 30 years younger. "That sounds like fun. I wish we'd had those when I was a kid. All we had were bean shooters and water guns."

"A bunch of guys have them. We're gonna play war tomorrow down in the woods by Gutweiler's lake. You wanna come along and play?"

"Oh, cripes no. I'm not gonna play war with a bunch of high school kids."

"No. A bunch of the guy's dads are gonna do it, too. It's kind of like a father/son thing, but since my dad doesn't live here, I thought maybe you'd want to take his place."

"How many are going to be there?"

"Oh, I think there are about ten, so far... eleven if you come, and maybe a few more."

"But I don't have a paintball gun."

"You can use Caleb's. This is just for high school kids. He's too young. He already said you could use it."

Well, it seemed that I no longer had an excuse to keep me from it, and actually, it did sound like fun. "Well, okay. Count me in."

"Cool. We gotta get some groceries, and afterwards, I'll let you try Caleb's gun... so you know how to load it and stuff."

"Groceries? What do we need groceries for?"

"Well, we're all gonna bring some stuff, and then after we play paintball for a while, we'll have a cook out," Thunderfoot explained. "It'll be a real bonding thing."

Well, I guess I could afford a few groceries for a *bonding thing*.

We went to the grocery store and got some hotdogs, buns,

chips, and a twelve-pack of soda, and then stopped off for Caleb's paintball gun and headgear.

Thunderfoot showed me how to load and shoot the gun, and before long, I had just about used up the entire carton of 200 paintballs.

"We're gonna have to go get more balls, and get our air tanks filled," Thunderfoot said.

So off we went to the paintball shop, and then we were ready for the "bonding experience".

The next morning was nice and cool, and a little cloudy, so I put on a heavy sweatshirt and my camouflage bib overalls over it. I put my camo shirt on over the bibs, slipped into my leather hunting boots, and took a pair of leather gloves to protect my hands. When I put on the facemask, I looked like a camouflaged version of Darth Vader. I was admiring my outfit when Thunderfoot came stomping through the front door. He was dressed almost exactly like me.

"Luke. It is your Destiny!" he said in his Darth Vader voice.

"I've waited for a long time, Obewan."

We both laughed like grade school kids as we walked to the van and headed to Gutweiler's.

"This is gonna be a blast," Thunderfoot said.

As silly as it seemed, I was just as excited as him, and it did seem like it would be a lot of fun.

When we got to the lake, there were already seven other father/son pairs there, and within a few minutes, three more arrived. I knew all of the dads and most of the boys, and soon we were all chatting about our adventure that was about to begin.

One of Thunderfoot's friends went to the family car and brought out two flags stapled to laths. One was a blue bandana and the other was red.

"One team will take the red flag and the other blue," he said, setting down the rules of the game. "One team will go out in the woods and find a place to hide, and ambush the other team hunting them. When one team captures the other's flag, the game is over. Then we'll change – the second team will hide and the first team will find them. If you get hit by a paintball, you're dead. You have to stop shooting and lay down. No cheating." He looked at all the old guys. "Understand?"

"Who's on who's team?" one of the dads asked.

"How about old guys against the young guys?" one of the kids said.

"Okay. That sounds good to us," I said, nodding to the other dads. They all nodded in agreement. "Who hides first?"

"We'll go hide first," Thunderfoot said. "Give us ten minutes before you come looking for us. No cheating."

All the young guys trotted off into the woods. The other dads and I chatted about our tactics, feeling pretty good about our chances with these rookies. We probably had a hundred years of hunting experience between us, compared to a few dozen years that the boys had. We decided to split into two groups and try to locate them without being seen, and then flank them and hit from behind.

The ten minutes were up. We split up and my group took the flag. We started off in the direction that the boys had gone, sneaking through the woods silently, looking for some sign of the other team.

We had gone several hundred yards when I noticed a big brush pile up ahead in the woods. I gave a hand signal to the others, and they nodded that they had seen it, too. It looked like the perfect place for the boys to be hiding. I looked across the woods and got the attention of one of the fathers in the other part of our team. I motioned to the brush pile, and just as I did that, I noticed movement in the brush. Ah ha! I signaled him to skirt to the right while we went left, flanking the boys on either side.

Both halves of our team slipped off and slowly made our way around the brush. As we went through the woods, I caught a glimpse of the red flag stuck in the ground behind a bunch of brush. This was too easy.

Once we were around the backside of the brush, I signaled our other half to advance, and we rushed forward toward the unsuspecting boys ahead of us. As we got to the brush pile, we began shouting and shot paintballs at the two sentries that were guarding the flag. Both of them took direct hits, with about 4 or 5 paintballs exploding on their shirts. One fell down and the other just stood there.

We all stopped and took a good look. The two boys didn't have any legs. They were just two shirts and helmets propped up on sticks. The flag was a red handkerchief tied to a stick. "What the...?"

Then, without warning, pain exploded in my back as half a dozen paintballs smashed against my shirt. Then another half dozen hit me in the legs, and one nearly took the gun out of my hand. The rest of the fathers were hit at the same time, and in an instant, the boys dropped down from the trees above us and grabbed our flag. "You lose, old guys!"

The rest of the fathers and I just stood there, dumbfounded. "You can't do that!"

"What?"

"You can't climb in trees and take off your shirts and make dummies."

The boys were laughing their heads off. "Why is that? Nobody said anything about decoys and climbing trees."

The two boys who had donated their shirts now crawled from under some heavy brush and retrieved their paint-covered clothes. "Boy! You old guys got bamboozled," one of them laughed.

The other dads and I stood there trying to figure out how we had been outsmarted... by kids.

"Well," one of the boys said, "let's go eat, and then you guys can hide and we'll find you."

Thunderfoot walked with me as we all went back through the woods to the parking area. "Think you're pretty smart, don't you?" I said.

He just smirked.

One of the dads had a portable grill, and between the ten pairs of dads and kids, we had enough food for about fifty people. But with ten of the twenty people being teenage boys, there wasn't much left over when we were done. We had a great time.

After the picnic mess was all cleaned up, we sat in the shade for a little rest before the next round of play. With heavy eyes, many of the dads were soon snoring. The boys let us snooze for a while, and then rousted us up and told us to go hide, so they could come and try to find us.

The other dads and I went into the woods, marching toward the other end of the lake.

"What do you think?" one of the dads asked.

"What about down on the other end of the lake where they planted the corn for the deer," one of the dads said. "There's still a lot of it standing... couldn't we hide in there?"

"That sounds like a good spot," another said.

The decision was made. The cornfield was our hiding place.

We hiked to the other end of the lake and came to the corn – about an acre. The DNR had planted it in the spring for the deer and squirrels and raccoons to eat, as they needed it. It also made cover for pheasants and other birds, as well as shelter and food for turkeys. And a good hiding place for ten old guys.

We maneuvered out into the middle of the field and formed a small circle, so we could watch from all directions. "They'll have fun trying to get us in here," one of the dads whispered.

We all felt pretty safe, hunkered down in the corn, waiting for the boys to stumble past.

Time wore on, and I was getting sleepy again. I looked over at the dad sitting closest to me, and he was nodding off. I threw a dirt clod at him and he woke up. He grinned at me and we both looked off into the maze of corn around us.

My butt was getting tired, so I slid down on my side and lay looking through the corn stalks, trying to see or hear the boys coming toward us.

My eyes flew open as I heard a sound that startled me. It sounded like a chain saw. Then there was another one just like it. I looked over at the dads on either side of me and both were sitting up rubbing their eyes. They had been sleeping, too. I looked at my watch. I couldn't believe we had been sleeping for half an hour.

"What's that noise?" I asked.

"Sounds like a chain saw, or an outboard."

"Or a four wheeler," the other dad said.

The sound was getting louder. It was soon obvious that the sound wasn't of two chain saws. It was two four wheel trail bikes, and they were coming right toward the cornfield.

All of the dads were getting to their haunches trying to see what was going on without showing themselves. Suddenly two four wheelers carrying the two drivers and two of our enemy troops came roaring into the cornfield. The two riders were wielding paintball guns and began shooting at the dads scattered throughout the corn. It all happened so fast that none of us had the chance to return the fire. The two attacking four wheelers made a u-turn at the end of the field and came back.

Two of the dads had been "killed" as the first attack came, and they lay "dead" in the corn. The other eight of us took off running from the attackers as they made their second run. As we cleared the corn at the end of the field, the other six boys began shooting at us from the tall grass at the end where they lay in wait. I was hit at least a dozen times, as was every dad in the field. We all fell "dead" as the boys came screaming from the grass to capture our flag.

"Game over! We win again!" they all yelled, dancing around like a bunch of savages.

All of the dads arose, covered with paint and feeling pretty foolish. "Nobody said you could go get four wheelers," one said.

"Nobody said we couldn't, either," said his son.

"Jeez! You guys don't play fair," I said.

"All's fair in love and war," Thunderfoot said, laughing.

I looked at the other dads, and we all had the same feeling that we had just been taken to the cleaners by our sons. "Well, you guys outsmarted us. Let's go home," I said.

We all started walking together down the dirt road back to the parking lot, but the boys were soon ahead of us, and the two on the four wheelers were already there. I got the attention of the other dads and pointed my paintball gun at Thunderfoot's butt. I nodded, and held up three fingers. Then two fingers. Then one. We all let loose a volley right into the butts of our kids.

"Yeouch! Hey! No fair!"

The boys were jumping up and down rubbing their backsides.

"That's not fair! You guys can't do that," one of them whined.

"Oh, you never said that we couldn't, did you? All's fair in love and war."

Well… it might *not* have been quite fair. But it sure made us all feel a little better.

Thanks, Thunderfoot.

Northern Adventure

We were enjoying the beautiful late October weather. Although there had been a few cold days, the fall had been unseasonably warm, and the forecast for the following weekend was a beauty. I happened to run into a friend at the hardware store one day, and he started telling me about how amazing the small mouth bass fishing was at this time of year near the cottage he owned in the Drummond area. Good friend that he was, he offered me the use of his cabin for the weekend.

I called Thunderfoot and told him I was planning a little trip, and to come over if he was interested. As I hung up the phone I looked out the window. Thunderfoot was already on a dead run across the back lawn. He burst through the front door a few seconds later. "So, where is this trip?"

"Jeez. That didn't take you long," I said.

"I'm a speedy guy when it comes to hunting or fishing. Which one are we doing on this trip?"

"Well, I think a little of both," I said. "You know Jim, don't you? He's got a cabin up near Drummond, and I was thinking of going up there this weekend. We can hunt ducks during the morning, then fish for small mouth during the day, and then hunt ducks again in the evening. That is, if you're interested."

"When are we leaving?" he said.

"Oh, so you approve? I was thinking Friday after school. We'll get up there pretty late, so maybe we won't get an early start Saturday morning. But we'll still hunt and fish Saturday, and part of Sunday, and then we'll come home. Not a big trip, but I think it would be fun."

"Let's make a grocery list," Thunderfoot said, "and I'll get my stuff over here later. Then all we gotta do is jump in the van on Friday, and off we go." It seemed that groceries were always his first concern when we were packing.

Thunderfoot raced home from school on Friday afternoon,

changed into his traveling clothes, and was at my house a few minutes later. Everything was ready and loaded in the van. We had decided to take the van because it got much better gas mileage, and with the back seats removed, we could take a nap if we got too tired to keep driving the entire six hours to the cabin.

We loaded up Katy and Kirby, and off we went. Katy came along so she could retrieve our ducks – if we got any – and Kirby came along for the ride. He had some Golden Retriever in him, but one of his parents was probably a Collie, and he didn't like swimming in the cold water, and he didn't have a clue about finding a dead duck. But he liked to ride, and he would have been horrified to be left behind.

Dusk came pretty early at that time of year, and by then we were getting into the "northy" woods. At home, our hills were full of oak, hickory, maple, and pine trees. But this far north, there was only flat ground, pines and poplars. The biggest hills were just slightly rolling high places, left over when the glaciers had passed and scraped the land down to the remaining sandy soil.

We stopped at a hamburger joint and ordered from the drive through window. The dogs were barking with excitement, and the kid at the other end of the speaker had a little difficulty hearing our order. When we drove up to the window, he was rubbing his ears. "Jeez. Your dogs about made me deaf," he said, good-naturedly.

He handed me the bag of goodies and our drinks, and then he smiled politely as I handed him the dog's dish for some water. "I can't fill that. My boss would have my head," he said. "But I *can* give you a large cup of water."

"Boss must not be a dog guy," Thunderfoot said, shoving a handful of French Fries into his mouth.

We pulled into the parking lot and ate, sharing our meal with the dogs. I had ordered a hamburger for each of them – Kirby's with no pickles – and an extra order of fries that they shared. They loved trips like this.

Then off we went, once again, into the darkness.

Thunderfoot and the dogs were sleeping, and I was getting a little drowsy, too. I closed my eyes for just a second, and abruptly found myself on the shoulder of the road. I jerked the steering wheel back to the left.

Thunderfoot sat up. "Did you fall asleep?" he asked.

"Yeah. I'm getting real tired. You wanna drive?"

"Not really. There's lots of deer up here, and I'm afraid I'll crash and then you'd never let me hear the end of it."

"Well, then we'll have to pull over and sleep a while," I said.

We were just outside of a little town that was built right on the shore of a small lake. A sign pointed the way to the town park, so I turned. Just down the street we found a nice little park with picnic tables, a beach, a toilet and changing house. "Let's just crawl in the back and take a nap," I said.

"Sounds good to me," Thunderfoot said, yawning. "I'll take the dogs out for a potty while you get out the pillows and blankets."

A makeshift bed in the back of the van was ready when the three of them returned. Everyone was ready for a nap. We all climbed in, and I pushed down the buttons on the doors, to make us snug and safe. The dogs snuggled down between us, and soon we were all sleeping.

I awoke a couple of hours later to the overhead light in the van coming on, and then off again. I sat up and saw Thunderfoot in just his under shorts and barefoot tiptoeing across the cold grass to the toilet. I lay down again and started to drift off, when a devilish idea just popped into my head. I sat up again, and snapped down the lock on the door. Then I watched as he tiptoed back to the van. I lay down and pretended to be asleep. My eyes were open just enough to see what he would do. He grabbed the door handle and pulled. Nothing happened. He pulled again, and then he realized it was locked. He stood there for a bit, and gave it one more unsuccessful try. Then he tiptoed around to the other side and pulled on that door handle.

Locked!

By now he had his arms wrapped around his chest, trying to ward off the cold night air. He went to the sliding side door of the van – it was locked, too. I could tell he was getting worried. He cupped his hands around his face and pressed it up to the window, trying to see inside. I heard him talking to the dogs: "Kate. Come pull this thing up," he said, pointing to the door lock button. Kate just yawned and laid her head back down. Thunderfoot was jumping up and down, shivering as he pulled on the door handle again.

By then I was laughing so hard, the entire van must have been shaking. I tried to pretend I was still sleeping, but he could see my sides heaving with laughter.

"Oh, you're real funny," he whined.

I tried to lie still, but Kirby got up, went to the window and looked out at Thunderfoot. "Hey, Kirby, buddy! Pull this thing up, will you?" Thunderfoot said, once again pointing to the door tab. Kirby just stood there, and then he licked the window.

Thunderfoot rapped on the window. "Come on, I know you're awake. I'm freezing out here."

Finally, I felt sorry for him and I acted as if I just had awakened. I sat up and looked around. "What are you doing out there?" I said, trying to sound surprised.

"If you don't let me in," he said, "I'm gonna strangle you in your sleep next time I get a chance."

"Well, get in. I'm not stopping you."

"The door's locked... as if you didn't know."

"Oh, maybe Kirby did it. He must have been worried about where you went."

"Kirby, my butt. Now let me in. I'm freezing!"

I reached over and lifted the lock tab. Thunderfoot climbed into the van and quickly slid under the blankets. He pulled Katy and Kirby down to snuggle on both sides of him. "Jeez! I almost froze to death out there."

"Well, I didn't tell you to go running around in the night

almost naked," I said.

"Oh, you're a barrel of laughs," he said. "Why don't you go back to sleep and shut up?"

"Ooo. Touchy," I teased.

"Just wait," he said. I heard him mumble something about shaving off one of my eyebrows as he snuggled under his blanket. I was probably in for some retaliation, but oh, it was worth it.

I just about jumped through the window A few minutes later when he put his ice cold feet on my back. "There! See how cold the grass is?" he said.

I guess I deserved that.

We woke up early, but we got to my friend's cabin just a little too late for the early duck hunt. "Well, let's have a good breakfast," I said. "Then we'll go down to the river and see if the smallies are hungry."

We made a huge breakfast of bacon, eggs, pancakes, and toast – enough for the dogs to each have a big plateful, too. After the kitchen was cleaned up, Thunderfoot took the dogs for a walk, so they would be ready for a nap while we went fishing. I didn't want to take them to the river for two reasons: Katy would be in the water all the time, scaring the fish; and there were a lot of bears around – I didn't want the dogs to get them riled.

I made a fire in the fireplace while they were gone, and when they returned, both dogs picked a spot in front of the warm fire. They were sound asleep before we walked out the front door.

"Jim told me the river is about three quarters of a mile north," I said. "It's like a big trout stream, but instead of trout, it has smallies and northerns. He said spinners and small crank baits are all we need."

Thunderfoot went to the driver's side of the van. "I'll drive while you pick out a few lures. How about putting them into one of those little plastic boxes, so we don't have to be lugging a tackle box along."

That sounded like a good idea. I sat on the floor in the back of the van and sorted out a few lures. We hadn't driven very far when Thunderfoot turned right onto a narrow road.

"Is this three quarters of a mile?" I asked.

"Pretty close. It's the only road I've seen on the right."

I went back to the sorting, and then I heard a lot of leaves scraping and brushing on the sides of the van. "Pretty narrow, isn't it?"

"Yeah, it is. But most of these roads into lakes are like this," the driver said.

The brushing and scraping got to be real noisy. "Are you sure this is the road? It seems like it's getting pretty narrow."

"Well, it is narrow. But I think it's right," Thunderfoot replied.

When I finally I had the small pocket tackle boxes ready, I climbed up between the seats and sat down on the passenger side. There was a trail ahead of us, but it was just barely wider than the van. It looked like it hadn't been traveled in years.

"Whoa. Wait a minute. This isn't a road."

"Well, it was a lot wider back farther, but it's gotten pretty narrow, now."

"Stop. Let's walk ahead and see. I don't want to find out that it just ends, and then have to back all the way out," I said.

He stopped and turned off the engine. I tried to open my door, but it would only open about four inches before it hit a tree. It was the same on Thunderfoot's side. "We can't open the doors," he said. "How're we gonna get out and look ahead?"

"Pop the tail gate door," I said. He pushed the button and the tailgate snapped. We crawled through the back of the van, and pushed it opened. "Whew, at least we can get out of here."

We made our way through the trees and brush to the front of the van, and then followed the "road" about twenty feet where it stopped dead against a big spruce tree.

"Well, there's the end of our road," I said.

"Who would make a road like this?" Thunderfoot said. "Just

go in half a mile or so and stop."

"What do you mean? Half a mile? Are we that far in?"

"Yeah, I think so... maybe a little more."

"Oh, boy. We're gonna have to back the whole way out."

"I guess so. There's no place to turn around," he said. "You drive."

Oh thanks! That's just what I wanted to hear. We got back in through the tailgate and Thunderfoot pulled it shut. I got in the driver's seat and he knelt in the back and tried to guide me as I backed through the trees and brush.

It was slow going. Many times I had to stop and pull forward because I had gotten off track, and one of the mirrors was against a tree, or the rear bumper had smacked into a tree that was quite close to the trail.

The *Mother of all Cricks* lodged in my neck by the time we finally reached a place wide enough to turn around. Thunderfoot climbed back up to the front. "Whew, that was pretty tight," he said.

"No kidding. It's a good thing I'm not fussy about my van, or I'd be going nuts about what's left of the paint job."

"Oh, that'll buff right out," Thunderfoot said.

We pulled out onto the road again, and about fifty feet farther, there was a gravel road to the right – *and a sign* that said "To the River."

"That other one must be that road less traveled... that Robert Frost was talking about," Thunderfoot laughed.

A ways down the road we came to a beautiful little stream. The road continued on over a bridge, but we could see no reason for going any farther. We pulled over and parked, took off our shoes, put on our hip boots and gathered up our fishing rods and little plastic tackle boxes of lures.

"I think I'll cross the bridge and fish that side," Thunderfoot said.

"That's a good idea. I'll fish this side," I said.

The river was like something from a movie, about ten yards

wide with crystal clear rapids tumbling over boulders. Parts of it were bordered with trees right down to the water's edge, and gravel bars out in the middle. Other places were more open with grass and brush along its banks, and shallow enough that if you couldn't make your way along the banks because of brush, you could just wade along the edge of the water. It meandered back and forth for as far as I could see.

Thunderfoot emerged from the brush on the other side. "This is just about perfect," he called out. "What do you want to do? Go upstream or down?"

"Let's go upstream, today," I said. "Maybe tomorrow we can try downstream."

He signaled an okay, and we started working our way up the river, casting to pockets behind boulders – likely looking eddies where a smallie might be – and casting to the bottom of riffles where the water dumped into a small pool. It didn't take long until Thunderfoot let out a whoop, and a nice small mouth bass made its first jump, and then took a screaming run downriver with his spinner. The fish jumped another half-dozen times during the fight, and finally Thunderfoot brought it up to his feet, reached down and lipped it. "Look at this beauty," he beamed, holding up the little bronze torpedo.

I was just about to compliment him on his fish when one hit my spinner and almost took the rod out of my hands. It made a jet-like run upstream and jumped three times in about three seconds before it made a run back toward me. I reeled as fast as I could, caught up to the fish and turned it. It jumped again, fighting, but I soon had it lying on its side next to my feet. It was a twin to Thunderfoot's fish. I took the hook out and slid it back into the water.

By then, Thunderfoot was upstream from me, wading along the shoreline toward a bend in the river. There was a deep-looking cut along the bank on my side, so I stepped out of the water and worked my way past it so Thunderfoot could cast to it. I emerged from the brush about ten yards beyond and stepped into the river again, casting up toward some boulders. Thunderfoot, meanwhile, was standing on the point at the bend, casting toward the opposite bank. He quickly had a strike and began playing a nice fish. I had a strike just then, too. My fish jumped and put up a good fight until I finally got it close enough to pull it out of the water. I released the fish and waded upriver to cast again. I turned to see if Thunderfoot was still fishing the point.

Sure enough, he was in knee-deep water at the point, fighting another fish. I was just going to start upstream again when I saw something black moving through the brush near the point. I stopped and looked more carefully, and then I realized that a pretty large black bear was tramping through the willows right toward Thunderfoot. I wasn't exactly sure what I should do. I was afraid that if I yelled, it might startle the bear into running Thunderfoot over. So I just stood there, waving, trying to get Thunderfoot's attention.

He was intent on his fishing, but after a few long, nervous moments, he looked my way and saw me waving. He raised his hand, returning the wave. I pointed behind him. He looked confused and shrugged his shoulders. I pointed again, and made a gesture with my arms, trying to convey the idea that something big was there. He turned slowly toward the bank, and just as he did, the bear stood on its hind legs, looking through the willows right at him, from about ten feet away.

Thunderfoot froze. The bear dropped back down on all fours and took a couple of steps forward. Thunderfoot began backing away. The bear heard him splashing in the water and stood up again to see *what* he was. That did it. When the bear stood up the second time, Thunderfoot waded backwards as fast as he could go, right into the deep hole on my side of the stream. The water was about mid-chest depth, but that didn't stop him. He kept wading and sloshing backwards until he was up against the bank. When he felt the bank against his back, he threw his fishing pole up into the weeds, climbed up out of the river, and took off running through the tall grass for the van.

The bear watched him go, calmly walked down to the river, got a drink, and then ambled off into the woods. I just stood there quietly enjoying the entire performance.

I fished a while longer, and then I decided to see if Thunderfoot had stopped at the van, or if he had kept running all the way back to the cabin. I picked up his rod and reel and strolled back downriver to the parked van. Thunderfoot was sitting on the floor with all the windows rolled up and the doors locked, peeking out the rear window.

He reached to unlock the door and whispered, "Get in... and lock that door behind you!"

"What? Are you afraid that the bear knows how to open car doors?" I laughed.

"I'm not taking any chances. Did you see that thing? Jeez! I'm lucky I'm not bear supper right now! Did you see him stand up and charge?"

"See him charge?" I was laughing so hard I could barely get my breath. "He wasn't interested in your scrawny body. All he wanted was a drink of water."

"Yeah, right! He looked pretty hungry to me. Besides... what do you know? You were a long ways from him. I was right there, looking him right in his evil eye."

"If he'd taken a bite of you, he would've spit it right out," I laughed.

"Oh, real funny," Thunderfoot pouted.

"I really don't think he intended to bother you. He was just out for a drink of water, and you just happened to be where he was going," I said.

"Well, let's go back to the cabin. I need some dry clothes," he growled.

"You probably need some fresh underwear, too."

"Oh, ha, ha!"

We drove back to the cabin. Thunderfoot changed into dry clothes and hung his wet ones on a clothesline strung between two pine trees. We had some lunch, fed the dogs, and settled down for a little nap before the evening flight of ducks.

The little duck boat tipped up against the backside of the cabin was longer than the inside of the van, so we had to leave the tailgate up, but didn't have far to go and we'd drive slow. When the boat was loaded, we changed into camouflage clothes, grabbed our hip boots, shotguns, and shells, put the dogs in the back with the duck boat, and headed out for the evening hunt.

Katy and Kirby were all excited about going someplace, even if they didn't know for sure where. We drove down a little country road to a small lake. The dogs jumped out and immediately ran around exploring. We unloaded the boat and the rest of the gear, called the dogs, and pushed off for the cattails on the opposite shore of the lake.

We hid among the cattails, and pulled some of them across the open boat to camouflage it better. Then we just settled back to wait for some evening ducks. Katy watched the sky for her first duck. Kirby curled up in a ball and took a nap.

It didn't take long for a small flock of Wood Ducks to slip over the tops of the trees and circle the lake. "There, to the right," Thunderfoot whispered.

I nodded. The ducks circled again, right over us. We both rose up and shot. The ducks went from four little steady targets to a swarm, flying every which way as they scrambled for altitude. I missed with my first shot, but one fell with my second. Thunderfoot missed both the first and second, but got one with his third shot. "Kate, go fetch," I said.

Katy jumped into the water and swam out toward the first duck. She picked it up and swam back, got her front paws up on the side of the boat, dropped the duck in, turned and went after the second duck. Now Kirby was awake. He sniffed the duck, sneezed, and curled up again for another nap. Apparently, he wasn't interested in getting wet. Kate came back with the second duck and we helped her back into the boat. Of course, she brought a lot of water in with her, so now there was a puddle in the bottom of the boat. Kirby got up and moved closer to Thunderfoot where it was still dry. "Kirby's not real excited about hunting, is he?" Thunderfoot said.

"Nope," I laughed. "His hunting is mostly for a place to sleep."

After a couple more flocks had flown past, it was time to call it quits. I rowed across the lake and let the dogs out of the boat, drug it onto the shore, tipped it and drained the water out. We loaded up and headed back to the cabin.

I made supper – steaks and raw fried potatoes – while Thunderfoot cleaned the ducks and fed the dogs. It had been a long day for us, and after we ate, we were feeling pretty tired. "I think it's time for bed," Thunderfoot said.

"No argument from me."

We let the dogs out for a potty break, and then the four of us settled down for the night, Thunderfoot and I in the bunk beds, and Katy and Kirby sprawled out in front of the fireplace.

It was still dark when my alarm went off. Katy was hogging my bed – stretched out taking her half out of the middle, leaving me on a little sliver. "Kate, move over!" I said. She grumbled and groaned but moved a bit so I could straighten out my legs. "Hey, wake up, there's daylight in the swamp."

No answer. I pushed on the mattress above my head. "Wake up, lazy. Time to go hunting."

"You know, you can sure be irritating so early in the morning. How can anyone wake up and be so cheerful?"

"I'm going hunting, and if you want to go along, you'd better get up, or I'll go without you."

"Well, if you put it that way… okay, let's go," Thunderfoot said. He hopped down from the top bunk.

We washed up and went to the van. We'd hunt for an hour or so, while the morning flight was on, and then come back for some breakfast.

We went back to the same lake and got in some pretty good shooting, collecting two more ducks for our bag. Then we went back, cleaned the birds, and had a big breakfast.

Thunderfoot kept the dogs entertained while I was washed the dishes. "Well, what do you think?" I asked. "A couple hours of fishing before we head for home?"

"Fishing? Where?" he said.

"The stream we fished yesterday."

"Are you insane? There are hungry bears out there. I'm not going near that place again."

"Oh, don't be such a baby. Those bears won't hurt you."

"Easy for you to talk. You're almost the size of a bear. I'm just a snack size."

I laughed, and then I decided it was fine with me if we prepared for the trip home. It was a long drive; we could take our time to enjoy scenery that we had missed on the way up during the night.

"And besides… I need to do some homework before school tomorrow," Thunderfoot said.

"Oh, you just remembered that, did you?"

"Yes, I did. And you know I'm a very conscientious student. I want to get good grades to make my mom happy."

I just shook my head. Now I had heard it all.

Thanks, Thunderfoot.

Covered Coveralls

Thunderfoot and I were getting our deer hunting gear laid out for opening day. As usual, before a big hunt, he stayed overnight at my house in the spare bedroom that he had claimed as *his room.* He kept several changes of clothes and had a lot of his junk stored there, so, for all intents and purposes, it *was* his room.

He was making sandwiches and bagging up cookies as I laid out my clothes and boots. All of his outer clothes, his gun, shells, and other gear were all piled up and ready to go.

"You'd better go and roll up some TP," he suggested.

"Oh, yeah! I can't go without that," I said. I went into the bathroom and unrolled a long strip of toilet paper, rolled it up into a small roll, and stuck it into the pocket of my jacket.

"You got enough? You know how you always have to go when you get to the woods," he said.

"I think so. There's always leaves in an emergency."

"Oh, yuck," he groaned.

I turned on the radio to hear the weather report. The weather lady was talking about possible rain, and temperatures in the upper 60s, possibly low 70s.

"Holy smokes. It's gonna be warm tomorrow," Thunderfoot said.

"Yeah. I don't think I want to wear my insulated pants and coat. I'll cook in them."

"I've got that thin jacket I can wear over anything, so I'm in good shape," Thunderfoot said. He packed the sandwiches into a couple of duffle bags.

"You know, I've got those old red coveralls. Maybe I can just wear them… so I won't be so hot."

"You can't wear red. That's illegal."

"Yeah, but if I wear a blaze orange vest over them, I'm okay. One half of the top of me in blaze orange is all that's required."

"Yeah, that might be a good idea. After we meet Jerry and Scott at noon, and make some drives, you'll be cooked in those heavy clothes."

I found my old red coveralls and an orange vest, and transferred the stuff from the pockets of my heavy jacket and pants. Now at least I wouldn't get overheated.

It was still quite dark outside when the alarm went off. Thunderfoot and I ate a quick breakfast, and then off we went to the woods. We were hunting on the high bank near the area where we usually hunted ducks. There were two nice alfalfa fields for us to watch, and even better for me, it was only a short walk, on flat ground to my stand. I was getting to like flat land hunting more, rather than climbing the hills that seemed to be getting steeper every year.

I carried a lawn chair to my stand under a huge white pine, cleared off the branches in a five-foot area and settled down. The blanket of needles under my feet felt like a carpet. It was still dark and the wind was blowing just a bit, making mournful sounds through the pine branches, but it was a real cozy spot. I slid down and leaned back in my chair, and closed my eyes just for a second.

Quite surprised to see that it was fully daylight, I opened my eyes again when I heard a thudding noise. I looked out into the alfalfa field; two big does and a really nice buck had made the noise that awakened me. They stood about forty yards away. My heart beat a little faster, and then I realized that my gun was laying on the blanket of pine needles on the ground. Slowly, I moved my right arm off the chair rest and toward the gun. The deer watched as my hand got closer, and just as I reached it, their tails went up and they bounded off into the edge of the woods.

I didn't bother to jump up and make chase. They were headed right toward Thunderfoot, across the lane and at the other end of the woods, watching another alfalfa field. I waited and listened, but there was no sound of gunfire. I grinned to myself, thinking that Thunderfoot was probably asleep, too, and the deer had probably tiptoed right past him without waking him.

Oh well. No hurry. It was opening morning. Lots of time left.

I did pick up my gun and lay it across my lap. I was just finishing a sandwich and a cookie when a coyote trotted across the field, and a few minutes later, six turkeys ambled out of the woods, picking their way across the alfalfa, having their breakfast. A couple of hours later, two does snuck across the other end of the field, but no more bucks showed themselves.

I was enjoying the morning when I heard leaves crunching and saw Thunderfoot coming through the brush toward me.

"Seen any?"

"Yeah," I said. "Real early, but I was dozing. They came your way... did you see them?"

He shook his head. "Yeah, but not till they were almost in the woods. I was resting my eyes, too. I heard them and woke up, but it was too late. My gun was laying on the ground, anyway."

I laughed. "We seem to hunt alike."

"Well, it's almost noon," Thunderfoot said. "Let's go back to my house. Mom said she'd make lunch for us. Jerry and Scott will meet us there. We'll hunt some more this afternoon."

"Sounds good to me.

I picked up my gear and my chair, and we walked down the lane to the truck. When we got to Thunderfoot's house, Jerry's old beater of a pickup was already there. He and Scott had been on stands all morning without any shooting, either.

"You guys see any?" Jerry asked.

"Yeah, but we were both snoozing, and neither of us shot," Thunderfoot said.

Scott and Jerry laughed, and couldn't resist giving us a lot of static about being such poor hunters.

"Just wait till this afternoon," Thunderfoot said.

Thunderfoot's mom had a huge pot of chili on the stove, and a big plate of ham and cheese and a couple of loaves of bread on the table. "Sit down and make some sandwiches," she told us. "I'll dish up the chili."

She sat the bowls of scalding chili in front of us and we all dug in. The chili was hot in both ways – scalding hot off the stove, and spicy hot, too. But it was delicious after a morning of fresh air. I had two bowls, and with a little coaxing, I was talked into a third.

"Boy! That is the best chili I've had in ages," I said.

"You'd better watch out with that stuff," Thunderfoot warned. "You know how those kidney beans react with you."

"Just be sure to stay upwind of me," I said.

"No doubt about that!" he said, laughing.

After we ate, we made our plans for the afternoon. A patch of big pine trees on the edge of town usually had a few deer in it. With only four of us, we'd be better off sticking to a smaller woodlot to make a drive. We decided that Jerry and Scott would go to the east end of the pines and find a couple of places to sit. Thunderfoot and I would go to the west end and do the same. Then, at 3:30, Thunderfoot and I would walk slowly through the pines, hoping to scare out any deer toward Jerry and Scott.

"You guys watch for us at about 4 o'clock," I said.

"Okay. We'll be ready," Jerry replied.

Off we went in the two pickups. Thunderfoot and I parked along the highway and walked along the fence at the end of the pine plantation. Thunderfoot stopped about a third of the way in and looked at his watch.

"I've got 1:44," he said.

"Okay. I'll set mine for that, too. We'll start walking at 3:30 sharp. But take it easy, and don't rush," I told him.

He nodded an okay. I walked on for a while, found a nice spot, and sat down.

Of course, with a full belly and a nice sunny afternoon, my eyes soon began to get heavy. I was at a nice big tree with a cushiony bed of needles on the ground, and I couldn't resist the temptation of a little nap. I was dreaming about deer and ducks, and then all at once I felt like I was having a heart attack. I woke up, sweating, and realized that my heart attack was really heartburn from the chili.

My stomach was churning and I thought I was going to blow up. Oh, boy! I had an upset stomach. I would have given anything for a *Tums*. I looked at my watch. It was nearly 3:30 already, so I stood up and carefully tried to let a little gas slip out, just to take off the pressure. I felt a little better.

It was time to start the drive toward Scott and Jerry. I walked slowly, working my way to the east. As I walked, I must have stirred up the chili again, because I soon had some terrible gas pains again. I stopped, concentrated, carefully vented and moved on.

Now I was half way through the woods, and suddenly I had a pain like what I imagined it would be like to give birth. I doubled over in pain and tried to bleed off a little more gas. But I knew that the previews were over. The big show was inevitable, and it was not far off.

I looked around for a log to sit across, but found nothing. The danger of an unwanted discharge was getting closer with every step, so I decided that the moment had come to release the beast, and by that time, it was almost too late. I laid down my gun and unzipped the front of my coveralls. Underneath was just a tee shirt and a pair of jeans, so I hurried the coveralls off my shoulders, dropped my jeans and let fly.

Because of the tremendous backpressure, it didn't take long for the job to be done. I reached in my vest pocket for my roll of TP and took care of things. When I bent over to pull up my pants, I saw what had happened. In my haste, I hadn't thought about the coveralls lying on the ground behind me. The backpressure had been great, but not great enough to take the main event past them.

"Oh, no," I groaned.

Well, there was nothing to do now but to get them off. I removed my boots and carefully slid my feet out of the legs of the coveralls. I used a stick to roll them up into a ball, and tied my deer dragging rope around them. I picked up my gun and started off through the woods again, dragging my coveralls behind me.

When I reached the other end of the woods, I heard voices.

"Maybe we should look for him... maybe he had a heart attack or something." It sounded like Jerry talking.

"He's probably in there someplace... sleeping," I heard Thunderfoot say.

"I'm not sleeping," I announced as I emerged from the woods.

"Jeez! You took long enough. What you been doing?"

"I just took my time," I said.

I had left the coveralls at the edge of the woods, planning to return later to get them... to save myself a little ridicule.

"Well, okay. Let's go," Scott said.

We started walking toward Jerry's truck when Thunderfoot stopped abruptly. "Hey, where's your coveralls?"

The other two stopped and looked me up and down, too. "Yeah. You were wearing coveralls when you went in there."

My brain was working overtime trying to think of a plausible explanation for why I was without my outer clothes.

The others just stood there waiting for an explanation.

"Well, I had a little accident with them, so I left them behind," I said.

"What did you do? Rip them?" Scott asked.

Thunderfoot began laughing like a fool, staggering around and clutching his belly.

"He pooped them. I'll bet you a dollar he pooped them."

The other two began laughing, too, so I hiked back a few yards, picked up the rope and pulled my bundle toward the truck. They all howled like mad when they saw me dragging the coveralls out of the woods.

"Ho, ho! Is that a buck or a doe?" Thunderfoot gasped between laughs.

"Need some help taking that to the locker?" Jerry said.

I just ignored their sophomoric behavior, walked to the truck and got in the passenger seat. Jerry was going to take me to my truck, and then I'd come back to pick up Thunderfoot.

When I drove my truck back, Thunderfoot and Scott had hoisted my bundled coveralls over a branch of a tree with the rope, and tied a deer carcass tag on the zipper.

"Come over here and stand by your trophy," Thunderfoot said. "I'll get the camera and take your picture."

Sometimes, he could be such a wise guy.

Thanks, Thunderfoot.

Lutefisk

Winter was just around the corner, and Thunderfoot had agreed to help me with my winterizing chores. There were still a few leaves to finish raking, some pots to move to the greenhouse, and most important of all, we had to winterize the pond in the back yard.

Pond might be a bit of a misnomer. Earlier in the summer, he and I had built *Lake* Thunderfoot, with some potted water lilies in the water, some arrow root plants, and, of course, some bluegills. The instructions that had come with the pond liner said to remove about half of the water and the pump, and leave it that way for the winter. So, that was our main chore for the day.

I saw Thunderfoot coming across the back yard. "Hey. You ever ate lutefisk?" he asked as he came through the front door.

"Nope. Why?"

"My grandpa gave me two tickets to a lutefisk dinner tonight. I thought you and I might go to it."

"Why isn't grandpa going?"

"He has to go to some meeting, but he already bought the tickets, and he doesn't want them to go to waste."

"What about your mom?"

"She said she doesn't like it."

I had never tried lutefisk, but I'd heard from some of my friends that it was great, and from others that it was awful. "Do you know what it is?" I asked.

"It's fish, isn't it?"

"Yeah. It's dried cod that's been soaked in lye," I said.

"Lye? Don't you make soap with that?"

"I guess they used to. I've heard it's good, and I've heard it's nasty. I really don't know, for sure, what it's like."

"Well, let's try it," Thunderfoot said. "We got free tickets."

Well, how bad could it be? I agreed that I'd go with him to

the supper.

We started our chores for the day out in the yard. By a little after noon, we had finished and I offered to make lunch, but Thunderfoot just wanted a snack, to save room for the lutefisk.

"I love fish," he said, nodding his head. "I don't want to miss out, so I'm gonna go *real* hungry."

We goofed around cleaning the boat and straightening up the garage for the rest of the day until it was time to go to the lutefisk supper.

The supper was at the Five Points Lutheran Church – a country church way out in the middle of nowhere. We knew *about* where it was, and when we came closer to the area, we saw signs pointing the way to the lutefisk supper.

"Wow! This must be a big deal," Thunderfoot said. "They've got signs all over the place."

When we topped the next hill, there was the church, sitting next to a small cemetery, and a parking lot with about a hundred cars in it.

"Holy smokes. Look at all the cars," Thunderfoot gasped.

"No foolin'. People must come from all over the place for this stuff. Maybe it's better than I've heard about," I said.

Kids with flashlights were directing cars to parking spots. People were going to and coming from the church it in steady streams. We parked and walked toward the church. As we got closer, we both began sniffing the air.

"Whew. What's that?" Thunderfoot said.

"It smells like a dead carp on a sandbar," I said.

"I hope that's not what were eating," he whispered.

"Me too."

We went in the door of the church and the aroma was even stronger. I looked at Thunderfoot and he just shrugged his shoulders. A man inside the church directed us to the pews in the main part of the church. "The next seating will be in about twenty minutes," he said.

"Seating?" I asked.

"Yes, we can seat about forty people at a time. You can wait in the church, and when the last group is finished, you can go down to the basement to eat. This will be our twentieth seating today."

"Twentieth? You mean there have been eight hundred people here to eat?" Thunderfoot asked.

"Oh, yes. We started at eleven o'clock this morning. By the time we're finished, we usually will have served about a thousand people."

We were both kind of amazed at those statements. We walked into the church, found a pew and sat down. Soon we were chatting with some people in the next row.

"So, this is your first time eating lutefisk?" the man asked.

"Yeah, my grandpa usually comes, but he couldn't make it, so we're using his tickets," Thunderfoot said. "Where are you folks from?"

"We're from Janesville," the man answered.

"Janesville! That's a hundred miles from here. Are you just visiting the area?" I asked.

"No, we drove up here just for the lutefisk," the man replied.

An older couple was sitting behind us, and the man smiled and said, "My wife and I are from Green Bay. We drove down here just for this, too."

Thunderfoot looked at me. "Maybe we've been missing out on something really good all this time."

I was beginning to think that he was right.

A few minutes later, the man from the front door stepped in front of the pews and told us that we could go to the basement and be seated. We got up with all the rest of the people and walked down the stairs to a big room that had long tables set up with plates and silverware and everything we would need for our lutefisk supper.

We sat at the table with the folks from Janesville and Green Bay, and within just a little while, the ladies of the parish started bringing bowls and platters of food to each table. First came a big bowl of mashed potatoes, and one of meatballs. Then came some green beans and one of corn. Then a girl brought out a plate of sweets and another brought bread and rolls. Finally, like a king entering his court, a lady brought out a big bowl of lutefisk and handed it to Thunderfoot. "Here, young man. You can start the main course."

The lutefisk *looked* kind of like fish, but it had a jellylike wiggle to it as Thunderfoot took hold of the bowl and spooned a medium sized chunk onto his plate. He had a worried look on his face as he passed the bowl to me. "Here. Have some lutefisk."

I was careful to take a piece that was not too big. I slid some of the wiggly stuff onto the plate and quickly passed it to our Green Bay friend. He shoveled about four big pieces of the stuff onto his plate and passed it on. The rest of our tablemates did the same.

The rest of the food was passed around and when we all had some of everything, we began eating. I cut off a small piece of fish and put it in my mouth, just as Thunderfoot did the same.

As soon as I bit down on the lutefisk, I knew why it wiggled so much. It was like tough jelly – like fish-flavored rubber bands. My throat constricted as my stomach tried to keep my mouth from sending the strange stuff down to it. I chewed and chewed and did my best to try to swallow it. I looked at Thunderfoot and he was doing the same, chewing like he had a hand grenade in his mouth. He looked at me with horror in his eyes. Both of us chewed for a long time, and we finally managed to swallow the lutefisk.

"How do you boys like the lutefisk?" Mr. Green Bay asked.

"I think somebody should be put in jail for doing that to perfectly good fish," Thunderfoot said.

Green Bay burst out laughing, and soon the whole table was in stitches over Thunderfoot's remark.

"It's an acquired taste," Green Bay said.

"How long have you been eating it?" I asked.

"Oh, for about thirty years," Green Bay said.

"You must be a glutton for punishment," Thunderfoot said.

Again the whole table had a good laugh.

I ate some of the meatballs and potatoes and gravy just to get the taste of the fish out of my mouth. The rest of the food was great, and both Thunderfoot and I ate several helpings of the other stuff, but we politely passed on extra helpings of lutefisk.

I hated to leave the fish on my plate, so I kind of hid it under some beans and potatoes. I could see Thunderfoot was doing the same thing. But our friends at the table ate lutefisk until I thought they would all blow up and make a terrible mess. Finally, we all were full.

"Well, what do you guys think? Will you be back again for lutefisk?" Green Bay asked.

Thunderfoot glanced my way. "I don't know about Dan, but I believe this will be my first and last time for it."

"I sure don't want to hurt anybody's feelings," I said, "but it would take a bunch of big, mean guys to ever make me come to another lutefisk supper."

"Big guys with big guns," Thunderfoot added.

Well, at least we gave it a try.

Thanks, Thunderfoot.

Finders Keepers

Our first day of ice fishing season was upon us. The morning was clear and crisp after a fair snowfall. I saw Thunderfoot pulling one of those little plastic sleds across the back yard on his way to my house. The sled was loaded down with his ice-fishing bucket, rods and tip-ups, propane stove, and medium size cooler, all tied down with bungee cords.

"You ready to go?" he said, huffing and puffing into the living room.

"Yeah. All I have to do is put on my jacket and boots. You've got lunch, right?"

"Yeah... I told you I'd make the lunch today, and we're gonna feast," he said grinning.

We loaded the ice shanty, his sled and all our gear into the back of the pickup, and off we went to the river bottoms.

I was never sure why, but we always started fishing at the same slough known as The Camp each year, as did most of the local fishermen. There always seemed to be good action there for the first month or so, and then, as the season went on, we moved on to the others – Puffenrots' or Kendal, and then Gutweiler's toward the end of the season – always in that same order. For some reason it had been this way for years, and so it was no surprise to see a dozen cars and trucks in the parking area at Camp. We unloaded our gear and I pulled the sled while Thunderfoot pulled the shanty down the bank and onto the ice.

We surveyed the lake, decided on a spot to fish, and started to get organized. Thunderfoot drilled four holes in a line, so we could fish in the warmth inside the shanty set up over them. Then he drilled a couple more holes for tip-ups a short distance away, making sure they were in line with the window in the side of the shanty so we could keep an eye on them.

Meanwhile, I set up the shanty and slid it over the holes. I put our gear inside and lit the propane stove so the shanty would get warm. I carried the minnow bucket to where Thunderfoot had drilled the tip-up holes and set the tip-ups, baited with golden shiners.

In just a little while, we were snug in our shanty with the heater keeping us warm, buckets lined up so we could fish with two poles each, and with the outlook of a great day ahead. The wind was blowing outside, and some of the other fishermen were braving it in the cold, but we were as comfortable as if we were sitting in the living room at home.

Thunderfoot pulled a nice bluegill from the hole, and soon we were catching more bluegills of various sizes, quite regularly.

"Flag!" Thunderfoot yelled as he looked out the window.

I zipped open the door of the shanty and we both ran to the tip-up. The line wasn't moving, so we knelt down and stared at the icy water in the hole, waiting for the Northern to make his move.

No movement.

"Lift it and see if there's any weight," I said.

Thunderfoot took off his gloves and carefully tested the line. "Nope. Nothing."

He pulled up the line until the golden shiner was just a few feet from the hole. "Probably the wind," I said.

We re-set the tip-up and went back to the shanty. When Thunderfoot was in and settled, and I had zipped the door closed, I reached down to pick up my poles. Only one was lying on the floor of the shanty.

"Hey. Did you pick up my other pole?" I asked.

"No. What would I want with another pole?"

"Well, it's gone. Crap! It must have gone down the hole."

"Probably a big bluegill... or a bass took it," Thunderfoot said.

Well that peeved me just a little. I had an extra pole along, but of course, the missing one was my favorite. I got out the extra pole, rigged it up and began fishing again.

We fished for another couple of hours with fair action and a couple more false alarms from the tip-ups. Thunderfoot decided it was time for lunch. "Just wait till you see what I've got here," he said. He reached over and tipped the heater on its side. It was a thing called a Heater/Cooker – it doubled as a heater and a cook stove. Just by tipping it to the side made a flat surface for a cooking pan.

"I made this last night," he said, sliding a pot of chili out of the cooler. He set the chili on the heater; in a few minutes the shanty smelled like diner. "Mmm, that smells good," I said.

When the chili was hot, Thunderfoot dipped out each of us a big bowlful. It was fantastic, and it really hit the spot on such a cold day.

When we had finished our chili, Thunderfoot rummaged in his cooler, put a small frying pan on the stove and poured in some cooking oil. Then he dropped chopped onions into the sizzling oil. When the onions were partially cooked, he laid two big hamburger patties on the stove, and once again the aroma was wonderful.

It was getting a little smoky in the shanty; I unzipped the door part way to let out some of the smoke and heat. It didn't take long for the burgers to fry, and in short order munched on some great sandwiches–ala Thunderfoot.

Just outside the door there stood a big guy with icicles hanging from his beard, and a frozen-looking sandwich in his hand.

"If you guys don't close that door and keep that smell inside, I'm gonna have to leave," he said.

"Oh. Sorry," Thunderfoot said. "What smell is it that you don't like?"

"It's not that I don't like it, but I'm sitting here eating a frozen baloney sandwich, and the smell of your food is driving me nuts."

"Oops. Sorry," Thunderfoot said. "We've got plenty of chili left. You want a bowl?"

"Sure, I'll take one," Grizzly said.

"Yeah, I will too," a fisherman a short ways away said.

"How much you got?" another asked.

Well, it didn't take long for just about every fisherman on the ice to line up for a bowl of chili. Luckily, Thunderfoot had packed a whole package of plastic bowls and spoons.

Lunch hour over, we went back to fishing. By mid -afternoon the sun was shining and the wind had died down a bit. It was pretty nice outside the shanty. "I'm goin out and fish a few new holes," Thunderfoot said.

"Yeah, me too. It's nice out there now," I said.

We cut some holes and sat down on our buckets to fish. We hadn't been at it long when Thunderfoot started to laugh. He was holding a fish, hanging from his line just above the water. A second line from the fish's mouth went down into the hole.

"Finders, keepers?" he asked.

"Depends on what you found," I said.

He raised his fish, and up came the line and my pole that had disappeared earlier during the tip-up false alarm.

"Holy cow! My pole!"

Sure enough, my jig was in the fish's mouth, along with Thunderfoot's jig, and there was my pole hanging from a blue gill the size of the top of a pop can.

"Yeah, sure. A big bluegill or a bass," Thunderfoot laughed.

We removed the hooks from the little bluegill and Thunderfoot was about to toss him down the hole.

"Stop. Let's keep him," I said.

"What for? He's too small."

"Not for eating," I said. Let's put him in the aquarium, and next spring he can go out in the pond in the back yard. A Northern'll probably eat him this winter if we throw him back. He'll have a safe home in the pond."

Thunderfoot put the little fish in the minnow bucket for the ride to his new home. "I've thought of a good name for him, too," he said.

"What's that?"

"Gilbert."

"Gilbert the Blue Gill. That's good," I said.

We fished a couple more hours and then gathered up our stuff. We loaded everything on the folded down shanty, and as we walked off the ice toward the truck, Grizzly called out: "Hey, kid! C'mere."

Thunderfoot walked over to the man. "Here," Grizzly said, handing him a dollar. "For the chili – it really hit the spot."

"Oh, you don't have to pay for it. I had plenty," Thunderfoot said.

"Take it. It was worth that, and more. Next time, bring some extra hamburgers, and I'll buy one of those, too."

Thunderfoot thanked the man, and before he got off the ice he had nine dollars in his pocket from other fishermen who had sampled his chili. He was looking kind of smug as he walked up to the pickup to help me load the shanty.

"What did those guys want?" I asked.

He put out his hand holding a fist full of dollar bills. "They like my cooking," he said.

"Well, that was nice of them, and nice of you to do that in the first place. I guess one good deed deserves another."

"Yeah, I guess so," he said grinning. "Maybe I'll make a sign for the shanty, and start a new business."

"Just as long as you don't start charging me," I said.

"I'll just put yours on account," he said, and slapped me on the back.

Thanks, Thunderfoot.

Wheels

I was just about to drift off into an afternoon nap when I heard the loud vroooom, vroooom of a car in the driveway. I knew who it was. He had been waiting quite a while for this big day. There sat Thunderfoot in his new car. He waved for me to come out and have a look.

"Come and see my new wheels," he said as I stepped out onto the porch.

"Jeez! It looks like a racecar."

"You bet! And it runs like a racecar too."

He had been saving his money for the last two years for a car, and he had finally found the one he wanted, and the one that he could afford to buy. I kept trying to steer him toward something small with a tiny engine, that wouldn't go past about 50 miles per hour. Of course, he wanted just the opposite.

The car was a Dodge Charger, and it looked like something that should have been on a racetrack instead of in my driveway. It was gold, with stripes down the side, and it even had a couple of stripes from the windshield to the front of the grill. It sounded like a racecar, too, as Thunderfoot kept gunning the engine and making it roar.

"Turn that thing off. You're making me deaf," I said.

He grinned, shut off the engine, and stepped out of the car. "Well what do you think of her?"

I looked it over, and while I checked out the upholstery, he popped the hood. "Look at this engine," he said.

I tried to act impressed as I stared into the engine compartment. The extent of my knowledge about cars and how they ran was confined to the fact that gas went into the hole in the back, and the key started it. If it didn't start, I called someone to fix it. "Yeah, that's a big one," I said.

"It's got some real kick to it."

"Yeah, well you'd better be careful with it... at least until you get used to driving it. It's supposed to snow tonight, so take it easy."

"Yes, Mom."

He was grinning as he dropped the hood. "I'll be careful. You know I didn't save for two years just to wreck it the first day."

"Yeah, I know. I just worry that you'll get hurt," I said.

"Don't worry. Jerry and Scott and I are going to take her for a spin tonight, and we'll be careful. I promise."

I went back into the house, and he went to show off his car to anybody else that would look at it.

It started to snow later that afternoon and it kept on snowing all evening. I spent a quiet evening with a book and the dogs, and after I had taken them out for their last potty session, I went to bed. As usual, about two thirty I had to get up to use the bathroom – one of the joys of getting older.

When I was finished in the bathroom, I turned off the light, opened the door, and ran right into a man standing in the hallway. I jumped back and shouted something incoherent at him, and began to look for something with which to defend myself. My shouting woke up the dogs and they came barking and growling from my bedroom, and the dark, quiet house quickly evolved into bedlam. I tried to grab the intruder in the dark, and then he started yelling at me. "Wait, wait, it's me!" Thunderfoot yelled.

I stopped short and turned on the light. "Holy Criminey! What the heck are you doing here? You almost gave me a heart attack," I said.

"You! Jeez! I about pooped when you came out of there and attacked me."

"What are you doing here at two thirty in the morning?" I asked again.

"I had a little problem with the car, and I came here to see if you can help."

Then I noticed that he was dripping wet and shivering. "What happened? Why are you all wet?"

"Well, Jerry and Scott and I were out driving around and we came to this place in the road where you had to turn right or left. But it was real slick, and we went straight. We went through a fence and out into a field."

"Good God! Are you okay?"

"Yeah. But the car is stuck in the field."

"Where are Jerry and Scott?"

"They're out on your front porch."

"Go and bring them inside before they freeze to death," I said.

He went to the living room and called to his pals to come in. They both looked like drowned rats, too, wet from head to toe.

"You guys get those wet clothes off, and I'll get you something dry to put on," I said. I went to the bedroom that Thunderfoot used when he stayed over and found some of his tee shirts and jeans. Jerry and Thunderfoot were about the same size, but Scott was a little huskier, so I found a pair of sweat pants for him. I got out some towels and took them to the boys. The three of them were standing in their underwear, shivering like crazy. "You guys jump in the shower for a few minutes and warm up, and then put on these dry clothes," I said.

They all trooped off to the bathroom, and while they were taking turns in the shower, I gathered up all the wet clothes and tossed them in the dryer. Then I put a big pan of water on the stove to make some hot chocolate. By the time the water was hot, they all were wearing dry clothes and had warmed up a bit. The hot chocolate finished the job.

They were sitting side by side on the couch, and I was sitting across from them in my recliner. "Well, you guys have been busy tonight. Where did you wreck?"

"Out by Sand Branch creek," Scott said.

"You walked all the way from there?"

"We didn't have much choice," Jerry said. "It was that or sit there in the middle of the field for the night, after Mario Andretti, here, drove us through the fence."

"Well, we'd better call your folks and let them know where

you are, so they don't worry," I said. I stood up to get the phone.

"Uhhh, we can't do that," Thunderfoot said.

"Why?"

"Well, I'm supposed to be staying over at Jerry's, and he's supposed to be staying over at Scott's, and Scott is supposed to be staying over at my house."

"So you little connivers fixed it so you could stay out all night and not get caught?"

"Yeah, and it would have worked, too... if we hadn't crashed."

"Well, I'll help you get the car out of the field, but not until morning. You guys can sleep here, and we'll see what we can do then, okay?"

They all agreed. Thunderfoot went to his room, and I found some pillows and blankets for Jerry and Scott to sleep on the sofa that opened to a bed. I went back to bed, and the house was dark and quiet once again.

The next morning I fried a pound of bacon, scrambled a dozen eggs, and toasted a loaf of bread. My young midnight hikers polished it all off in just a few minutes. Their own clothes were dry by then, so they got dressed. I put on some boots and found extra ones for them, and off we went to rescue Mario's racecar.

The snow had stopped falling, but the roads were still covered. In a short time we got to the scene of the wreck. "How fast were you going?" I asked as I peered at the car sitting in the middle of the field, about fifty yards from the highway.

"A little too fast, I guess," Thunderfoot said, grinning.

"Will it run and drive?" I asked.

"Yeah. It's not hurt... just some scratches on the hood where we went through the fence."

I contemplated the situation and decided it would be easier to get the car out from another road on the back side of the field. The car was closer to it than it was to the road we were on. "I'm going down to the house and tell them what's going on," I said, "and meanwhile, a couple of you go out there and hook this chain under the car someplace on the frame. One of you can come with me to open that gate on the ridge road."

Jerry went with me, and I drove down to the farmer's house and explained what we were doing. The farmer said that if I couldn't get them out, to come back and he'd come out with his tractor. Jerry told him that they would be back and help repair the fence. The farmer was real nice about it. "That would be just fine," he told Jerry.

I drove back past the field and stopped at the ridge road. Jerry opened the gate and I drove through, gunning it a little because it was kind of steep. I stopped about half way up the slope and waited for Jerry to get back into the pickup. Then I gave it some gas and began to climb up the steep road. I got almost to the top and the tires began spinning. "Uh, oh," I said. I gave it a little more gas, but that only caused the truck to slide sideways, over the side of the hill. I braked and we stopped.

"We've got problems," I said.

Jerry nodded. "See if you can go backward," he whispered, as if talking out loud would cause us to slide down the hill.

I put the truck in reverse and gave it a little gas. We started to slide again, and now we were even closer to the edge of the bank.

"That's not going to work," I said.

We sat there, afraid to move, trying to think of a way out of our predicament. "I'm afraid we'll slide over the edge if I try to go any farther."

Jerry nodded, his face nearly as white as the snow.

"But we gotta do something," I said.

I put the truck in Low and gave it a little gas. We moved uphill about a foot and then the truck started sliding over the edge. It only took a couple of seconds for us to slide down the hill sideways, but it seemed like hours. Jerry and I were both screaming like thirteen-year-old girls at a horror movie. When we reached the bottom, the truck tipped up on its side, hovered there a few seconds, and then fell back onto its wheels. Jerry was almost sitting in my lap by then, and when we stopped, he let out a breath like he had been holding it for hours.

"Holy smokes! I don't believe we did that," he said.

I could barely speak, let alone release the steering wheel. "W... w... we almost tipped this thing over," I managed to say.

We sat there a few moments, recovering from our trance-like stupor, when Thunderfoot started blowing the horn on the racecar. Jerry gave me a big grin. He slid over to the other side of the seat. "I think we'll go out through the hole in the fence," he said. I nodded and grinned, too.

We drove along side the hill to the pasture where Thunderfoot and Scott were waiting. "Jeez! What took you so long?"

"We had a little adventure trying to get to that ridge road," Jerry said.

"Yeah... just a tiny flaw in our plans." Jerry and I laughed, but Scott and Thunderfoot, though, failed to see the humor in the joke.

We hooked up the chain to my trailer hitch, and although it took some time and effort, I managed to tow the racecar back toward the hole in the fence, and we finally got it back on the road. Thunderfoot started it up and vroomed the engine. It seemed to be okay to drive.

"Okay," I said. "You guys go down to the house and see when he wants you to come and help him fix the fence. I'm going home."

The boys all thanked me and I drove away. I was still shaking from the ride over the side of the hill.

About mid-afternoon, the phone rang. It was Thunderfoot. "We got the fence fixed and the car is okay... except for two big scratches on the hood where the barbed wire scraped it."

"Well, that's good. And it's even better that you guys didn't get hurt."

"Yeah. That was pretty stupid, to take the car out on a snowy night. Maybe I learned a lesson... you think?"

I grinned. "Maybe. At least, I hope so," I said.

"You going anyplace tonight?"

"Nope. Why?"

"The guys and I are coming over. Don't make any supper. We're buying."

"Ok. See you then."

A couple of hours later, the three of them got out of the car in my driveway. Jerry and Scott were each carrying a huge pizza box, and Thunderfoot had a case of sodas. They came in, took off their shoes and coats, and we all sat around the kitchen table, laughing and talking and eating pizza.

"That was pretty cool of you not to nark on us last night," Jerry said.

"Yeah. Thanks for that, and for a hot shower, dry clothes and a warm bed," Scott added.

Thunderfoot just punched me in the arm. "These guys don't know you like I do," he said. "That's why I hang around with you. You're a pretty okay guy."

I grinned at him. "And the best fisherman in town, too."

He grinned. "Second best."

Thanks, Thunderfoot.

Runaway Ship

When it came to fishing, Thunderfoot and I really didn't care what we caught. We enjoyed fishing for anything that swam in the area lakes and rivers. No matter if we were fishing small mouth bass or carp, as long as they pulled on our line, we liked it. If we had to choose a favorite, though, it probably would have been the spring walleye.

There is nothing like sliding the boat across an icy landing and into water that has chunks of ice floating in it, and then feeling the faint tick of a walleye inhaling your jig, especially after a long winter of fishing through a hole in the ice. Walleye fishing was our first chance to get out and fish on *soft* water again.

The first places to fish each year are below the dams on the Mississippi and Wisconsin rivers. Due to the fast moving water, the ice melts sooner below the dams, and they're the first places to see boats each spring. I had received a call from a friend who lived near Genoa. He told me that the dam was open and the boat landings were free of ice. So, Thunderfoot and I were heading for the big river at first light for our first day of open water fishing. Riding between us, with his head tipped back, his mouth open, snoring loudly, was Thunderfoot's buddy, Scott, who often went with us on our adventures.

We arrived at the river and prepared the boat for it's first launch of the year. Someone had scattered pea gravel and salt on the landing ramp, so it was quite safe backing up to the edge of the water, where we slid the boat off the trailer and into the river. I jumped in the boat while Thunderfoot parked the truck, and Scott held onto the bow rope. I wanted to be sure the motor would start before we got away from the landing. It started right away, and it was nicely warmed up by the time Thunderfoot sprinted back from the parking lot. "Cast off, mate!" he said to Scott as he climbed into the boat.

We idled away from the landing out into the current, and then motored upriver to the dam. We weren't alone, as there were already twenty or more boats already there. When we got up into the pack of boats, I stopped the motor. Thunderfoot jumped up onto the front seat and lowered the bow mount trolling motor and worked us downriver through the maze of other boats. I didn't have my line in the water very long when I felt that slight tap on my jig. I set the hook into a walleye of respectable size.

"Ah! Boy that felt good," I said as I lifted the first fish of the season into the boat.

Just as I said that, Scott set his hook into another fish, and just a second later Thunderfoot did, too. They glanced at each other with that competitive look in their eyes, and both began reeling as fast as they could, eager to be the first with his fish in the boat. Thunderfoot's fish was rather small. It came up fast, and he won the challenge. "Okie, dokie, Scotto," he said with a huge grin. "You buy the ice cream!"

"That's okay," Scott replied with a smile. "It's worth a couple of ice creams just to be here on a beautiful day like this." He enjoyed the fishing too much to let a little thing like buying ice cream bother him.

It was, indeed, a beautiful day. The sun was up over the hills, now, and the air was warming into the 50s – just about perfect for a day of spring walleye fishing.

We drifted slowly downriver until we were no longer getting bites. I started the big motor again, and we went back to the dam and started another drift. It didn't seem like much time had passed when Thunderfoot announced that he was famished. I checked my watch – it was already past noon. We pulled over to the shore, drug the boat up on the sandbar, stretched our legs and ate some sandwiches.

While we were eating, Thunderfoot took notice of the western sky and said, "Boy, those clouds over there look like they're gonna rain or snow on us."

Sure enough. A bank of really dark clouds was rolling in, and they looked wet. "Well, we've got plenty of fish right now, but I'd like to fish a while longer," I said. "We'll keep an eye on the clouds, and if they look like they're gonna rain on us, we'll get out of here."

I took over the trolling motor and Thunderfoot ran the gas motor when we went back on the river. I was on my pedestal seat fishing, running the trolling motor, and minding my own business when I heard Thunderfoot say to Scott, "Crack kills."

They both laughed.

Then Scott said, "Say no to crack."

Another big laugh.

I turned around. "What are you guys talking about?"

They were snickering and Thunderfoot pointed to my lower back. "Every time you lean over, don't you feel a draft?"

I reached behind me and then I understood. My jeans had slid down a little, and my butt crack was showing, and they were making fun of me. "Quit picking on my butt crack. My jeans just don't stay up very good... I'm all belly and no butt."

"Well, from where we're sitting, there's enough of your butt showing that it makes us just about lose our sandwiches," Thunderfoot teased.

I laid down my pole, stood, and hiked up my pants. "There. Now you ladies won't have anything to whine about."

"Thanks. You're so kind."

I have had a problem with my pants sliding down for most of my adult life. I'm kind of built wrong for good pants position. I'm top heavy, with a much smaller behind than I have belly, and there's just no way to keep my pants from sliding once in a while. I'm not to that stage, yet, when I want to wear them up under my armpits, so I just have to put up with a little slippage now and then.

We fished for about another hour, and then the wind picked up, swirling around a few snowflakes. "Let's reel up and get out of here," I said. "If it starts snowing heavy like it does sometimes in the spring, I'd rather be on the other side of the big hills between here and home before the roads get slick."

The boys agreed. We reeled in our lines and headed back to the landing. By the time the boat was on the trailer, heavy snow was coming down. Luckily, enough salt on the landing kept it from getting slick, so we made it up from the water and onto the highway with no problems.

We had planned to drive downriver to Lynxville, then up the Lynxville hill, and on home. But by the time we got there, the snow was piling up on the road. "Boy, I wonder if we should try to get up that hill?" I said.

"If we don't, we have to go all the way to Prairie du Chien," Thunderfoot said. "That's a lot longer road home."

We stopped in Lynxville to take a better look at the road. The route we were to travel went up the side of a huge Mississippi bluff. About three hundred yards up the steep incline, the road took a sharp turn to the left and continued up the backside of the bluff. That was the problem. To make the left turn, you had to slow way down and lose all of your upward momentum.

"Well, what do you guys think?" I asked.

Thunderfoot walked up the road a little ways and scraped his foot through the snow. "It's only six inches deep. We can make it."

"Okay. Let's go before it get any worse," I said.

We began the climb, and it was going quite well up to the turn. I didn't want to go too fast, but I had to keep moving upward. As I slowed down turning into the sharp curve, the wheels started to spin. "Uh, oh." The truck slid sideways and came to rest up against the left bank at a right angel to the boat.

"Oops. That didn't work too well," Thunderfoot said.

I applied the emergency brake, and we got out to look over the situation. It was not good.

"There's no way to keep going up," I said. "We'll have to unhook the boat, get the truck turned around and go back down."

The boys agreed. "Scott, you get in the truck. We'll unhook the boat and lead it down the hill. Then you turn the truck around and meet us at the bottom. We'll hook it up again and go home by way of Prairie du Chien."

Scott nodded okay. Thunderfoot and I went to the back of the truck, unhooked the lights and safety chains, and then I said to Thunderfoot, "Hang on tight when I take the hitch off the ball."

Thunderfoot nodded.

I opened the latch and we lifted the trailer tongue of the off the ball. The boat rolled backward and we walked with it, one of us on each side, holding onto the trailer tongue. "This isn't so bad," Thunderfoot said.

We had started at a brisk walk, and soon we were trotting behind the boat. "Hold back on it! It's going faster!" I was starting to pant.

Then our trot increased to a fair-paced run. "I'm holding as much as I can," Thunderfoot said. There was a little panic in his voice. "I can't keep it slow. It's gonna get away if we don't run with it."

We ran as fast as we could, doing our best to keep the boat from veering off the road and crashing over the side of the hill. Then, just when I thought it couldn't get any worse, it got worse. My pants began sliding down off my butt. "Oh, no! My pants are coming down!" I yelled. Then they slid a little farther, and then they dropped to my knees. I was running as fast as I could, taking one-foot-long steps because my pants were now around my ankles, acting like a prisoner's leg restraints.

Thunderfoot was panting and laughing as we ran, me with my pants flopping along on the roadway. "Say no to crack!" he managed to get out between laughs, glancing over his shoulder at my long underwear – that was now sliding down just as my pants had done.

We were both laughing, and we could hardly hold onto the boat, but we finally reached the bottom and stopped the trailer against a mailbox post. There I stood, snow blowing around me, snot running from my nose, steam rising off my bare butt, and my pants and underwear in the snow. Thunderfoot was lying on the road laughing so hard I thought he was going to have a coronary.

Just then Scott drove up behind us. He beeped the horn and rolled down his window. "Say no to crack!"

I brushed off some of the snow from my pants and long johns, and got them back to where they were supposed to be. We all sat and laughed until I thought I was going to be sick.

"It's good nobody else was coming up this road," I said.

"Yeah," Thunderfoot laughed. "They'd have probably driven right over the side if they saw you coming down the hill like that!"

We maneuvered the boat trailer around with the tongue pointing in the right direction, hooked it up to the truck again, and drove down into Lynxville. We stopped at one of the local restaurants for a bite to eat, and to hear the weather reports.

"The road's closed to Prairie," the owner said.

"Oh, great," I moaned. "We can't get up the hill, and the highway is closed. What do we do now?"

"The motel has a couple of rooms left. Want me to call?"

The owner called the motel and confirmed a room. We had our meal, and then there was nothing more to do but to sit out the storm until the next morning.

"I'll call my neighbor to take care of the dogs; you boys call your moms and let them know we're all right."

After we ate, we drove the short distance to the motel, packed our fish in snow, and went to our room. Thunderfoot and Scott shared one double bed, and I had one to myself.

When we were all snug in bed, I turned out the light. "Well, that was pretty fun," Thunderfoot said.

"Yeah. That was great," I replied.

"From where I was sitting, it wasn't very pretty," Scott added.

"Yeah," Thunderfoot said. "From what I saw, it was pretty terrifying, too. I'll probably have nightmares, so if I yell out during the night, you'll know I'm reliving it."

It was quiet for a few minutes and then Thunderfoot yelled, "Say no to crack!"

Wise guy.

Thanks, Thunderfoot.

Snow Day Fun

It was a typical spring snowstorm. Just when we thought the green grass and leaves were right around the corner, a heavy, wet snow fell, and by morning there was nearly a foot of it on the ground. Thunderfoot came over for breakfast. Since earlier in the week we had planned to go turkey scouting this Saturday morning. Of course, turkey scouting was cancelled, so we were trying to come up with something else to occupy the day.

Thunderfoot wanted to get the boat out and go on the river for some walleyes. "No way," I said. "I'm not dragging the boat through all that snow and salt just to find out that the boat landing is snowed under."

"Well, what're we gonna do all day?"

"Go out and shovel the driveway," I said. "I'll think of something while you're shoveling."

He grumbled and griped, but he went out shoveling, and he took the dogs with him. They loved playing in the snow. Thunderfoot threw shovels of snow at them as they ran past. The driveway wasn't getting much cleaner, but the three of them had a great time.

Then they all came bounding through the front door amid a shower of snow and water. The dogs shook off their wet coats and laid down for a nap, exhausted. Thunderfoot pealed off several layers of wet clothes, and while I hung them up to dry, he disappeared toward my room. I noticed that his wet socks I was hanging were *my* socks. "Hey! What are you doing with my socks?" I asked.

"What do you mean?"

"Why were you wearing my socks?" I said, walking into his bedroom. He was just putting on a fresh pair. They were mine, too. "And why are you wearing my socks again?"

"Yours are nice and new. Mine are all thin and full of holes," he said.

Well, that explained why I was always out of fresh socks. I had just bought two dozen new pairs, and now I knew I wasn't just imagining that they disappeared right before my eyes. "Guess what you're getting for Christmas next year," I said.

"Oh, I don't need any new socks," Thunderfoot replied. "I just got a bunch of new ones a couple of weeks ago."

Real funny.

"So, what're we gonna do?"

"How about we clean out this closet in your room and find the Monopoly game?" I said.

"Okay. I'm a master at Monopoly."

We opened the double closet and started sorting through all the saved stuff. It was stacked full of junk on top of more junk.

"Jeez! When's the last time you cleaned this out?" he asked.

"I've been putting stuff in this closet since I moved here, and I don't think I've ever taken anything out."

"Oh boy! A treasure chest," he said.

We dragged boxes out and opened them to see what was inside. It was a mess. "Get the big trash can from the shop," I said. "We're gonna throw about half of this junk away."

Thunderfoot brought in the can and we began sorting stuff from the boxes. He opened one that was full of tubes of oil paint and brushes. "What's all this?"

"Oh, I attempted to learn to paint once," I explained. "I thought it would be nice to be able to paint pictures like those wildlife artists do, but I'm no good at it."

"Did you try?" he asked.

"Yeah. Look at that," I said, pointing at a canvas covered board that was under the box. He pulled out the "painting" and started to laugh. "Jeez! It looks like a road-killed duck."

I looked at the horrible attempt at painting and quickly tossed it into the trashcan. "Not one of my better skills."

Next was a box full of old papers from school. "You planning on a new career as a student?" he asked.

"Throw them."

I was sorting through a box of puzzles and games when Thunderfoot found a little shoebox with a shoestring tied around it. "What's this? Your pet turtle?"

"Marsha! That's Marsha," I said.

I carefully opened the box, and there, wrapped in a tiny piece of flannel blanket, was Marsha – my bunny rabbit from when I was a little baby.

Thunderfoot picked the artifact out of the box and began laughing. "What is this supposed to be?"

"It's a rabbit. It was my favorite toy when I was a little kid," I said, admiring Marsha.

"That's a rabbit? It looks more like a bean bag."

Well, I had to admit, Marsha bore little resemblance to a rabbit anymore. Actually, my mom and grandma had thrown away the real Marsha while I was taking a nap. She had become so dirty and ragged that they didn't want me to play with her anymore. They stitched up a chunk of cloth, stuffed it with cotton, sewed on two mismatching buttons for eyes, and told me they had washed Marsha, and now she just looked a little different. I must have been very gullible at that age, because I bought the deception and accepted this beanbag as Marsha, despite the fact that Marsha used to have rabbit ears and now she had no ears at all. Many years ago my mom had dropped her off at my house, thinking I would like to have her – I guess for my old age, when I was senile. I put Marsha in the closet, and she had been there ever since.

"Garbage can?" Thunderfoot asked.

"Not on your life!" I said. "Marsha goes back on the shelf." I carefully wrapped poor Marsha in her little flannel blanket.

Thunderfoot shook his head sadly. "So obviously deranged," he whispered.

Our next great find was a box that held about fifteen bottles of cologne. "Wow! A stink-me-pretty treasure chest," Thunderfoot said. He began opening the bottles that had been on the shelf for twenty years or more. "Hai Karate, Brut, English

Leather – boy, these are real antiques," he said.

"One year I happened to mention that I needed some after shave," I said. "I got about twenty bottles of it for Christmas... a lifetime's worth. I guess I just stashed some of it away and forgot about it. You can have it if you want."

"Oh, boy. Thanks. If I want to smell like a grandpa, I'll be all set. Thanks, but no thanks. I think it needs to go in the can."

I agreed.

Thunderfoot was about to pull another box down when he jumped back. He ran to the hall closet, grabbed a can of Raid, then to the kitchen and tore off about ten feet of paper towel.

"What are you doing?" I asked.

"A huge spider is up there," he said.

He sprayed the Raid into the box, and then carefully opened the lid. With the paper towel wrapped around his hand, he slowly reached in and grabbed the stunned spider. It was a tiny little thing, about the size of a match head.

"Jeez! I thought you found a tarantula," I said, laughing. "That's just a harmless little spider.

"There's nothing harmless about a spider – any size."

We opened some more boxes, ever vigil for another spider attack. By the time we had gone through the last box, the garbage can was full, and the closet now had a lot of room for more good junk – when I got some. I began putting away the keepers, and Thunderfoot decided it was time to start lunch.

"There's some ham and cheese in the refrigerator," I said. "Get out the bread and butter and mayo, and we can have sandwiches and salad."

I heard him rummaging around in the refrigerator, and soon after, I heard the microwave beeping. I put the garbage can back in the shop and went into the kitchen. A cup was going around and around in the microwave. "You making hot chocolate?"

"No. I wanted some boiled egg for my salad, so I put one in a cup of water to boil."

"Can you do that?" I asked.

"Sure. Why not? You can boil water in a cup for coffee or chocolate. Why not boil an egg in one?"

Just then there was a loud POP! The microwave window instantly turned a pale yellow. Thunderfoot ran over and opened the door to stop the cooking. "Oops. I guess you were right." The entire inside of the microwave was covered with partly boiled egg, eggshell, and hot water. "Who would guess that one little egg could make such a mess?" he said, grinning.

"Well, so much for that idea. I guess the microwave needed cleaning anyway. Now it'll get done for sure."

After we had eaten our lunch, cleaned up the dishes *and* the microwave, we set up the card table in front of the TV and started a game of Monopoly. We spent the afternoon buying and selling property, and watching TV guys catching fish on the outdoor shows. Outside, the snow continued to pile up and it was dark. "You staying over tonight?"

"Yeah, I guess so. I'll call Mom. What's for supper?" he said.

I went to the freezer and pulled out a package of walleye fillets. "Shore lunch for supper," I said.

Thunderfoot grinned. "Well, that's okay by me. Let's look at the pictures of that last trip to Canada while the fish thaws out."

So, as evening came, we reminisced about Canada and ate an *indoor* shore lunch. Sometimes it doesn't take much to have an interesting day, especially when you can share it with a good buddy.

Thanks, Thunderfoot.

Turkey Trouble

When you apply for a turkey permit, you have a choice of the area and the time periods that you wish to hunt. Thunderfoot and I usually filled out our applications so that we covered all six time periods. We picked our favorite area as our first zone choice, and the other side of the river as our second choice. This year, I had chosen the first, third and fifth periods, and Thunderfoot had chosen the second, fourth and sixth.

My permit arrived in the mail, and then I saw Thunderfoot trotting across the back yard carrying his envelope. "What did you get?" he asked as he came flying through the door.

"Third period," I said.

"Bummer. I got first and fourth."

"You got two? You lucky little cuss! I've gotten two only once in my life."

"You just gotta know how to fill out the form," he said grinning.

It was only a little over a week until the first season, so we started making plans. We always hunted together, and that was the reason we tried for different seasons, so we could hunt more times. It really didn't make any difference to me if I shot a turkey or not. I just loved being out in the woods at dawn, listening to the gobbling – the sounds of hens and toms talking back and forth. The idea of fooling a big tom into making him think I was a turkey was the real reason I liked the sport so much. Fooling any wild critter with a call, like a turkey or a duck, just made it the sport for me. It was always exciting just to see them coming in. Killing the bird or ducks wasn't so important – fooling them into thinking I was one of them was the fun part.

"I think we should go up on the hill and wait for some gobbles on the first day," I said. "Then we can work our way to which ever side they happen to be on."

"Yeah, that's a good idea. They like that hilltop for strutting in the early morning sun."

We had this turkey thing down quite well. Of course, we had been hunting the same area for six years, so we knew the turkeys and their habits.

We had everything prepared, and the night before opening day Thunderfoot stayed over at my house so we'd be ready for an early start - at least an hour before first light. The hilltop that we liked to hunt required climbing a long, steep logging road, and it took us - well, it took *me* - quite a while to get to the top without having a coronary. Thunderfoot, on the other hand, was barely breathing hard when we reached the hay field at the top.

We had a quick breakfast of cereal and toast, loaded his gun and our turkey vests into the back of the truck, and off we went through the darkness to our favorite hunting farm. We parked near the milk house. Our friend Ken, who owned the farm, knew we would be there this particular morning, so we just left the key in the truck and began sneaking up the hill on the logging road.

Thunderfoot was carrying his shotgun, and since I didn't have a permit for this season, I only had my calls and a decoy in the back of my vest.

To those non-turkey hunters, I should explain a turkey vest. It's a wonderful invention that allows a turkey hunter to carry all of the toys it takes to get a turkey close enough to shoot, keeping his hands free. Our turkey vests are made of camouflage material with about a dozen pockets of all sizes to hold calls, gloves, hand warmers, candy bars, water bottles, head nets, shells, and the big pouch on the back will carry a decoy or two. If the hunter gets a turkey, it will fit in the pouch and can be lugged out on the hunter's back rather than carrying it. The vests also have a seat cushion attached to the back with a strip of nylon. While you are walking, Velcro holds the cushion up inside the vest against your back. When you get to where you want to sit, you pull the seat free, and let it flop down so you can sit on it. What a great idea.

We had climbed about half way up the logging road when I felt a little backpressure in the nether region. "Oh, boy. I think I'm gonna have to visit Mother Nature," I whispered to Thunderfoot.

"What a surprise," he whispered. "How many times have we gone hunting when you *didn't* have to do that?"

"Well, I can't help it. When it's time, it's time."

He just shook his head. "Let me get up the road a ways before you start."

I stopped and took off my vest and found my handy dandy little roll of toilet paper in one of the handy dandy pockets in the vest. I always had a little roll of emergency paper with me. I spied a tree broken off about two feet from the bottom, but it was still attached to the stump, probably broken when logs were skidded down the road many years ago. It was about eight inches thick and looked sturdy enough for a perfect place to sit and ponder the mysteries of life.

The broken tree was right on the edge of the road, right above a steep bank, so everything would drop away from the road and not offend my sensitive hunting partner.

I unhooked my bib overalls, lowered my boxers and sat down on the log, sliding across it far enough to get my business done. I put my elbows on my knees and relaxed. I was in about mid-deposit when the tree made a slight cracking noise. I tried to hurry. I was just about to stand up when the log cracked again, and both the tree and I went over the bank backwards. I rolled over backward about three or four times before I came to rest at the bottom of the hill. The log rolled down, too, and stopped when it hit my shins.

I was sitting there on the bare ground trying to get my bearings when I heard Thunderfoot chuckling. He was peering down at me over the edge of the road, sitting there with my pants around my ankles. "You think you could make a little more noise?" he whispered. "There are a few turkeys over across the river that didn't hear you."

I ignored him, got myself up, and brushed off the dirt and leaves that covered me. Thankful that I had missed my deposits and that none of that stuck to me, I used my paper and situated my pants. Then I had to walk all the way back down to the end of the road and climb the hill again to where I had taken my fall. When I got there, Thunderfoot was leaning against the tree, just shaking his head. "I swear. I should get college credit for this."

"Oh, dry up," I said. "Let's go hunting."

"Let me go first," he said. "I don't want to take the chance of you tipping over and knocking me all the way down the hill."

I socked him in the arm.

We finally reached the edge of the field, sat down, and waited for some birds to begin tree gobbling. Tree gobbling is just what the words imply. The toms roost together in one or several trees that are close together, and the hens do the same, somewhere nearby. When there is just enough morning light, the toms gobble from the tree, to let the hens know where they are, hoping the hens will fly down from their roost to where the toms are waiting. The hens, too, make a yelping sound to let the toms know where they are. That's the sound a hunter makes, trying to convince a tom that he is a hen that can't find her mate, so he should come to find her. If it's done right, you fool the tom into coming to you, and you get your bird. It works sometimes, and sometimes it doesn't, but it's lots of fun trying to make the toms come to you.

We sat and listened. Soon we heard a soft yelp from a hen down in the valley below us. In just a short while, a tom gobbled on the ridge just behind us. Then, seconds later, another one gobbled from the same area. Soon there were half a dozen toms gobbling and several hens yelping. "Wow. They're hot today," Thunderfoot said.

The gobbling went on for about ten minutes, and then it got quiet again. "They're flying down," I whispered.

We listened some more, and we heard a gobbler again, but then he was part way down the side of the hill toward the calling hens. "Let's sneak over to that point," I whispered. "When the toms are finished with the hens, they'll come up here and strut in this field.

Thunderfoot nodded and we snuck toward the point of the hill. We had seen birds in the field at mid-morning many times, and we figured these would soon be there, too. Turkeys are birds of habit. They do much the same thing every day, so if you watch them enough, you can predict what they'll do, and when. Tom turkeys like to strut in an open field, where the hens can see how beautiful they are. They puff all up and walk around like they're saying, "Look at me! Look at me! See how big and strong I am."

When we got to the point, we heard a gobble down below us. "They're with the hens," I said. "Get down in that clump of brush, and I'll sit here behind this big log." Thunderfoot nodded, snuck down about ten yards from me, and sat down in a brush pile. I staked the hen decoy I had in my pouch about ten yards in front of Thunderfoot, snuck back up the hill, flipped my seat down, and sat comfortably next to a big log. I sounded a soft yelp every ten minutes, or so, and after about an hour, the gobbles from down the hill were getting closer. I wished I could have sat with Thunderfoot to make sure he was ready, but there wasn't enough room in the brush pile for two, so I had to hope he was watching in the right direction, and that he would see the birds when they came.

The gobbles gradually got louder, and then I could see a big tom, in full strut, coming right to us. I quit yelping and watched. The tom strutted up to the disinterested decoy, making his drumming noise, parading back and forth, working himself silly trying to impress it. Then two more toms came up and stood, watching the show. They were a little smaller and probably younger, and were not allowed to participate. The strutting tom was the dominant bird and they had to wait their turn in the pecking order. (The turkey world has its hierarchy, and both toms and hens have a boss and underlings.)

It *was* quite a show, and I almost forgot about Thunderfoot. "He must be enjoying the display, and waiting for his shot," I thought to myself.

The tom turkey kept working to get the hen to submit to him, but she ignored him. Finally, he let his feathers down and stood there, looking at her. One of the other toms raised his feathers about half way, and boss tom chased him off down the hill. Tom number three followed, and all was quiet.

It wasn't much of a surprise to find Thunderfoot snuggled down, sound asleep and snoring quietly in the brush pile. His gun was lying beside him, so I slowly and carefully pulled it out from the brush and slid the safety off. Then I aimed at a clump of weeds a short distance away and pulled the trigger.

Thunderfoot came awake quite abruptly, just about jumping out of his shoes. He scrambled around, searching for his gun, not even noticing me behind him.

"Looking for this?"

He spun around and glared at me. "What the heck are you trying to do? Give me a heart attack?"

I was laughing so hard I couldn't answer.

"Jeez! I almost wet my pants! Are you nuts? Shooting a gun like that when a person is... oh, no. I was asleep."

"Yes you were, Sleeping Beauty."

He shook his head. "Don't tell me. Did a turkey come?"

I nodded. "Three of them came."

He hung his head. "How far?"

"See the decoy? One was there, and the other two were just five feet to the left."

"I suppose you're gonna tell everybody that I fell asleep and missed a turkey."

I shrugged my shoulders. "Not unless I hear that you told someone about my backward summersault down the hill, sans pants."

"Deal," he said, offering his hand.

We shook and then collected up the decoy. By now, it was close to lunchtime, and we were both pretty hungry. "Let's go back for some lunch, and maybe a nap," I said.

"Lunch... good idea," he said. "But for some reason I'm not real tired, though." Big grin.

Well, we didn't want to get a bird the first day, anyway. What would we do the rest of the week.

Thanks, Thunderfoot.

A Howling Good Time

Thunderfoot and I had spent the five days of his turkey season working on a group of toms that just wouldn't cooperate with us. Maybe it was stubbornness, or just a lack of any new ideas, but we had tried just about everything – without success.

Now it was my turn. The two-day wait between seasons had made me think about options, and I decided to leave the old spot and try for some new turkeys, elsewhere. Early on my first morning of hunting, we trekked up a logging road to another field at the other end of our hunting farm.

"I don't know if this is such a good idea," Thunderfoot whispered when we stopped for a breather. "We *know* there are turkeys over on the other hill. What if there's nothing up here?"

"If we don't hear or see any, then we'll try someplace else tomorrow," I whispered. "I just want to let those other birds rest for a while. I think we pestered them enough last week."

He shrugged his shoulders, and again we started walking toward the top of the hill. A few minutes later, we stopped again, trying to decide where to place our decoys and get set up for dawn. It was dark – really dark. The moon and stars were completely blanketed by clouds. The eastern sky hadn't started to brighten yet, and dawn was at least a half hour away.

"Let's cross the field and sit on that point that comes down from the woods... where we sat one time last year," I whispered.

Thunderfoot nodded. We walked across the hay field as quietly as we could. We were about halfway across when a coyote began howling just down the hill from us. Then, two or three more began howling all around us. "Holy smokes. Those are close," Thunderfoot whispered. He moved a little closer to me.

The howling became louder, and then some of the coyotes started yipping and barking. Thunderfoot stood right against my side, looking all around us. "Did you want to hold hands?" I whispered.

He turned to me with a look on his face that I thought might suggest that he *did* want to hold my hand. "No. But I don't want to get too far away, either," he said.

"Those coyotes won't hurt us," I said. "They probably smell us, and when one howled, the whole pack started. I'm sure we're not in any danger."

But Thunderfoot wouldn't move. He stuck to me like a wood tick. He matched me step for step all the way as I walked to where I knew we would find a point of woods that protruded down into the other side of the field. The point was a good spot to sit and watch for turkeys.

As we got close to the point, I stopped to try to ponder our position. Thunderfoot plowed into my back. I turned and stared at him. "Would you like a piggyback ride?"

"No, I wouldn't like a piggyback ride. What do you expect? You stopped without warning me."

"Maybe I should get some brake lights for the back of my hunting coat."

"Oh, you're such a comedian. I'm just about sick from laughing."

I could just make out the point up ahead, and we walked to it. "I'll put the decoys out," I said. "You clear out all the branches and leaves so we can sit."

"I'll help you with the decoys, and then we can come back here."

"I don't need any help with the decoys. What's the matter? Are you still scared of the coyotes?"

"Shut up! Let's get the decoys out."

We put out three decoys, returned to the point, and made a makeshift blind. I stood my gun against a tree and sat down on my vest seat. Thunderfoot didn't have his gun since it was my season, so he flipped his seat down and sat right next to me.

"Would you like to sit on my lap?" I said.

He gave me a dirty look. "Kinda touchy this morning, aren't you?"

"Touchy?" I said. "You're the one who seems to be nervous. You still worried about a coyote carrying you off into the woods? The Dingo ate my Baybeee."

"Oh, dry up and watch for turkeys," he whispered.

"It's so dark I can't see the decoys. How do you expect me to see a turkey?"

No answer.

We sat side by side, and after several minutes the sky in the east turned to a dark blue from the pitch black it had been. Soon after that we could see the silhouette of the other ridge, and gradually the dark blue faded to gray as the sky brightened to daylight. And with the daylight came the yelping from a bunch of hens in their trees, and a couple of gobbles off in the distance.

"Well, there's a couple of toms up here," I whispered.

Thunderfoot nodded.

The initial gobbling was all that we heard. Everything was quiet – no turkey sounds – only birds chirping and squirrels chattering. I brought out my favorite call and made a series of yelps, and then settled back to wait.

"Look," Thunderfoot whispered. He nodded ever so slightly. "Over to the right."

I looked carefully, and instead of turkeys, two does were coming across the field toward our decoys. "Well, at least we have *something* to keep us entertained."

We watched the deer eating alfalfa, working their way across the field. Every so often they stopped, raised their heads, carefully listening and looking around to make sure they were safe. The does fed right among our fake turkeys as if they didn't mind them at all. As they came closer, Thunderfoot whispered, "Well, there goes that theory that turkeys have chased all the deer out of some places."

I nodded in agreement. "Yeah, these seem to be pretty happy

feeding next to turkeys."

By then, Thunderfoot must have felt safe from the coyotes, because he had moved away from his position of nearly sitting in my lap. "Feel safe now? You're pretty far away. Don't you think a coyote might be lurking around here?"

"Oh, you're such a smart butt."

Just then, one of the deer raised her head and sorted. The other one looked in the same direction. Abruptly their tails went up, they took a couple of hops to the right, and ran across the field toward the woods.

"What the heck was that all about?" I whispered.

"I don't know. Something must have scared – look, look!" Thunderfoot said with excitement, nodding and pointing to the left end of the field.

Two coyotes came on a dead run, hugging the ground as low as they could, crossing the field in just a couple of seconds. When they reached the decoys, the closest one pounced on one of the plastic hens. Thunk! The decoy tipped over with the coyote right on top of it. But as soon as he had the decoy in his grasp, he turned it loose like it was on fire. The coyote jumped about three feet in the air and made an about face. The second coyote understood what his friend had conveyed, and they both raced off back to where they had come from.

We both started to laugh. "Holy cow! Did you see that coyote turn that decoy loose?" Thunderfoot said laughing. "He reminded me of Wiley Coyote with that look on his face like 'Oh No!'"

"Wow," I said. That was worth getting up early. You don't see that every day."

"No foolin! That was great!"

By now it was late morning, and it looked as if it were going to turn into a pretty nice day. "My butt's getting tired," I said. "Let's pick up the decoys, get something to eat, and then get out the boat and try for some Northerns and Bass."

"Hey, now that sounds like a good idea."

We picked up the decoys and hiked down the hill back to the truck. While we drove back toward town I said, "You were pretty spooked when those coyotes were howling, weren't you?"

"No… I was just fooling around," he said.

"Yeah, sure you were. Then you go up there tomorrow by yourself, and I'll hunt someplace else."

He stared at me. "Boy, you're such a funny guy. You just make me laugh all day… Not!"

Well, *I* thought it was kind of funny.

Thanks, Thunderfoot.

Woof, Woof

With our first two turkey hunting seasons a memory, it was a three-week wait until Thunderfoot and I could hunt again. Thunderfoot had received two permits, and his second one was for the very last season of the year. The late seasons took a little more luck than the first because most of the hens were nesting by then, and there were fewer toms still in the mood to look for them. Of course, when you did find a lovesick tom, he was pretty easy to lure with the decoys.

But, in the meantime, we had to find something to keep us busy.

"Let's check those old night crawlers in the shop refrigerator," Thunderfoot said.

"I doubt that they're still alive."

"Well, if they are, we can go down by the bridge and soak them for a while and see what's biting. It's better than sitting around doing nothing."

I had to agree with that. In the back of the refrigerator we found the bait bucket that we had stored away last fall. I opened it expecting a nasty smelling mess, but the dirt was still moist, and when I shook it a bit, a nice bunch of fat night crawlers came to the top. "Wow, they're in good shape," I said.

"Let's go see if we can catch something," Thunderfoot said, grabbing a couple of my fishing poles and heading for the truck. We stopped at his house to pick up a couple of his poles, and soon we were at the riverbank just above the bridge.

We carefully stepped down over the rocks and boulders that had been dumped on the shore to keep the riverbank from washing away. I was especially careful on those rocks – concerned not only about falling and breaking my neck, but also about the snakes that liked living among them.

"What? You scared a rattler is gonna grab you?" Thunderfoot teased with a big grin.

"It doesn't have to be a rattler. I see any snake and I'm outa here."

He laughed and called me a sissy, but I ignored him.

At the river's edge, we each found a nice flat rock to sit on, far enough apart that we had room to fish, but close enough to share the one container of night crawlers. We baited our hooks and tossed our lines out into the water. It didn't take but half a minute and I caught a small sheepshead. "First soft water fish of the year," I said, swinging the fish past Thunderfoot so he could get a good look.

"You're not gonna count that little thing are you? You must really be desperate to win an ice cream to keep that little thing."

I just smiled, and a few minutes later, I caught a nice walleye. Thunderfoot was still waiting for his first bite. Then just as I released the walleye back into the river, he had a jolting strike on his pole. He set the hook, and the fish began pulling line off his spool. "Holy cow! It's a huge one!" he shouted.

His fish put up a good fight and it seemed to just dog down, staying on the bottom. "Are you sure it's a fish? Is it pulling?" I asked.

"It doesn't seem to be swimming, but I can feel it shaking its head and pulling. It's like he's hanging onto the bottom."

Finally, his line started to move. He pulled and tugged, and gradually gained some line. We could see it swirling just below the surface, but I couldn't figure out what kind of fish it was. It seemed long and skinny and dark colored, and it made me think it might be a flathead catfish. "Maybe it's a small flathead," I said.

"It's too early for them, isn't it?"

Just then the fish came to the top and Thunderfoot dragged it up on the rocks. "What the heck is that? Hey! My fish has legs!"

The fish wasn't a fish at all, but a salamander called a Mud Puppy. The twelve-inch-long creature had dark brown/black mottled coloration, four legs with very sharp-looking claws, a big mouth full of teeth, and it was very, very angry.

"That's a Mud Puppy!" I said.

"Jeez! It's an ugly critter. How am I gonna get if off my hook?" Thunderfoot said.

"Just grab it like you do a catfish and take it off," I said bravely.

"Oh, just like that," he said as the Mud Puppy hissed and crawled around on the rock, trying to get back into the water. "Here. If it's so easy, you do it," he said, and he swung the nasty little critter over at me.

The Mud Puppy landed right at my feet and immediately grabbed my right pant leg with its teeth. Once it had a good grip, it grabbed hold of my leg with its front feet and dug its claws into my jeans. Of course, meanwhile, I was trying to get up off the rock and make tracks away from the little monster.

"Holy cow! It's got me!" I shouted. I began kicking, trying to dislodge the critter, and the harder I kicked the harder it held on. Meanwhile, Thunderfoot was rolling on the rocks laughing.

The Mud Puppy let loose with its jaws and climbed a little farther up my leg, like it thought it was going to sit in my lap. That did it. I gave a mighty kick and off it went, right into the river… along with my right shoe.

Thunderfoot was laughing so hard that he couldn't sit up, and when my shoe flew off into the water, I thought he was having a stroke. The Mud Puppy's teeth must have sawed through Thunderfoot's line, because when it hit the water, the line went limp and Mr. Puppy was gone.

My shoe floated for a couple of minutes, and then sank below the surface. I sat with my head between my knees, hoping that The Big One wasn't going to hit just then.

When the excitement finally settled down, Thunderfoot was able to sit up. Tears still streamed down his face. "Holy smokes. That was the funniest thing I've ever seen. Your shoe flew halfway across the river."

My heart rate had slowed down, and I had to laugh, too. "Jeez, you little snot. Why'd you throw that ugly thing over here? I about had a heart attack."

"You said it was easy to take them off. I thought you wanted to show me," he said, laughing again.

"It's a good thing I went to the bathroom before we left home."

We both had another good laugh.

We caught several more fish, but thankfully, no more Mud Puppies, and after an hour, we climbed up over the rocks to go home – me with one bare foot. When we got to the grass on the bank above the rocks, I stopped, took off my left shoe, and threw it in the river.

Thunderfoot began laughing again. "You should have saved it, just in case you ever lose a leg."

I grinned at him. "That's a cheery thought. But with you around, it's probably just a matter of time till I do," I said. "With my luck, I'd lose the wrong leg, and the shoe wouldn't do me any good anyway."

"Hey! I've never even come close to making you lose a leg."

Just give him time, I thought.

Thanks, Thunderfoot.

Sneak Attack

We had been anxiously waiting for the final spring turkey season. Thunderfoot had a second permit, so with him as the gunner, we were off to the turkey woods again. It really didn't matter to me that I couldn't do any shooting. I loved the springtime, and I never got tired of trying to fool a turkey. But the later seasons required us to get up at an ungodly hour. It was light a few minutes earlier each day, and by the sixth week of turkey season, it seemed like we were getting up in the middle of the night to be ready by dawn.

In the month since our last turkey outing, I had made a major purchase and was anxious to try out my new hunting toy. For the past several years, turkey-hunting blinds were becoming quite popular. These were little houses made of camouflage fabric that would hide the hunters from the sharp eye of the turkeys, and could be set up and taken down in just a few minutes. They featured several windows that could be zipped open, and through which the hunters could shoot.

I had postponed buying one because the early models seemed a little complicated to set up, especially in the dark woods. It appeared to be more trouble than it was worth. The second reason keeping me from getting one was that I just couldn't believe that a turkey would come close to something the size of an outhouse that hadn't been there in the woods the previous day. I was quite certain they would steer clear of a blind, and I had a hard time accepting this new idea.

But, after dozens of conversations with hunters who used the blinds, I was finally convinced. "They'll walk right up to it and don't worry a bit," one of my friends told me. "They don't see it as a threat." Well, I decided to get one, and we would try it out on opening day of the last season.

"This'll give us a chance to move a little, and to get a good shot without being seen," I told Thunderfoot as we drove through the darkness toward our turkey hunting farm. "And a turkey coming in from behind won't see us moving, either."

"I think it sounds great," Thunderfoot said. "And if you get tired, you can lay down and have a nap, and if you move, you won't spook my turkey."

"He might hear me," I said.

"Not if I pinch your nose shut." Big grin.

We got out of the truck at the farm and closed the doors as quietly as possible. We put on our vests, Thunderfoot uncased his gun, and I slung the blind over my shoulder. It weighed only a few pounds, and folded up, it was the size of a golf bag with a similar strap that allowed me to haul it easily on my back, keeping my hands free to carry a gun, if I had been carrying one.

We hiked the path to the area that we liked to hunt. "We've got about a half-hour till light," I whispered. "Let's set up the blind here in the corner of the field."

Thunderfoot nodded.

I opened the drawstring on the end of the carrying bag and slid the blind out onto the grass. It looked kind of like a short, fat umbrella without a handle. A couple of pulls, and a tug here and there, and it popped up, ready to use. Its shape was a geodesic dome, and I had to tip my hat to whoever designed this neat little house. We zipped the door open and crawled inside. There was plenty of room for the two of us, and there could have been a third hunter. With twelve small windows spaced around it, we had our choice of shooting ports. Each window was covered with a screen of camouflage netting, and the idea was to shoot right through the netting. The turkey would never know we were inside the blind.

"This is just too cool," Thunderfoot said.

"It would be better if we had some chairs."

"How about those folding lawn chairs? Aren't they still behind the seat in the truck?" he said.

"Yeah! I forgot about them. They'd work great."

"I'll run back and get them," Thunderfoot said.

"No, you wait here. I'll go. You're the one with the permit. I'd hate to have a turkey come by while you were gone and not be able to shoot it," I said.

Thunderfoot nodded an okay.

I slipped through the door and looked at the sky. The east was beginning to brighten and the sky was turning blue. It wouldn't be long before it would be light enough for the turkeys to fly down from their roosts, and I wanted to be back inside the blind before they started moving around.

I hiked back to the truck. We had two of those new space age chairs that folded up into a small package, and opened to a real comfortable chair with a backrest. We used them a lot for fishing at the riverbank, and they would be perfect for the turkey blind.

I slung the chairs over my shoulder and started back to the blind. Daylight was here and I was surprised how fast dawn had turned to daytime. As I approached the rise in the field, about halfway between the truck and the blind, I slowed my pace, crouching down and kind of waddling, just in case there were any early turkeys in sight. I peeked up over the grass on the rise and sure enough, there was a tom turkey standing in the edge of the field about a hundred yards from Thunderfoot and the blind.

I lay down in the grass and watched, not able to move any closer without spooking the bird. And then I heard a "yelp, yelp, yelp." Thunderfoot had seen the bird and was calling from the blind.

The tom turned and looked at the blind but didn't move toward it. We hadn't had time to put out any decoys, so I guessed that the tom didn't see any girl turkeys that interested him. Then he puffed up and displayed his pretty feathers, strutting down the hill toward the ditch at the bottom of the field. Thunderfoot called again, but the tom now had his eye on something that did interest him, and he wasn't having anything to do with that invisible hen.

I looked toward where the tom was headed, expecting a hen

to be waiting for him. But all I saw was a rusty old milk can lying partly buried in the edge of the field. The tom pranced around the milk can, displaying his feathers. I laughed to myself. That stupid tom must have thought the milk can was a hen. So much for detailed decoys.

Thunderfoot yelped again, but tom wasn't interested. I lay there watching the tom, and then I could have sworn that the blind had moved from where it had been originally. I must be seeing things.

I looked back at the tom, still strutting back and forth, trying to impress the rusty milk can, and in the corner of my eye I noticed the blind moving. It rose up about six inches off the ground, and then I could see Thunderfoot's feet moving under it, toward the tom. He was trying to sneak up on the turkey, staying inside the blind. I could hardly believe my eyes!

I kept watching. Every time the tom would turn and strut, Thunderfoot moved the blind five or six feet closer. With a couple more moves he would be in range.

Actually, he moved three more times. The blind was just about twenty yards from the tom when I saw the gun barrel slide out one of the windows. There was a puff of smoke, and then the sound of the blast reached me. The tom lay on his back, flapping his wings. The kill was complete. Then the blind moved rapidly across the remaining pasture, flipped over, and Thunderfoot emerged pick up his bird.

I could see his grin from a hundred yards away. He held up the bird and gave me thumbs up. I returned the gesture.

There didn't seem any use in carrying the chairs to the blind now, so I left them in the grass and walked across the field to Thunderfoot and his bird.

"You crazy little fool. I can't believe you got away with that!" I said laughing as I slapped him on the back.

He grinned. "There's more than one way to skin a turkey."

"I think that's a cat, but I get your idea."

We folded up the blind, slid it back into its carrying bag, and walked back to the truck. "That's a pretty cool new toy we've got," Thunderfoot said.

"Yeah, I guess so. I wonder if the guy who designed it ever thought it would be used for *sneaking up* on a turkey?"

"Probably not. But he doesn't know me," Thunderfoot said.

Obviously, he doesn't.

Thanks, Thunderfoot.

Just Plumb Foolishness

"The toilet won't go down!" Thunderfoot yelled from the bathroom.

"What did you do?" I asked.

"What do you think I did? That's kind of a stupid question."

"Jeez! Now's a great time for this. I'm gonna be late as it is."

"Hey, it's not like I did it on purpose. This isn't the first time it got plugged, I bet," he said defensively.

He was right. My toilet plugged about twice a year, right on schedule. It was because several years ago, I had cut a section out of the pipe running from the house to the septic tank so I could put in a drain from the spare room. At the time, I was using the spare room as a makeshift workshop for my business. Some time later, I moved to a larger shop and just cemented over the opening in the room, but left the T in the pipe. Now, at about six-month intervals, paper and other debris gathered in that T area, and eventually it plugged. In fact, I was so tired of going to the hardware store and renting a toilet snake, that I just bought one so I had it when I needed it. Of course, it always seemed to plug at the most inopportune times.

"Well, you'll just have to not use it till I get home," I said.

"I can fix it… I've seen you do it before."

I'd have rather waited until I returned home that evening, but I didn't have a lot of choices. I had to be at a meeting that would last most of the day, and Thunderfoot was dog sitting for me. He didn't have school, and he was usually at my house anyway, so it worked out nice for him to stay there with the dogs.

"Get the snake out of the shed," I told him.

While I prepared my papers and a few other things for the meeting, Thunderfoot trotted out to the boat shed and found the sewer snake and a big pair of heavy black rubber gloves that I wore when I was clearing out the sewer pipe. I went to the back of the house where he already had the clean-out access opened up.

"All I do is run this down the pipe and ram it back and forth till it clears up… right?"

"Yeah. Just go slow and don't wreck anything."

"No faith in me." He shook his head. "Just go… and don't worry about this. I'll take care of it."

"Ok," I said. "I'll see you later. " And off I went.

The meeting broke for lunch so I thought I'd call home to see how the plumbing job was coming along. The phone rang, and rang, and I was about to hang up when Thunderfoot finally answered, panting like he had been running.

"Hi. Where were you?" I asked.

"I… uh… I was out back."

"Doing what?"

"Just about to finish up with the plumbing."

"You're still doing that? What's the matter? Did you have trouble?"

"I've got it under control. What time are you gonna be home?"

"Maybe about six. Are you sure everything is all right?"

"Don't worry. I'm just about done. See ya later." He hung up.

For some reason, that call didn't reassure me, but it wouldn't help to call back, so I just went back to the rest of the meeting.

The meeting was finally over at almost five o'clock, and the drive home took over an hour. When I pulled into the driveway, I was surprised to see my brother's pickup parked there. I was also surprised to see the back yard lit up with floodlights!

My brother came walking around the house wearing an amused grin on his face. "Don't get excited," he said. "Thunderfoot had a little trouble with your sewer and he called me to give him a hand."

"A *little* trouble?"

"Yeah, well, you know that V-shaped handle on the sewer snake? The thing that you squeeze to grip the snake?"

"Yeah, I know. It slides up the snake as you go so you can use it to push easier," I said.

"Well," he went on, "Thunderfoot forgot about that, and he put the V-handle down the pipe. Of course, it went okay as long as it was going down, but when he tried to pull it back out, the V caught in the pipe and he couldn't get it out."

"Oh cripes! I thought he knew how to use it," I said.

"Well, the V got stuck in the pipe way out near the tank, so he called me and I came over. We decided that the only way to fix it was to dig up the pipe, cut if off, pull the sewer snake out from there, and then put in a new piece of pipe."

I just shook my head. Such a simple job… and now such a big one.

"It took a little longer than we figured, so I went home and got my floodlights," my brother said. "He's been pretty worried that you'd be mad, so go easy on him."

"Ok," I said. We walked around the house.

Well, when we reached the back yard, Thunderfoot was lying on the grass next to a trench about six feet long, by about a foot and a half wide – very much resembling a grave. His hands were folded across his chest, as if he were ready for burial.

Despite the mess in the yard and my being a little peeved that he hadn't listened to me, I had to laugh.

"Just roll me in when you're ready," he said with his eyes closed.

We all had a good laugh.

"If you'd been just another twenty minutes later," he said, "I'd have had it done."

"What did you think? That this *grave* wouldn't catch my attention?"

He shrugged. "I guess not. But I thought maybe you wouldn't come in the back yard till the grass grew back."

I cuffed him on the head. "I'm not that senile!"

They had the new piece of pipe and a couple of rubber couplers that would splice it into the old one, and in a short while, everything was fixed and we started filling in the hole. My brother stayed with his lights until we finished, and then he went home.

"Thanks for helping," Thunderfoot said as he left.

"No problem." He grinned as he pulled out of the driveway.

"Well," I said. "I suppose you're faminished."

"No foolin," he responded. "Plumbing is hard work."

"Go order a pizza and I'll pick it up... on my way to the hardware store to pay for the pipe and connectors."

"Okay," he said, and then he hesitated. "I hope you're not mad at me."

"No. I guess not. You did your best, and besides... now that T is gone. Maybe we won't have to do this again."

"Yeah, that was my plan," he said, grinning from ear to ear.

Sure it was.

Thanks, Thunderfoot.

Night Fishing

"A kid at school was telling me about fishing for bass at night up at Blackhawk Lake," Thunderfoot said as we drove down the road.

"At night?" I said. "Remember the time we went fishing at night and I ended up in the river?"

"Yeah, but that was a long time ago. And you do this from a boat, so you won't fall in so easy."

"Oh, sure. But if I fall in, I'm gonna be in lots deeper water. What did this kid tell you that makes you think we should do this?"

"Well, he said they go up to Blackhawk at night and use top water baits – Hula Poppers, and Buzz Baits, and Jitterbugs. Y'know, there's lots of bass there, and he says they catch some huge ones at night."

"Why would it make any difference? Why would the big ones bite better at night?" I asked.

"Well, he said the big ones just feed at night, and that's why they're big, 'cause nobody fishes much for them at night."

He was deadly serious. Then he got me with the clincher.

"He said they catch some big walleyes at night, too."

Now, as much as I like to fish, for any kind of fish, I like fishing for walleyes better than any other. All fish are fun to catch, but walleyes had always been my favorite. I think it goes back to when my dad took me walleye fishing when I was a little kid. For some reason, I was pretty good at it, and over the years, walleyes have become my fish of choice. Blackhawk Lake had a good population of big walleyes.

But it was hard for the fisherman to find them at Blackhawk because there was no normal walleye structure, as it was pretty much that way in most man-made lakes. They're like big featureless bowls of water with weed beds that extend out from the shore for thirty or forty feet, until the water gets too deep for them to grow. Walleyes that live in these lakes are usually weed-oriented fish. They lie in the weeds during the day, and then feed along the weed bed edges at night when the light is low. They're really hard to catch – almost impossible in the daytime.

"Walleyes, too?" I asked.

"Yup. Lots of them five or six pounds... and bigger. He says they are laying on the bottom stacked up like cordwood."

Hmm. Maybe this was worth a try, after all. "Well, the season opens Saturday. I guess we'd better try it Saturday night," I said. "That is, if you don't have a hot date."

"There's no date hot enough to keep me from fishing," he said grinning.

Good boy.

Living along the Wisconsin River as we did, we enjoyed open season on all fish, except Muskies, all year long. The Wisconsin and its sloughs didn't have a closed season like the rest of the inland lakes and rivers where it closed in the fall for bass, northern, and walleyes. That made it nice for us. For the rest of the State, the game fish season opened on the first Saturday in May, which was the upcoming weekend.

Saturday came and we got the boat ready for night fishing. We didn't want a lot of extra junk in the way when we stumbled around in the dark, so we put away everything that wouldn't be used. We each rigged up four rods and reels with top water baits on three for the bass, and deeper running crank bait on the others for casting along the weeds for walleyes.

We filled the lantern with fuel and put new batteries in our flashlights. Then we waited for it to get dark.

It was rather eerie to see an empty parking lot at such a popular lake. Most of the time it was full of cars and trucks, and someone was always waiting to put a boat into the water or to take one out. But now, when we backed the boat down to the water's edge, we had the entire lake to ourselves, and I didn't have to hunt for a place to park the truck. In just a little while we were motoring out across the water.

"Let's head over by the dam," Thunderfoot said. "My friend told me that's a good area to fish."

I used a spotlight to navigate along the shore, and up ahead, past the picnic area and the swimming beach, I could see the dam. I stopped the motor, shut off the spotlight, and lit the lantern that bathed the boat in bright light.

"Okay. Let's try for some bass first," Thunderfoot said. "I guess we just cast out and reel back. These baits make a lot of fuss on top of the water, so I guess that's how the fish find them."

"Well, we'll see," I said.

We began casting and it didn't take long to discover that our lantern was creating a problem. Within five minutes after lighting it, there were about ten thousand flying bugs in the boat, landing on us and crawling all over us. They were everywhere!

"Boy! That light has got to go!" I said.

Thunderfoot shut off the gas valve and the light slowly died out. After a few minutes, our eyes adjusted and we went back to fishing again.

"How we gonna know where we're casting?" Thunderfoot said.

"I guess we have to listen for a plop. If you don't hear the bait hit the water, you know it's on land."

After many casts, we were both getting weeds on our bait. I turned on the spotlight and saw that we had drifted into the weeds next to shore. "Back us up with the paddle. We're in the weeds."

Thunderfoot grabbed the paddle. Soon we were making plops in the water again. A few casts later, I was reeling back, listening to my bait gurgling on top of the water when there was a huge splash and I felt a tug on my line. I set the hook and missed, but my bait came sailing back through the darkness and hit me right in the throat. "Arrrgggghhh! I'm wounded!" I yelled.

Thunderfoot turned on his light and helped me get the bait untangled from my shirt. Luckily, the hooks hadn't stuck into my neck, but my line was a hopeless mess of tangles, so I retired that pole.

A few minutes later, Thunderfoot missed a fish, too, and his Moss Boss came back, hit the side of the boat, and broke in half. Now he had half a Boss on the end of his line. He, too, retired that pole.

In the next half hour, we each managed to get another pole hopelessly tangled, and we still didn't have any fish. I turned on the spotlight and pointed it down into the water. We happened to be right along the edge of the weeds, and sure enough, there were twenty or thirty walleyes lying in the sand, just at the edge of the weeds. I could see the glow of their translucent eyes. "Holy smokes! Look at those walleyes," I whispered.

"Why are you whispering? Do you think they can hear you?" Thunderfoot grabbed his deep running crank bait pole. "Shut that light off before you spook them. Let's try to cast right along this weed line and see if we can catch one of them." He was excited.

Well, casting along a weed line in the dark isn't as easy as it sounds. If we cast too far toward deep water, we were out of walleye range. If we cast too close to the weeds, we got our baits full of grass. It only took about ten minutes to figure out that this was more difficult than it seemed. And in another ten minutes, we had our deep running poles tangled up beyond repair, especially in the dark.

"Well, that worked good," I said. "I've got one pole left that isn't tangled."

"Me too. Let's try some other area for bass."

I started the motor and found our way to an area where we had once caught many smaller bass in the daytime. I shut off the motor and the light, and we started fishing. Thunderfoot had a fighting fish on his hook almost right away. When he just about had it to the boat, it got off. When it spit the hook out, the bait went flying through the air and wrapped around the end of his pole about fifty times. "Well, stick a fork in me. I'm done," he said.

I laughed. "Don't worry... I've been too lucky with this bait. I'll be tangled soon, and then we can go home."

Two casts later, I didn't hear a plop. "Did you hear that hit?"

"Nope. Not a plop," he answered. "How close are we to shore?"

I turned on the light. We were only a few feet away from the bank. "A little too close," I said.

I reeled up, and then I could tell that my bait was hooked on something on the shore. "Be a pal and climb out and get that bait for your daddy."

He laughed. "Yeah, right. I'll hold the boat while *YOU* go look in the woods for *YOUR* lure."

He pushed us up to the shore with the paddle and I jumped out onto the bank. I reeled and walked and followed my line up to the trees. Of course, my lure was about fifteen feet from the ground in a tree. "It's up in a tree," I said.

"And that's my problem... how?"

"You're littler. You can climb trees better. Come here and help me," I pleaded.

"Oh, jeez! I swear, I should get college credit for working with the handicapped," he grumbled.

I heard him jump onto the shore. He came to where I was, and then, in just a few seconds he was up the tree and had my bait free. "Now, can you reel it up? Or do I have to do that for you too?"

"Oh, don't be such a smart pants."

I reeled up and shined my spotlight so he could find his way back down. When we walked back toward the shore, I shined the light on the bank. No boat. "Where's the boat?"

"I left it right here on the bank," Thunderfoot said.

"Did you tie it up?"

"No. I just pulled it up to the bank."

I pointed the light out onto the water, and there was the boat, about twenty feet from shore.

"Oh boy. Now that's a dilemma," he said.

"Well, you're gonna have to go get it. You let it get away."

"I wouldn't have let it get away if you had been able to climb that tree and get your lure."

"Well, one of us has to go out to get it."

"Rock, paper, scissors," he said.

I hated rock, paper, scissors. I always lost. But we had to do something, so Thunderfoot counted to three and we both opened our hands to paper.

"Tie."

"One, two, three." I figured he'd go with paper again, so I went with scissors. He had rock.

"Rock breaks scissors. Have a nice swim."

"I don't suppose you'd like to go for two out of three," I said.

"Not a chance. Kindly fetch my conveyance, my good man."

I took off my clothes and piled them on the bank. To say the water was cold is an understatement - it was icy - and I was wading in thick weeds that harbored who knows what kind of slippery, slimy critters. When the water was up to my belly, I had to swim, but then I was free of the weeds and out in the open water - water that was full of big walleyes with big teeth. My imagination was running full tilt as I reached the boat. Of course, graceful as I am, I couldn't pull myself up over the side, so I had to tow the boat back to shore. Thunderfoot, helpful as he was, shined the spotlight on me as I plowed through the water.

I finally staggered up onto the shore, and I was about frozen. Thunderfoot had all he could do to keep from busting out laughing. He must have felt a little sorry for me, though, because he took off his sweatshirt and dried off my back, and then gave it to me so I could dry off the rest of me.

When I was dressed again, we climbed into the boat. I

started the motor and shined the spotlight out onto the water. Surprise, surprise! Fog had settled in during my little rescue mission, and now the entire lake was covered in thick, white mist. "Oh, boy! This just keeps getting better all the time," I said.

"There's a streetlight at the boat landing," Thunderfoot said. "I guess we gotta just cruise along the shore till we see that."

We motored slowly for over twenty minutes until we could just barely see a bright spot in the fog. Thankful that it was the light at the landing, we pulled up and Thunderfoot held the boat's rope while I backed the trailer down to the water. A few minutes later, the boat was loaded and tied down, and we were on our way home.

"Turn that heater up," Thunderfoot said.

"Oh? Cold are you? You should have been in that water if you think it's cold here."

"Well, you were the one in the water, so I'll have to take your word for it," he said grinning.

We drove on toward home. "Well, I think that's enough night fishing for me," I said.

Thunderfoot laughed. "Yeah, I think we'd better stick with daytime fishing from now on. We can get into enough trouble in the daylight, without stumbling around in the dark, too."

"One thing about it – I managed to get a bath both times," I said, thinking back to another night fishing trip when I fell into the river.

"Yeah, you have a thing for night time swimming. And from what I saw of you tonight, you'd better stick to that. If anyone saw you in the daylight, they'd run for their lives."

"Are you saying that I'm not swimsuit model material?"

"Not even close."

Thanks, Thunderfoot.

Thunderfoot Trump

It seems that every small town in America has something that makes it famous. There are "Capitals Of--" everywhere, and they range from Wild Turkeys; to Czechs; to Norwegians; to Mushrooms. Of all the things that a small town could lay claim to fame, our town chose the Morel Mushroom.

The Morel is a spring mushroom that is considered a delicacy by millions of people. They grow in many places around the world, but are particularly abundant in the area of the Wisconsin River valley where we live.

The reason they are so abundant is because of Dutch Elm disease. A few decades ago this tree disease spread through the mid-west and killed off the majority of the elm trees that grew along shady streets, in parks, and on the hillsides and in the valleys. There were thousands of dead elms in the woods, and a morel mushroom loves nothing better than one of these dead trees for a host.

As a morel pops out of the ground, it opens its porous skin and releases thousands of tiny spores into the air. These spores sail on the wind and eventually fall to the forest floor. If they are lucky, they fall near a dead elm, and then they feed for the next several months on the energy that is being released by the roots of the dead tree.

The following spring, if conditions are right, the spore has been transformed into a morel mushroom, all scrunched up in a little ball just under the surface of the ground. When the air warms enough, and there has been enough rain, the mushroom swells up and pops up out of the ground, releasing its spores, and continuing the cycle.

Somewhere, at some point in time, a person who was either really brave – or really hungry – picked a few of these ugly little fungi, took them home, and ate them. He found them to be quite tasty, and from then on, the Morel was considered a delicacy. Of course, with the large number of mushrooms that were found each spring around all those dead elm trees in the area, someone decided that it would be a good thing to have a celebration honoring the Morel. And thus, our town became the Morel Mushroom Capital of Wisconsin.

One of the things that happened when this festival began was a surprising rise in the value of a bag of Morels. For years, my friends and I had loved to pick Morels in the spring, for fun. It was a great time of year to get out into the woods after a long winter, and it was an activity that allowed us to get some exercise and enjoy nature. But after the first couple of years of the Morel Festival, the mushrooms suddenly became very pricey. Instead of *giving* them to your friends and neighbors, you now *sold* them to the tourists who came to the festival. I guess that's called American Capitalism.

Surprisingly, more people came and the Morel Festival became more popular, and soon the price of Morels was at a point that made you scratch your head in wonder. And that was on Thunderfoot's mind, too, as the upcoming Festival drew near.

"You got a scale that I can weigh mushrooms on?" he asked.

"Yeah, I've got that digital fish scale that's really accurate. Why? You don't have any mushrooms."

"But I will have by the weekend."

"They've been kind of scarce, so far," I said. "We need some rain to make them pop."

"I'm going out after school tomorrow, and then every day after that till Saturday when the Festival starts," he said.

"Well, I've seen you hunt mushrooms," I told him. Don't plan any purchases based on your earnings just yet. You haven't found any, so far."

He gave me one of those "Ye have little faith" looks. "Don't worry. I'm gonna scour every tree on Ken's farm. I'll be rich when this is over with."

I didn't get too excited about his enterprise, and by the next day I had forgotten about it completely. I was getting dinner ready when he came through the front door carrying a plastic grocery sack that looked pretty light.

"Well, Rockefeller? Make a million on Morels today?" I asked.

"Oh, dry up!" he whined. "I walked about ten miles and all I found was three little ones."

I peeked in the sack at the three little baby Morels at the bottom. "You should just take a sandwich bag. It would look fuller."

He gave me a look that had murder in it. "I just can't find these dang things," he said. "I don't know what I'm doing wrong."

"Are you looking for dead trees?"

"Yeah, I'm looking everywhere. I just walk and look at the ground, and I look at all the trees."

"You're wasting your time looking all over the place," I said. "You have to find *dead* trees. That's where they are."

He looked at me pitifully. "Will you come tomorrow and show me?"

"Yeah, you poor thing. I'll help you."

Big grin.

I picked him up after school the next day, and we headed for the hills. "You work down that hillside," I said pointing to the hill below us. "I'll drive out to the end of that field and work on the other side. Then we'll meet somewhere down there and see what we've found."

Off he went and I drove out across the field on the worn path that our farmer friend had made when he planted and harvested his crops. I parked, got out of my truck, and studied the hillside I was planning to hunt. Along the side of the hill I could see the branches of a dead tree sticking up through the green leaves of the other trees around it. I headed toward it.

When I got closer, the tree looked good. It had been dead for three or four years, as the bark was just beginning to peal off and hang. That was the perfect age for a mushroom tree. Too young and the wood was too hard, and no nutrients were leaking out into the soil. Too old and the tree was used up. This one looked to be just right.

I walked up to it and looked at the ground around it. It took a couple of minutes before I saw the first Morel, and then, as I carefully walked around the tree, I saw that there were Morels all over. I decided to wait for Thunderfoot so he could see what the right tree looked like.

I sat on a stump and after a few minutes I saw him sauntering through the woods. His mushroom sack was still sticking out of the back pocket of his jeans, so I knew he hadn't found any yet.

"Hey! Find any?" I yelled down to him.

"There ain't no mushrooms on this farm."

"Come on up here," I yelled.

He climbed up the hill grudgingly and soon he was standing in front of my stump.

"No luck?" I asked.

"I found one of those ones that grow on the side of a tree."

"Did you look at dead trees?"

"I didn't see any dead trees."

"See any dead trees around here?"

He looked around the area.

"Look closer," I said.

Then he saw the dead tree right behind me. "Oh, yeah. There's one right there."

He was standing there looking up at the branches of the tree, and his right foot was about ten inches from a nice Morel. "They aren't up in the tree," I said. "Look on the ground."

He began looking all over.

"If that was a rattlesnake, you'd be dead," I said, pointing to the ground at his feet.

Then he saw the Morel. "Holy smokes! I was almost standing on it."

He bent down to pick the mushroom when he saw another, a few feet from it. Then he saw two more sticking up from under a leaf. He was scurrying around like a chicken chasing a grasshopper, picking mushrooms like they were going to sprout legs and run from him.

"Come and help me. There's millions of them!"

I worked my way to the opposite side of the tree, and after about twenty minutes, we had found all the mushrooms that were there. "If you come back here in a couple of days, there'll probably be more, too, so keep this place in mind and check it again."

He nodded.

"So, now do you think you can find them?"

"Now I know what to look for. Jeez, I saw a tree like this back down there. I'm going back." And off he went.

"I'll meet you back at the truck at about six," I shouted to him.

He just waved over his shoulder.

I hunted for another hour and then walked back to the truck with a bag full of nice mushrooms. It felt good to sit and enjoy the sun as it dropped into the west. A short while later Thunderfoot came huffing and puffing up the hill with his nice bag of mushrooms. "Boy! I'm gonna come back tomorrow. I've only covered about a fifth of this woods."

"Well, tomorrow you can come alone and spend all the time you want."

We went home, put the mushrooms into the bottom vegetable compartment of my refrigerator, and covered them with a damp piece of cloth to keep them moist.

The next day he came through the door just as it was getting dark. "Look at these. Jeez! I'm gonna be rich."

He had a sack and a half of nice mushrooms that we added to the ones already in the refrigerator. This went on for the next three days, and my refrigerator was getting pretty full of mushrooms. Luckily, the first day of the Festival was the next day, so I hoped he'd have luck selling them, and give me back my fridge.

Thunderfoot came over early the next morning. We rigged up a basket that we could hang on my digital fish scale and weighed out the mushrooms into one-pound bags. There were nearly ten pounds.

"How much are they paying for them this year?" he asked.

"I've heard about $15 a pound so far."

"Holy smokes! That's... mmm... carry the four... that's $135 plus what I can get for the part of a pound." His grin was bigger than the trunk of an old elm tree.

"Why don't you set up a card table in front of the store and sit there and see what happens?" I said.

He made a little cardboard sign and sat down at the table with his bags of Morels. About an hour and a half later he came running into the store. "I'm out of mushrooms already! I'm going to the woods!"

He was gone all day, and that evening he came over with a little more than five pounds of mushrooms. "There's not one mushroom left on that whole farm," he said. "I must have walked fifty miles today."

I had to admire his energy. I helped him weigh them, and when he added the new ones to the leftovers from the last batch, he had six bags of mushrooms that each weighed a pound, plus a few extra. "Just put an extra one or two in each bag," I said. "After tomorrow all the tourists will be gone and nobody will pay for them, so you might as well give them a good deal."

He agreed, and added the bonus mushrooms to the bags.

The next day he set up his mushroom business and sold out before the crowd had even begun to gather for the big parade – the culmination of the Festival.

"Another $90," he said, proudly showing me a wad of bills.

"Jeez! You did good," I said.

"Not bad. Not bad at all," he replied.

"So, Mr. Trump... what are you going to do with all that money?"

"Well, I've decided to finance an expedition to the upper part of Lake Michigan over Memorial Day weekend," he said.

"Really? What kind of expedition will that be? You and your knot head buddies chasing those northern girls?"

"Nope. This money isn't going for girls. It's for a trip to remember for a pretty special guy and me."

I wasn't sure what he was talking about. "Trip to remember?"

"Yeah. Since I'm gonna graduate in a few weeks, I thought maybe me and my best buddy should take a good trip and try to catch some of those Lake Michigan walleyes like we did a couple years ago. This money will be for that... I'm buying this time."

I didn't know what to say. The thought of a trip to Lake Michigan for walleyes was a great idea, but the idea that it may be one of our last trips together made me choke up. My eyes got a little full.

He put his arm around my shoulder and gave me a squeeze. "Whatya say?"

"I'd say you're quite a kid."

"The feeling's mutual," he said.

Thanks, Thunderfoot.

Gullible

Thunderfoot and I were on the road again, headed to the upper peninsula of Michigan for a long weekend of fishing. It was the last weekend before his graduation from high school. For me, it was a bittersweet trip, as I knew things would change after that. But I put that in the back of my mind and concentrated on having a great time of fishing for walleyes on Lake Michigan.

We had been to this area a few years earlier, enticed by watching a TV show about the place called Little Bay de Noc. That time we had caught many beautiful walleyes, and I had even taken a dip – though not on purpose – in the big lake. It was such a fun trip that we had been talking for the past two years about doing it again, and now we were on our way.

Thunderfoot had amassed quite a nice little bankroll selling morel mushrooms a couple of weeks earlier, and he had decided to use the money for this trip. This was a completely new experience for me. I argued that I could pay like I usually did, or at least share the expenses, but he insisted. "Hey, this is free money," he had said. "America is a great place. You can go out in the woods and just pick up money, so I think we should use it for a fun time... not on something like clothes or books." I guess that made sense, but I still felt funny about him paying. It had always been my treat for the past six years, and it was hard to change that old habit.

Thunderfoot had called ahead to rent a little cabin at a resort that was right on the water. In fact, there was a dock right in front, so we could just tie up the boat each evening instead of loading it on the trailer.

He grinned as we pulled into town. "Any chance you'd like to stop for tacos?"

"No way, Jose!'" I said laughing. On the last trip to this place, he had talked me into tacos that upset my stomach, and the end result was me falling into the lake while attempting an emergency potty maneuver over the back of the boat. I wasn't taking any chances with tacos this time.

"How about Mac's? It's right up ahead," I said.

"Mac's, it is."

One thing about pulling an eighteen-foot boat was that the drive-through was out of the question, and regular parking spots were unusable, so we parked the boat in the back of the *McDonalds* lot. We brought our bag of burgers, fries, and cokes to eat out by the boat. On such a nice spring day we hated to be inside, and although I have never had any problems with anyone stealing from the boat, we felt better about keeping an eye on our gear that was just lying in the bottom. I hated to think of how much that would mess up our trip.

We were standing on either side of the boat, using the deck as a picnic table and chatting about fishing, when a gust of wind blew Thunderfoot's fries off the deck, scattering them across the parking lot. "Holy cow! My fries!" he shouted.

Just as he bent down to pick up the box, still containing a couple of fries, about twenty seagulls descended out of nowhere, squawking and fighting over the spilled fries. Thunderfoot put his arms up over his head and ran from the melee. "Holy smokes! They attacked me!"

I was laughing so hard I could hardly swallow the bite of hamburger in my mouth. The birds cleaned up every fry, and then one of them perched on the side of the boat, grabbed the half of the hamburger that Thunderfoot had left on the deck, and flew off. "Hey! Come back here you buzzard!" he shouted.

He saw me laughing, and then he began laughing, too. "Jeez! Those things came out of nowhere. I thought they were gonna eat me, too."

I finally managed to get my bite of burger down without choking. "It reminded me of an old Alfred Hitchcock movie, *The Birds*," I said.

"Alfred who?"

Generation gap.

"Well, I'm gonna go get some more lunch," he said. "I didn't get full on that one."

He came back with another bag of food in a few minutes, and it didn't take long for some gulls to start circling overhead, watching for another feast. Thunderfoot watched them for a while, and then he grinned, holding a French fry up in the air. Two gulls swooped down and hovered just above it, but neither one would take it from his hand. He tossed it into the air and one gull grabbed it in flight. The other tried to take it away, and then off they flew, squawking like crazy.

Well, that led to both of us tossing fries up and watching the gulls catch them, until we ran out of fries. "That is so cool," Thunderfoot said.

"Yeah, and a good way for us not to overeat."

We went to the cabin and launched the boat at the landing just a short ways down the lakeshore. Thunderfoot drove the truck and trailer back to the cabin, and I drove the boat to the dock in front. While I helped Thunderfoot unload our clothes and food, I said, "Think we should try to catch a few walleyes for supper?"

He put his arm behind his back. "Force me," he said.

I just barely touched his arm.

"Oh, okay. I give. I give. I'll go along," he said with a grin as big as Lake Michigan.

We fired up the boat and took off down the lake to fish some of the same places we had fished the last time we were at the Bay. We caught several smallish walleyes that would be just right for a meal. We motored back to the dock, tied up the boat for the night, and then cleaned the fish at the little fish-cleaning shack. The fresh walleye fillets made a wonderful supper with raw fried potatoes and baked beans – a feast fit for a king.

Thunderfoot decided to enjoy the view down at the lake while I finished cleaning up the kitchen. A few minutes later, he came back inside, went to the cupboard, and grabbed a handful of slices from the loaf of bread. "There's a bunch of mallards down there begging. I'm gonna give them some bread." He sprinted through the door. When I finished the cleaning, I walked down to the lake.

There was Thunderfoot standing by the shore with at least twenty-five mallard ducks surrounding him, quacking like crazy and gobbling up the pieces of bread he tossed to them. "Get more bread," he called out when he saw me coming. "These guys are really hungry."

I retrieved the rest of the loaf, and soon we were both feeding the ducks. Before long, a couple of seagulls noticed the free lunch, and they, too, were screeching and swooping down, trying to steal some of the ducks' bread. Within minutes there were two dozen more seagulls, and we were quickly running out of bread.

"I hope they get full," Thunderfoot said. "I'd hate to see them attack."

"I think we'll be okay," I said. "At least I will be. I doubt that they'll try to take something as big as me away to sea." He gave me a strange sort of stare, and then he decided I was kidding.

"That's it, guys," he said as he tossed the last scraps of bread. The birds searched the ground for another few minutes, and then the gulls soared off toward the lake and the ducks waddled back into the water, moving down the shoreline, looking for another duck lover.

We sat there and watched the sun go down, and although it wasn't very late, we decided to go to bed so we could get up early the next morning for a day of fishing.

Since we had given the ducks all the bread, we drove to a small diner just down the road and had a big breakfast of eggs, ham, fried potatoes, and a pancake on the side. We figured with all that food in us, we'd be able to last almost all day. It was a glorious morning and we set out onto the lake. We had decided that we'd just catch and release all the fish during the day, and keep a few toward late afternoon for supper. We didn't plan to take a bunch home. We were there just for the fun of catching them.

We used jigs and we were catching quite a few fish, but none that were very big. We noticed that several other boats fishing the area were trolling. Every once in a while we'd see one of them net a nice, big fish.

"Why don't we try trolling?" Thunderfoot said after we watched a ten-pound walleye come to the net.

"I hate to troll. You know that."

"Yeah, but they're getting those big fish, and all were getting are these little guys. Come on… trolling isn't so bad." He gave me one of his pitiful stares. "Wouldn't you like to see me catch a big one?"

He sat there looking like a poor little waif, so I said, "Okay. We'll try if for a while if you think we have to."

Big grin.

We each rigged up crank bait on a casting rod and reel, and let them out behind the boat about fifty feet. I drove the boat slowly down the lake… mindlessly trolling.

That's what I had always thought of trolling. It was mindless fishing. I just didn't see any skill in dragging bait behind a boat, hoping for a fish to bite on it. To me, casting a jig was the way to catch walleyes, and it always would be.

At any rate, we trolled, and then we trolled some more. As it was my usual luck when trolling, we caught nothing but weeds. Every so often our bait would drag through some weed beds, requiring reeling up and cleaning the junk off the lure. At least it gave us something to do to break the boredom.

Thunderfoot was about half asleep when I noticed his bait skipping across the surface. "Your bait is fouled with weeds," I called to him. "It's on top."

He looked back at his bait. "I thought that felt funny," he said as he began reeling it in. He had the bait about half way to the boat when I saw a seagull swooping down toward it. "Hurry up," I yelled. "There's a gull after it!"

Just as I said it, the bird hit the water, grabbed his bait, and began flying off. Thunderfoot's mouth dropped open. He held on for dear life and played the bird in the air, like he would a fish in the water. "Holy smokes! He's gonna take my rod!"

"Hang on tight!"

Right then I'd have given almost anything for a camera. There sat Thunderfoot with his feet braced against the front deck, reeling in a seagull, fifty feet above the boat, struggling like crazy to get away.

The fight went on for several minutes, and then we could see the bird was getting tired. "He's coming down easier now," Thunderfoot said.

"What are we gonna do with him when he gets here?"

"Grab him and take the hook out and let him go," Thunderfoot said as he reeled the bird closer.

As the gull got closer to the boat, I realized that it wasn't one of those little ones about the size of a pigeon. It was one of those giants that stand about two feet tall with a four-foot wingspan.

"That's one of those big ones," I yelled.

"Yeah, I noticed. But it's just a bird. How mean can he be?"

We'd soon find out. The bird was now only a few feet above the boat. I stood up and Thunderfoot led the flapping bird toward me. I grabbed its body and just as I did, it began slapping me in the head and face with its wings – it felt more like someone was slapping me with a couple of pine planks. I very quickly decided that this wasn't the way to subdue the bird, and I let go.

"You had him. Why did you let him go?" Thunderfoot yelled.

"He was beating me to death," I said. "I need something to throw over him to keep him from slapping me with those wings." I saw my jacket lying on the floor and picked it up. "Okay… bring him in again."

This time I wrapped the jacket around the bird's wings to keep him still. He struggled for a bit, but then he settled down. Thunderfoot's lure was in the bird's mouth and I was thankful that just one of the hooks was stuck in its beak. "Hold him tight and I'll take that hook out," I said as I handed the bird to Thunderfoot. He wrapped his arms around the bird and held him so he couldn't move.

Just as I took hold of the hook stuck in the bird's beak, he turned his head and clamped down on my index finger. "Yeouch! He's got me!" I yelled. Thunderfoot began laughing and almost lost his grip on the bird. I thought the gull was going to bite my finger off, but I pried with my other hand and finally got him to release my finger. "Jeez! He's got a bite like a snapping turtle."

I wasn't about to try that again. I found my needle nose pliers in my tackle box, got hold of the hook and popped it out of the bird's mouth. "Okay... let him go," I said.

Thunderfoot removed the jacket from the bird. It flapped its wings and flew off into the air.

"Wow! That was fun," Thunderfoot said.

Gull feathers were all over the boat, but it seemed the bird would be okay after his little encounter with us. Thunderfoot picked up my jacket from the floor of the boat and laughed. "The bird left you a little present," he said, opening the coat toward me. Sure enough, there was a big streak of gull poop decorating the lining.

"Looks like he wasn't very grateful for all my work getting that hook out," I said.

We had a good laugh, and then we decided that trolling was over for the day. We went back to our jig fishing and we soon had a mess of fish for supper. After we ate, we went down the road, bought a couple of loaves of bread for the ducks and gulls, and then had a good night's sleep.

The next day we fished until noon, and then it was time to get on the road for the long trip home. The highway runs right along the lake for many miles until it goes off to the west as it enters Wisconsin. Thunderfoot looked out at the lake as we drove along. "Probably the last time we'll see that together for a while," he said.

"Maybe so," I replied. "But if it is, we'll have some fun times to remember about it."

"Well," he said, "I didn't get a ten pound walleye, but I'll bet that gull was at least ten pounds."

"Yeah, no fooling. You're the gull champeene of all times."

He punched my arm and grinned. That about summed up our many trips together. Nothing more needed to be said.

Thanks, Thunderfoot.

It'll Be Easy

Thunderfoot careened into the driveway and came to a sliding stop, throwing up a big cloud of dust. He got out of his car, waving the dust away and coughing. "Jeez! Why don't you get this driveway fixed? It's making my car all dusty."

"Why don't you drive a little more sensibly so you don't make so much dust? And at the same time, you might not destroy what's remaining of my seal coating," I retorted.

"You mean there's blacktop under all this pea gravel?"

"Not blacktop – seal coating. It's a layer of tar with pea gravel rolled down on top of it. It's lots cheaper than blacktop. But it doesn't last forever, and it looks like I'm going to have to get it done again soon."

"How much does it cost?"

"It was $500 the first time, but I think it costs about $300 for the second coat. They don't have to use as much oil the second time."

"Why don't you just put on some of that black stuff from the hardware store?" Thunderfoot said. "I've seen lots of driveways that are all nice and black and slick looking, and they don't make so much dust when you drive in."

I shrugged my shoulders. "I guess I've thought about it, but I just never got around to it."

His face lit up. "Sounds like a good project for us," he said, nodding his head up and down.

While I would have liked to have the driveway sealed, I wasn't sure if it was one of those jobs that Thunderfoot and I should attempt. I tried to be obvious in my lack of enthusiasm.

But he persisted. "Let's go take a look at that stuff at the hardware store and see what's involved." It was obvious that he thought this would be a fun job, and I knew he would pester me until I agreed, so off we went to the hardware store.

Thunderfoot squatted down and began reading the

instructions on the five-gallon pails of driveway sealer. "How long is your driveway?" he asked.

"Oh, I guess maybe seventy feet," I answered.

"And wide?"

"Hmm. Part is wider than the rest... maybe twenty-five feet on the average," I said.

I could see him figuring and calculating in his head. "It should take about five of these five-gallon pails," he said. "And look! They're on sale, too!"

Sure enough, the sealer was advertised at only $8.99 per pail. Such a deal. "You really think we can do this?"

"Sure, and this will only cost you less than $50. Just think of the money you'll save. How hard can it be? We pour this stuff out and smear it all over the driveway, and presto! A nice, black, dry, dust free driveway." Thunderfoot had that look that told me his mind was made up, so I agreed. We loaded up five pails of the sealer on a cart. "We'll need some kind of brush or squeegee to put it on," he said, and went off in search of a clerk to show him what was available for applying the sealer. I pushed the cart up to the check out and waited. Thunderfoot came back carrying a long-handled brush with a squeegee on one side. "This is the gizmo we can use to squeegee it on or brush it on... and it's only $8.95," he said, gaily adding it to the cart.

"Is that all we need?" I asked.

"What about the pea gravel? Do you have a big broom to brush that off?"

I shook my head, and he trotted off toward the back of the store. In a little while he came back with a big, stiff push broom and laid it on the cart. It was $17.95.

"Is that it?" I asked.

He nodded yes, with a grin as wide as my driveway.

My *less than $50* investment had just risen to about $75.

I parked my truck on the grass and started to sweep all the loose pea gravel off the driveway with the big broom. It became quickly apparent that there was much more pea gravel than we had anticipated. I had only swept a few feet and there was already a big pile. "You better get the wheelbarrow and the scoop shovel," I said. "We'll have to haul this off."

Thunderfoot went to the garden shed, came back with the tools, and we scooped up the gravel. He wheeled it to the back yard, dumped it by the canoe rack, and by the time he returned, I had another pile ready for him. Two hours later, I was about ready for heart surgery; I had a huge blister on my right hand; and Thunderfoot was getting slower and slower on his trips to the back. "This is turning into one of those jobs from hell," I said.

"I didn't think there was so much pea gravel," he admitted.

"Well, we're gonna take a break," I said. "We'll have some lunch, and then I'm having a nap. This will wait a while." He followed me to the house and we made sandwiches.

It only took a minute for me to fall asleep in my recliner after all that hard work. I woke up about an hour later and saw Thunderfoot sweeping and loading more gravel. As much as I hated to, I went out to help.

It took all day to remove the pea gravel from the driveway, and when we were done, there was a pile that would fill a pickup truck.

"Who'd have thought there was so much?" Thunderfoot said.

It was too late in the day to spread the sealer, so we called it quits. We'd do it the next day. Thunderfoot went home, and I took a long, hot shower and sat down to rest. Every bone in my body ached.

Thunderfoot was bustling around in the kitchen before I was even up the next morning. The smell of frying bacon coaxed me to drag my aching muscles out of bed.

"Morning!" he said as I staggered into the kitchen.

"Morning," I mumbled. I gingerly sat down to eat. He was all smiles and chattered about how much fun spreading the sealer would be. I was still aching from the previous day and not nearly as chipper as him, but when we finished our breakfast, I drudgingly went with him to resume the work on the driveway.

"You know, there's a lot of dust and dirt on it," I said. "We'd better get that off or that stuff won't stick."

Thunderfoot nodded in agreement. Suddenly his eyes lit up and he trotted off to the garden shed. He came back with the leaf blower and a long extension cord. "Watch this," he said. He started the blower. Dirt and dust billowed and the whole yard was engulfed in fine dust from the pea gravel. He went back and forth for over an hour, and finally it seemed that the driveway was clean enough to spread the sealer.

When we opened the first bucket we could see that its contents had settled. After quite a bit of stirring with a stick, the black stuff seemed to be pretty well mixed, so I poured a puddle of the goop on the end of the driveway. Thunderfoot began spreading it out with the squeegee.

The instructions were to pour out a gallon, and that it should cover about ten square feet. Thunderfoot scraped and pushed and the gallon covered about three square feet. "Hmm. It doesn't go as far as it says it will," he said, looking down at the card table sized patch of glistening sealer.

"The driveway is too porous," I said. It soaks up a lot more. If it was newer seal coating, it probably would go farther."

"Well, let's use what we have and then see how much more we need."

By the time we had used up the five pails, both of us had sealer all over our feet and legs, and we were a long way from being finished – it had covered barely a third of the driveway.

"This is going to be a bit more of a job than we thought," Thunderfoot said scratching his head.

I just stared at him. I knew this had been a bad idea right from the start.

We went back to the hardware store and bought all the sealer they had in stock. They had more coming in a few days, so we took the six pails, raising my total investment to a little over $125. They covered the driveway to about the halfway point, and we were out of sealer again. "Well, we'll just have to finish next week when they have more at the store," Thunderfoot said.

We poured some paint thinner on an old tee shirt to scrub off the sealer from our hands and legs. It didn't come off very easy, leaving our skin quite red and sore. "Jeez, that stuff is tough," I said. "I hope it sticks on the driveway that well."

The hardware store clerk called the following Tuesday to let me know they had received more sealer. Thunderfoot and I drove up after school and I bought eight more pails. My total investment was now at about $200.

We unloaded the pails and Thunderfoot inspected the finished portion of the driveway. "That part we did really looks nice," he said.

"Yeah, it did turn out good," I said.

"Well, let's get these on and we're done."

"It's supposed to rain tomorrow, and the instructions say that it needs to cure for twenty four hours before a rain. Maybe we should wait till later in the week."

"Awe, hooey. It ain't gonna rain. Let's get it done."

Against my better judgment, I agreed, and we started pouring and spreading the sealer. It was almost dark by the time we finished and the air had become considerably cooler. "I hope it's warm enough for this stuff to dry tonight," I said.

"Oh, don't worry. It'll be fine," Thunderfoot said, surveying the finished job.

We put the equipment away for the night, and then scraped and rubbed ourselves raw again getting the sealer off our legs and hands.

I heard the first thunder about three in the morning. I lay there hoping against hope that the rain would hold off until the sealer had dried, but of course, it was raining a few minutes later, and it continued steadily all the rest of the night. That morning I went out to see how our newly laid sealer had faired.

I just about cried when I saw the driveway. The fresh sealer that had been applied the previous night had just melted away and was running off into puddles along the driveway and down the sidewalk. Now I knew why the stuff was so hard to get off our skin with paint thinner – it was water soluble, not oil based. The new half of the driveway was ruined.

I just stood there with rain running down the back of my neck when the phone rang.

"Did it get dry?" It was Thunderfoot.

"Nope," I said.

"Is it ok?"

"Nope."

"Oh, boy!"

A few minutes later he came through the front door shaking his head. "We shoulda waited, I guess."

I just nodded. "Want some breakfast?"

We were kind of quiet while we ate. Finally he said, "I'll pay for some of the new stuff to fix it."

"What?"

"I talked you into doing it last night. I'll buy the sealer to fix it."

As disappointed as I was that the job had been ruined, I had to smile at Thunderfoot's thoughtfulness. I put my arm on his shoulder. "I'll pay for it. It's not your fault."

"But – "

I shook my head. "Forget it. We'll let it dry out and then get some more sealer and do it again. It'll be all right."

Later that morning the rain stopped and we went out to look at the mess. Not only was the driveway a nasty looking mess, but now the sidewalk from the house to the driveway was covered with black tar, too. I was standing there staring at it when Thunderfoot suddenly got a look of inspiration on his face.

"Remember that building show where they put a new pathway over an old one? You know, they put sand down and then put those patio blocks on it, and it made such a nice sidewalk?"

"Remember the driveway project that was going to take five pails of sealer? And now we're going back for more and it will end up being about twenty pails instead of five?"

"Yeah, but that wasn't like this. We can measure... and find the right size blocks, and all it will take is a little sand, and we can get that off a sandbar down at the river for free, and then we can make this real nice sidewalk and..."

I turned away and went to the house for my checkbook. There was no reason to argue with him. I hadn't won an argument in over six years, so it was a waste of breath to even start.

When all was said and done, the job had required twenty-three pails of sealer, and I had just under $300 invested. But the driveway looked great. As for the new sidewalk, he hasn't mentioned it in a while, so I'm hoping he's forgotten about it.

One thing about him... he's never short on enthusiasm.

Thanks, Thunderfoot.

Remember That Time?

I had been thinking about this day for quite a while. On one hand I was happy for Thunderfoot, and on the other, I knew our friendship was going to undergo some changes. It was graduation day.

Thunderfoot had been working like crazy helping his mom get their house ready for the big party that would be held in his honor. But there was work to be done before the party, and poor Thunderfoot had been slaving all week to make everything perfect. His mom even made him paint the garage and the trim on the house. Of course, he tried his best to get me to help, but I wasn't about to let anyone sucker me into painting – especially him. I had cleaned up all of my lawn furniture and helped him haul it over to their yard to add to the tables and chairs that had been gathered from everyone in the neighborhood.

I saw him across the back yard on a ladder stringing those little clear Christmas lights through the trees so the party could go on into the evening. The yard looked great from where I stood, and I was sure his mom had made sure everything was just right.

The graduation ceremony was scheduled for two o'clock, so I tried to find something to keep myself occupied until it was time to go to the school. I had just started straightening up the boat shed when Thunderfoot walked across the back yard carrying a fishing pole and a coffee can that looked like it might contain fish worms.

"Whatcha doin'?" he asked as he walked into the shed.

"Just puttering. What are you up to?"

"I gotta get out of here for a while. I think mom's gonna drive me nuts."

"I thought by now everything would be clean and painted and ready."

"She keeps coming up with new stuff all the time," he said.

"She even made me clean up my bedroom."

"Well, I've seen your bedroom, and it probably needed a cleaning... if I remember right."

"I like having my stuff out where I can see it," he grinned.

His bedroom was, well, I guess the best word would be a disaster area. He had a perfectly good chest of drawers, but instead of putting the stuff away when his mom washed it, he chose to pile all of his clothes on the floor. Jeans were folded and piled in one spot, shirts in another, underwear another, and so on. "That way I can find just what I want without looking all over the place," he always said when I teased him about his messy hovel.

"Did she make you put your clothes away?" I asked.

"Yeah, but I fooled her. I just slid them under the bed."

"So, what did you have in mind with that fishing pole?"

"Let's go down to the bridge and just sit in the sand... bottom fish for a couple hours. I've got plenty of time before I have to be at school, and I want to get away to someplace quiet."

It sounded like a good idea to me, too, so I grabbed a pole and a little tackle box with hooks and sinkers, and off we went. We didn't even take lunch, so I knew that this was an impromptu trip.

When we crawled down over the bank to the sandy shore and picked a good spot to sit, two forked sticks were already sticking in the sand. "Must be a good spot," Thunderfoot said. "Somebody left their pole holders."

We baited up with a big fat worms, tossed our lines out into the river, set the poles in the forked sticks, and settled down to watch for a bite. Several minutes passed and I finally said, "Big day today. Are you excited?"

He shrugged his shoulders. "I guess. I'm glad to be finished with high school, but... things are gonna change, and I'm not so happy about that."

I saw his eyes were filled with tears. I slid over a little closer and put my arm on his shoulder. "Hey. It's not going to be the end of it. We'll still see each other and do stuff."

He nodded.

Just then I got a bite. I jumped back to my spot, grabbed my rod and set the hook into a small river shiner that came right in without hardly any fight. "Oh, boy! A trophy," I said.

Thunderfoot laughed. "Pretty much what you're used to catching, isn't it?"

I unhooked the fish and threw it at him. It glanced off his shoulder and into the river where it swam out of sight.

"We've caught some pretty good ones in the past few years, haven't we?" he said.

"No foolin'," I replied. "I hate to admit it, but you've become a pretty darn good fisherman. Of course, not as good as me, but close."

"I've learned a lot since that first time we went squirrel hunting," he said. "How come you decided to take *me* hunting? Lots of kids came into your shop?"

I thought back to the first time I'd met him six years earlier. "I don't know for sure," I said. "You just seemed like a nice kid. You were real friendly, and when you bought that beef jerky and tore it in half and gave your brother the biggest half, I thought that was pretty cool."

"You remember that beef jerky?"

"Yeah. I guess it just struck me as something that a nice person would do, and I guess that's why I asked you to go hunting with me."

"Boy! Remember that?" he said, grinning. "You went down the hill backwards into that fence. Jeez! I almost peed myself laughing. Then I chased that stupid squirrel for about a mile, and when I came back you were standing in your underwear trying to get your pants out of the fence."

"It's a wonder that you didn't take off and never get near me again, seeing me there half naked," I said.

"Jeez, that was funny. Bloop! Right over backwards."

"Well, I'm glad it happened if it made you think I was a fun guy, because from then on, we sure did a lot of funny stuff."

"Remember the ten gauge?" he said. "Holy smokes. I thought that thing broke my shoulder."

I laughed, thinking back to that frozen day in a goose blind at the Horicon Marsh when Thunderfoot and I were waiting for a goose to fly close enough. We each had a twelve-gauge shotgun, and I had my single shot ten-gauge along, in case the geese were flying extra high. Thunderfoot had pestered me all morning long to shoot the ten-gauge, and I had finally given in. But that gun weighed over eleven pounds and was about as tall as he was. He was still pretty scrawny, and he could barely hold the thing up, let alone shoot it. But he insisted. Finally, I told him to shoot a lone goose coming right toward us. He followed it until it was right over the blind, about forty yards up. When Thunderfoot touched off the three and a half inch magnum, the recoil came right down on top of his shoulder and snapped his head back. His thumb, wrapped around the stock, hit him right on the end of his nose. His hat popped off and landed out of the blind in the pasture. He lowered the gun, his eyes filled with tears, and he looked kind of bewildered. "I think I broke my nose," he said as tears streamed down his face. I was laughing so hard that I slid right down the wall of the blind and landed on my butt in the pile of empty shells and pop cans littering the floor. It was one of the funniest things I'd ever seen while I was hunting.

"Yeah, that thing had quite a kick," he said grinning. "And now, thanks to my good buddy, I've got a ten-gauge of my own, and I'm big enough to handle it."

"That was funny... you have to admit," I said.

"Yeah, about as funny as when you found that big snake in my mushroom bag," he said laughing. "Jeez! You almost had a heart attack."

"You little snot. I'm still mad about that. You know I don't like snakes. That was a mean thing to do."

"Oh, poor baby. I'm so sorry," he said.

I was thankful that he must have learned that I am afraid of snakes, and that had been the only time he pulled a snake joke on me. It was during spring mushroom hunting season, and I was showing Thunderfoot what they looked like on his first time trying to find some morels. In doing so, I had run across a little grass snake that made me scream like a teen-aged girl, and he thought it was real funny. Later, when we met at the truck, he dumped a big black snake in my lap as I sat on the tailgate waiting for him. Needless to say, I caused quite a scene, and lucky for Thunderfoot he could run faster than me, or I'd probably still be in prison for murder.

"When you screamed, that note was almost up there where just dogs can hear," he said.

"Oh, sometimes you're so clever."

Just then he got a bite. He grabbed his pole and set the hook into a good, fighting fish. "At least it's not one of those little minnows you catch," he said as he reeled in a good-sized sheepshead. "Baaa, Baaa. A sheeper." He removed the hook and tossed the fish back into the water.

"Remember that time you caught that sheepshead and used it for bait?" I said. "...When you swung it to cast it out in the river and you hit that old lady in the head with it?"

"Oh, jeez! That was so funny," Thunderfoot said. "Her son got really mad at you."

"Yeah. You took off and he thought I did it. I thought I was going to get a good beating. He was huge."

We had been fishing in early spring for walleyes on the bank below the dam. Thunderfoot was using crawlers instead of minnows because he didn't want to get his hands cold in the minnow bucket. There was a family above us fishing, too, and besides the mom and dad and two kids, there was an old lady, all dressed up in her 'Sunday Go To Meetin' coat and a hat that looked like a turban. Thunderfoot caught a sheepshead, and just then the dad above us caught a big, northern pike. Thunderfoot decided to put on a big hook, use the sheepshead for bait, and try to catch a northern. He got his pole all rigged up and cast side arm toward the river. About halfway through the cast, the sheepshead came off the hook and flew fifty feet up the riverbank. It smacked the old lady right in the side of the head, knocking off her turban. I couldn't help laughing, and her son, about six and a half feet tall and built like a linebacker, thought I had been the one who hit his mother with the fish. Of course, Thunderfoot took off down the bank for safety, and there I was, trying to decide whether I preferred getting beaten to death, or drowning in the cold water. We finally worked it out, but it cost me all of the walleyes I had caught – a small price compared to the cost of plastic surgery to re-align my nose that would have surely been altered.

"I could stand there for the rest of my life casting a sheepshead and never hit that lady again," Thunderfoot laughed. "That was one in a million."

"No kidding. A classic," I said. "I was scared that her son was going to kill me with his bare hands. In fact, you've just about scared me to death quite a few times."

"Oh, bull. When?"

"How about when you nearly ran my brand new boat up on the back of that pontoon?"

"Oh, yeah. You about pooped that time didn't you?" Thunderfoot laughed.

I had just gotten my brand new dreamboat – shiny, not a scratch – and we were taking it on its maiden voyage. All day long I had run the big gas motor when we moved from one fishing spot to another, and all day long, Thunderfoot had pestered me to let him drive the boat. Finally, I gave in and let him get behind the wheel. He fired up the 150 horses and drove us upriver to a new fishing spot. He had done a good job, so I decided to let him drive some more, and not long afterward, we were going along the channel, and he gave the motor a bit more gas than I liked. But he was having such a good time that I decided to let him go. When you drive a boat on a river, you use the same rules as on a highway. You keep to the right of the channel, and if you want to pass another boat, you pull to the left and go around. Well, there was a pontoon boat ahead of us, going much slower than we were going, and Thunderfoot yelled to me over the noise of the motor, "Can I pass him?"

I nodded and motioned to go to the left. He nodded okay. He opened up the motor a little more, and we were rapidly getting close to the pontoon. A pontoon boat makes a horrendous wake since it's shaped like a back yard deck rather than a boat, and suddenly we were right behind the pontoon, caught inside his wake. The guy on the pontoon turned and saw this huge boat bearing down on him, and he waved us off, trying to get Thunderfoot to turn. The problem was that Thunderfoot was trying to turn, but couldn't get past the big wake. I yelled at him to turn sharp and give the boat more gas, and just in time, we jumped the wake and went around the pontoon.

I made a cutting motion at my throat. Thunderfoot cut the engine back and we slowed to a drift. The pontoon went past just then, and the guy looked like he was heading for the cardiac unit at the nearest hospital. I was about to bawl out Thunderfoot for his mistake, and then thought better of it and explained the correct and ethical way to pass another boat.

"That was pretty exciting," Thunderfoot said as he set the hook and missed the fish that was biting.

"Yeah. I came close to a heart attack that time," I said. "Just about as close as when I found that rattler at Bogus Bluff."

"Oh, holy cow! I thought we were gonna have to get a block and tackle to drag your carcass out of that little cave," he said laughing.

My fear of snakes had made a little cave-exploring trip into quite an exciting adventure. Thunderfoot had heard the legend about counterfeiters and buried gold in a cave on one of the river bluffs. He talked me into going with him in the cave. We had started walking down a long passageway that kept getting progressively smaller. Before long we were crawling, and a little later, we were shinnying along on our bellies with rock walls pressing against us on both sides and above. Being a little full figured, I was beginning to worry about getting stuck, but Thunderfoot kept pushing me onward. The trouble was that my flashlight died, and he wouldn't give me the good one. So, the only light was that shining past me from his light. We came to a corner in the tunnel, and in the low light I suddenly saw a rattlesnake's tail just ahead of us. I panicked and tried to scoot backwards to get out of the cave, and after a few minutes of terror and shouting, I had the good flashlight. In the better light the snake's tail turned out to be part of a corncob. Of course, Thunderfoot had a great laugh over that one. He still points out killer corncobs to me every chance he gets.

"I've always thought about how mad the guys from the Rescue Squad would have been, if I had dropped dead in that cave. Imagine the trouble they'd have had getting my body out."

"Maybe we'd have just filled in the opening and left you."

I had a huge bite and set the hook, only to catch another of those little river shiners. "Boy! You've got the touch for catching those little guys," Thunderfoot said.

"It takes special skill to catch the little ones."

"Which are you more scared of?" Thunderfoot asked. "Snakes or horses?"

"Oh, no question there," I replied. "Snakes. Horses I can see coming a lot farther away."

"Boy, that time the horse chased you was funny."

"Yeah, that was a barrel of laughs."

The incident happened when Thunderfoot and I were rabbit hunting on his grandpa's farm. There was a good rabbit ditch on the back forty where treetops and stumps had been dumped for years. It made good cover for bunnies, and we usually had some good shooting when we hunted there. On this particular day, we were headed toward the rabbit ditch when I noticed a horse standing at the end of a fenced field. The horse watched us as we neared the fence and he perked his ears forward like he was trying to hear what we said. "That horse looks mean," I said to Thunderfoot. He laughed at me and called me a sissy, and then he started across the field. The horse watched him, but didn't bother him. When he got to the other side, he climbed over the fence and stood there, looking at me, wondering if I was coming, or not. I was not really enamored by horses – ever since I was a little kid, when the one I was riding had decided to lie down and scratch its back. Of course, that traumatic experience scarred me for life, and since then I had always been really hesitant when it came to getting near horses. Thunderfoot was taunting me, so I decided I'd take the chance. Naturally, as soon as I got about halfway across the field, the horse started after me, and I ended up on my back in a brush pile after vaulting the fence, attempting to escape.

"That was about the fastest I'd ever seen you move," Thunderfoot chuckled.

"I can be a speedster if the jaws of death are behind me," I assured him.

Just then he got a bite and caught a carp. "At least it's not a minnow," he said.

"Yeah, yeah. Just you wait. Sometimes smart guys get their just deserts, too."

"Like when?"

"Oh, I remember a kid that was acting pretty smart and got a mouth full of cow pee."

We both began laughing over that memory. I had taken Thunderfoot and his friend, Dillon, to the State Fair for the day. We had seen lots of cool things and eaten just about every treat that existed. After a few rides on some contraptions that made my stomach feel like a blender, I suggested that we look at some of the animals. In the poultry barn, Thunderfoot had pilfered an egg from a crate that held chickens, and a short while later, in the dairy barn, he had slipped it into Dillon's pocket and smacked the pocket with his hand. Thinking he had pulled a great joke, he ran off down the aisle with his mouth wide open, laughing, when a cow tethered to the wall suddenly slapped him in the face with her tail – that had just been soaked with a load of hot, fresh cow pee. Thunderfoot stopped dead in his tracks. He turned toward us, as if his arms and legs were suddenly sticks. "Ohmygosh! I got hit by cow pee!" Dillon and I – and everyone else in the barn – had a gut splitting laugh at poor Thunderfoot, and after we all recovered, we hosed him off, and hosed the egg out of Dillon's pocket. Thunderfoot was pretty upset with us for laughing, but we didn't care. We tormented him for the rest of the day. It was like Christmas for me, because I very seldom had a laugh on him – I was usually on the receiving end of the jokes.

"That was a pretty funny day," I said.

He shook his head. "Yeah, I guess it probably was. But, boy! That cow pee was nasty tasting stuff."

We chuckled at that for a while, and then he got a bite and caught another sheepshead.

"I wonder if your bowling ball is still out there," he said, nodding toward the middle of the river.

"I suppose it is," I said. "I guess it depends on how deep it went into the sand when it hit."

The bowling ball incident started out innocently enough when Thunderfoot was helping me with a bi-yearly cleaning of my junk closet on the porch. He found my old bowling ball. One thing led to another, and of course, he talked me into going bowling that evening. Needless to say, I was my usual, graceful self, and slid too far with my foot, doing the splits. I ripped the butt right out of my pants. Of course, this had to happen amidst a packed bowling alley, and my red plaid boxers now were in full sight. On the way home, I stopped in the middle of the bridge and unceremoniously dropped my bowling ball into the river. Poor Thunderfoot thought I had finally gone around the bend.

"You thought I'd lost it that day, didn't you?" I said.

"Close," he said. "I was glad there weren't any sharp objects in the car. By the way, speaking of things falling into the water, how about the time you did a back flip out of the boat into Lake Michigan?"

"Yeah, I remember that... and if I remember right, that was your fault."

He looked so innocent as he grinned at me.

Of course, he was referring to my famous Taco Bell incident, when we were at Little Bay de Noc on the Upper Peninsula of Michigan, fishing for walleyes. We had gone north to the big lake after watching a TV show about the good walleye fishing there, and during our stay, Thunderfoot had pestered me to stop at Taco Bell for lunch every time we drove past the restaurant. Finally, I gave in and filled my belly with tacos and other spicy food. That just about did me in. I spent a long night suffering from heartburn and frequent trips to the bathroom, and the next day when we were a long way from shore, I had an emergency call from Mother Nature. After arguing about going in to shore, I finally had decided to sit on the back of the boat and do my business over the side. It wasn't that I wanted to do it, but that I knew I'd never make it all the way to the shore. Of course, Thunderfoot couldn't let well enough alone, and just as I was baring my backside, he turned the back of the boat toward a bunch of other boats that were fishing in the area. In my haste to try to cover myself, I lost my grip on the motor and fell backward into the lake, with my pants around my ankles. Of course, he thought it was hilarious. The people in the other boats all had a good laugh, too. I guess it was a pretty good show.

"You just have no respect for your elders," I said.

"It's pretty hard to show respect for someone who is pooping over the end of a boat," Thunderfoot said, laughing.

He grabbed his pole and missed another bite. He baited the hook and tossed it out again. "That was the last crawler," he said.

"Well, I suppose we'd better get back soon, anyway. What time do you have to be at the school?"

"Graduation starts at two, so I have to be there at one-thirty."

We sat quietly for a while. I guess we were both thinking of the fun times we had shared, and how our relationship would change, now that he was finished with high school. The part time work at my shop wasn't enough for him to make a living, and he wanted to get out into the world and try new things. I understood how he felt, but it didn't make it any easier to think of him moving away.

"You know, we'll have to make plans for another trip up north," he said.

"Yeah. We should do that... maybe this fall, or next spring."

"We sure had a lot of fun those other times," he said. "That big moose trying to get in our boat... and the bears... and all of those good shore lunches... wow! That sure was fun."

I had to laugh when I thought about the funny things that had happened on some of the trips. The moose incident was pretty scary, but funny, too. Thunderfoot and I were fishing in Canada when he spotted a moose in a shallow bay, feeding on underwater weeds. We motored into the bay and then I oared us closer so Thunderfoot could get a picture. He was kneeling on the front seat and watching the moose through the camera viewfinder. "Go closer," he whispered. I moved us closer. "Closer," he whispered again. We were getting quite close, but I pushed on the oars once more and we slid through the weeds, coming to a stop about ten feet from the moose. Just then Bullwinkle rose up from eating weeds, saw us right there in his face, and he let out a bellow and charged the boat. I was oaring backward as fast as I could, and Thunderfoot was crawling backward in the bottom of the boat shouting at me to "Go fast – back!" Well, we got away, but he harped about me trying to get him killed for the rest of the trip. I reminded him that it was he who wanted to get closer. His excuse was that the moose looked pretty small in the viewfinder, and he didn't realize that we were *that close*. So, obviously, it was my fault.

"I just about had one of those very rare teenager heart attacks," he said.

"I still think you wet your pants," I laughed.

I had a bite and caught yet another river shiner.

"Jeez! We should skip graduation and go Northern fishing," Thunderfoot said. "You've caught enough bait for a whole day of fishing."

"It takes a lot of skill to catch those little guys with the little mouths. Those big sheepshead just swallow it, and that's why you can catch them… no skill required."

He threw a clod of mud at me and then set the hook and reeled in another sheepshead. "Well, that's the end of our bait."

"I suppose we'd better get back. Your mom is probably worried that you'll be late for your graduation. And after all the work she's done to get the house and yard ready, she'd *really* be mad if we skipped it," I said.

"Yeah, I guess so. Let's just sit and watch the river for a few more minutes," he said.

We sat side-by-side in the sand and watched the river drift by. A nice breeze and the gurgling water made the day seem so peaceful. I saw Thunderfoot's eyes were full of tears again.

"I'm gonna miss stuff like this," he said.

"Me too."

Thanks, Thunderfoot.

Pomp and Circumstance

I left my house a half hour early so I'd get a good parking spot at the High School for Thunderfoot's graduation. As I neared the school, I realized that everyone else must have had the same idea, because the school parking lot was full and the streets were full for two blocks around the school. I finally found a spot, parked and hiked to the gym where the ceremony would be held.

It was one of those spring days that, with just a little push, the weather could have turned hot and muggy. As long as the sun stayed behind the clouds it was comfortable, but as soon as it peeked out, the humidity rose and the air quickly became rather sticky. Of course, by this time of year I was used to wearing a tee shirt and shorts, so a shirt and tie with long pants was a little stifling.

I arrived at the gym and showed my Guest ticket to one of the high school boys who were acting as ushers. This ticket allowed me to sit in the chairs that were lined up on the gym floor where the families of the graduates sat. The rest of the onlookers had to sit on the bleachers, which was akin to a Chinese water torture. I've always thought that if you wanted to get information or a confession from someone who you suspected of wrongdoing, just make him sit on the bleachers to listen to hours of boring speeches. He'd confess in no time.

There was a hum of conversation; teachers and school administration people were hurrying here and there getting everything ready for the ceremony to begin. I saw Thunderfoot's mom and his brother, Caleb, sitting in the Guest section. They motioned to me. "Why don't you sit with us?" Thunderfoot's mom said. I squeezed down the row and sat.

"Thanks," I said. "How are you doing, Caleb?"

"Good. Are you coming to the party later?"

"Sure. Wouldn't miss it," I said.

Just then the choir came in and took their places on the risers behind the stage. Then the band filtered in, and soon everything seemed to be ready. The time was getting near for the graduates to come in, and I was getting a lump in my throat, thinking about this as being the end of Thunderfoot's high school career. How had it come so fast? It seemed like only yesterday that I had met him as a young boy, and now he was all grown up and going off into the world.

I guess I'm an old softie – always have been. Thunderfoot often made fun of me when I cried at a movie. I've always been that way, I guess. I can remember when Lassie came home... my gosh, I cried like a twelve year old girl. I'm one of those guys who gets emotional when the flag passes in a parade, or when a particularly patriotic song plays. I can't help it. That's just the way I am.

Just then the School Board members and the principal took the stage, and the crowd began to quiet. The band director raised his arms, gave the downbeat, and the band started playing the mournful chords of Edward Elgar's *Pomp and Circumstance*. Everyone's eyes turned to the entrance as the first pair of graduates slowly marched in. Everyone stood, and my heart was in my throat as the sounds of the music filled the gym. About midway in the line of graduates, Thunderfoot walked with his friend, Scott, at his side. They had been friends for years, and now they were taking their final walk together as classmates. They came down the right side of the gym, turned at the back, and then paraded up the center aisle between the Guest sections. Parents and friends were stepping out into the aisle taking pictures and movies, as their graduate passed by.

When he saw me standing there watching, Thunderfoot gave me a little wink and a grin as he and Scott came down the aisle. Try as I might, I couldn't keep a tear from running down my cheek. They passed by and took their places with the rest of the graduates. Then the speeches began.

It seemed like everyone in the class made a speech, and every teacher, every school board member, and maybe even some members of the audience might have taken a turn. One good thing about all those speeches was that I had the opportunity to get my emotions controlled and settled down a little. Finally, the speeches were over and the graduates were called up, one at a time, to receive their diplomas. As his name was called, Thunderfoot strode across the stage, not a scrawny little boy any more, but a tall, handsome, confident young man. He received his diploma, turned to smile at his mom and me, and then he went back to his seat and waited while everyone in the entire class received their diplomas. The principal walked up to the microphone and presented the graduates. The entire class stood up and cheered and threw their hats into the air. Some had smuggled in confetti and stilly string, and there was utter chaos for a few minutes. When that part of the celebration had settled down, the kids picked up their hats while the band began playing *Pomp and Circumstance* again, and they all filed out of the gym.

Once the graduates were all out, the guests and the rest of the people in the gym began a slow procession into the cafeteria where the graduates had formed a line around the outside of the room. It was mass confusion trying to find anyone, but eventually I saw Thunderfoot and his friends, Scott and Jerry, all standing together, shaking hands with people who were wishing them well. I made my way to the boys and shook hands with Scott and Jerry.

And then I came to Thunderfoot. I didn't want to embarrass him, so I offered my hand. He stared at it a moment, and then he threw his arms around my neck and just about dislocated my head with a bone-crunching hug. "You get more than a handshake," he said into my ear.

"I'm real proud of you, you know," I said.

"Yeah, I know."

I hated to let him go, as if this were the last chance I'd ever have to hug him again, but I knew there were people coming down the line waiting for their turn to congratulate him, so I let him go and stepped back. He gave me a grin. "We'll talk later."

I stayed at the cafeteria for a while, talking with friends, and soon the room began to thin out as people left for parties that were starting all over town. I went home and changed into shorts and a golf shirt – I thought a plain tee shirt was a little *too* casual. Then I walked across the back yard to Thunderfoot's house to join his graduation party.

The yard and garage were full of well-wishers and relatives. I met many of Thunderfoot's relatives, and I talked with his grandparents for quite a while. People came and went all afternoon, while Thunderfoot greeted everyone and was the perfect host. By late afternoon things settled down a little, and he finally had a chance to sit with me at the picnic table and catch his breath. "Holy smokes! I didn't know I knew so many people."

"You're such a popular guy, no wonder," I said. "So, what's on for tonight?"

"Some of my friends and I are going to a party at one of the kid's house out in the country. They're having a band and all kinds of stuff. We're all staying over night, so no one will be driving."

"That's a good idea."

"I didn't tell you before... I guess I just didn't want to finally say it. But I'm gonna be working this summer, out of town," he said. "Jerry and Scott and I got an apartment, and we're gonna work at that place where they build those two piece houses up in Lancaster. I hope you're not mad."

"Mad? Why would I be mad?"

"Well, I guess I thought you might be mad that I wouldn't work for you again this summer."

"Hey, I know you can't make a living working for me. It was okay when you were in school, but now you need something that'll make you more money than I can pay you. I'm not mad at all. I'm glad you got a good job so quickly."

Just then a car pulled in, and Scott and Jerry jumped out, and then a girl I had never seen before stepped out behind them. She saw Thunderfoot and waved and smiled at him.

I looked at him. "And that would be…?"

He flushed beet red. "A girl I met a few weeks ago."

"I see. Does this girl have a name?"

"Yeah, she does."

I waited.

"Oh! You want to know her name?"

Just then the girl strolled up to the table. Thunderfoot jumped to his feet. She put her arms around him and gave him a kiss on his cheek. He was so flustered he didn't know what to say, but he finally turned and said, "Crystal, this is my friend, Dan, and Dan, this is Crystal."

I said "hi" and Crystal said, "I've been wanting to meet you. Jamie talks about you all the time."

"I hope it's not *all* bad," I said, laughing.

"No, not at all," she said. Then she leaned to my ear and whispered, "Jamie thinks you're about the best guy in the whole world. He said you've done a lot for him, and you'll always be very special to him."

I just hugged her and said, "thanks."

"Uh, we're gonna go to the party now, okay?" Thunderfoot said.

"Sure. Don't let me stop you. And have fun… you only graduate from high school once."

Thunderfoot turned to Crystal. "I'll meet you in the car."

She said goodbye and walked to the car where Scott and Jerry were waiting. She waved as she got in the back seat. Scott and Jerry waved, too.

"Well, I guess I'll go then," Thunderfoot said.

"Have fun… but be careful."

"Yes, Mom!"

"You know what I mean. Don't do anything stupid."

He grinned at me. "I probably won't have to worry about that, as long as you're not there. Most of the stupid things that I've done in my life have been with you."

So, we *had* done some dumb things together. But at least we'd had a lot of fun.

He threw his arms around my neck. "Thanks for everything. I'll never forget all our good times together."

I put my arms around him and hugged him; I felt like my heart would break. "I love ya, kiddo," I whispered.

"Me too."

He walked to the car and got in the back seat with his new girlfriend. As the car pulled out of the driveway I saw his hand come out of the window and wave goodbye.

I thanked his mom for the nice party, and then I sauntered slowly across the back yard toward home. I had an empty feeling inside. I had known for a long time that this day was coming, but now that it was here, it was hard to accept. It would be really quiet without Thunderfoot in my life every day, as he had been for the past six years. Oh, sure, we'd still get together once in a while, but it wouldn't be the same. He had a new life ahead of him, and it would take him to faraway places.

I flopped down in my recliner and began idly paging through the latest copy of the newspaper. A classified ad caught my eye:

Seventeen-year-old Norwegian Boy desperately seeking Host Family. Enjoys fishing, movies, and skiing. Loves dogs and animals. Call 1-800-*-******

Hmm. That sounded interesting. I'd always thought it would be fun to host an exchange student. Maybe tomorrow I'd call and see what this program involved. It just might be a lot of fun.

Then, just as soon as I had that thought, I felt guilty. How could I be thinking of replacing Thunderfoot so quickly? Of course, *no one* could ever replace Thunderfoot, but this might be a way to put some new adventure into my life. An image of his face popped into my mind, and he had that grin that I had seen so many times. "Give them a call," he said. "It's okay – really – we'll still be friends no matter what." I smiled and picked up the phone. One thing I had learned from Thunderfoot was that no matter how old you feel some days, you always get a new shot of life with a kid around the house, and you never know when a little trip to the river or the woods will turn into a great adventure.

Thanks, Thunderfoot… for everything.

Last Thoughts from Thunderfoot

I remember the first time I met Dan. We had just moved to Muscoda, and my little brother and I decided to check out the fishing store just down the street from our house. When we walked in the front door, Dan was sitting behind the counter, sorting out piles of bills and writing them into a ledger. Instead of ignoring us, he smiled and said "hello" and asked if he could help us find anything special. I said "no" but then I asked if it was all right if we just looked around. He told us to go ahead and left us to check out the stuff in the store.

A while later, I bought a beef jerky, and we got to know each other a little. He seemed like a pretty nice man. After we left, I told my brother that I thought I'd like to get to know him. For one thing, he had a lot of good stuff in his store, and for another thing, he was friendly.

A few days later I took my dog over to meet him, and he asked me to go squirrel hunting with him, and that was it. From then on, we became good friends and, well, you know the rest.

Dan had a little mishap that first day of squirrel hunting. He ended up hanging backwards over a fence on the side of the hill. Instead of getting all mad and stuff, he laughed about it and apologized for having to cut the hunting trip short. Of course, his pants didn't have any back in them any more, and he had a bunch of cuts and scrapes that were bleeding pretty badly.

That day taught me that Dan had a good sense of humor and didn't take himself too seriously. And he treated me like an equal – not like some kid who didn't know anything. Of course, I *didn't* know anything much about hunting and fishing, but I soon learned, and boy, what fun I had learning.

I shot my first deer with Dan. I shot my first turkey with Dan. I shot my first duck, and my first goose with Dan. I caught my first of many kinds of fish. I went to Canada where I just about shared a boat with a huge moose. I went up north and almost was dinner for a bear. I saw Mt. Rushmore. I flew in an airplane and landed on the water. I helped Dan bury and mourn over three of his dogs that got old and left us.

We had so many laughs that I can't begin to remember them all. There were countless times when something I did ended up with Dan in the water, or rolling down a hill, or stuck in the mud. There were so many times when we started out right on track and ended up with a hilarious adventure. I was the cause of some of them, but Dan did his share of foolishness, too. He's just a big kid, really.

He got me back on some of my mischief, too. Like the time at the State Fair when I got hit in the face with a cow pee tail. He thought that was real funny, but then he bought me a new tee shirt. He got me almost every time we went fishing, and I had to buy ice cream because he caught the first fish of the day. Of course, I usually didn't take any money along, just because of that.

We shared a lot of funny, exciting adventures. But we shared a lot of quality time together, too. We sat in the duck blind watching sunsets turn to dusk and then night. We gazed out at a million stars and watched the Northern Lights from a dock on a Canadian lake. We felt the pride and majesty of Mt. Rushmore. We shared countless hours just sitting and watching nature, enjoying everything from the call of a turkey to a chickadee landing on our gun barrel.

Dan taught me a lot about hunting, fishing, and life. But he did it in a way that it wasn't like preaching. It was like learning by example. I learned that hunting is more than killing something – the hunt is much more important than the kill, and is much more memorable. I learned about hunting ethics, and the fact that a fair chase is more important than a full game bag. There were countless times when we could have shot a limit of ducks by just waiting until ten minutes after closing time, but instead of shooting late, we watched them land on the pond in front of the blind with our guns unloaded. There were many times when we could have shot a turkey from its roost as we snuck into the turkey woods. But what honor would there have been in that? How could we be proud of a trophy that we took unethically? The answer was, of course, we *couldn't* be proud of it, and so we didn't do it.

Before I met Dan, I thought that any fish I managed to get to the shore was going home with me. Then I watched as Dan returned a fish back into the water, and smiled as he watched it disappear. He never told me that I should let any fish go, but after watching him release many big, trophy fish, I tried it, and found it to be a real good feeling. Now I keep some smaller ones for eating, and let the big ones go back, to fight another day and to give someone else the thrill of catching them. And, it's a good thing.

A hunting trip or a fishing trip can be memorable without a full limit of ducks or a big stringer of fish. Time spent with a good friend is just as rewarding as a trophy for the wall. The trophy that you save from these quality hunts and fishing trips will be in your memory forever.

Now things will change. Tomorrow my friends and I will move into our apartment and begin our new jobs. Tomorrow evening when I get home, I won't be able to run over to Dan's and see what he's got planned. I'll be too far away, but I'll think about him and I'll wonder what he's up to. I think he'll probably do the same, worrying that I'm okay and wondering if everything is going all right for me. It'll be strange not seeing each other every day, but we'll eventually get used to it.

We'll still see each other on weekends, and I'm sure we'll still have a few fishing and hunting trips together, but it won't be like it used to be. I guess this happens to everyone. Your situation changes, you move on, and life goes ahead. But no matter where I am or what I'm doing in the future, I know we'll still be friends.

When Dan first began writing down these stories many years ago, I thought he was wasting his time. Who would want to read about such simple things that we did? Who would see anything funny or exciting in them? They were just stories about a couple of guys who did things that most people do when they spend time in the outdoors. Well, I guess I was wrong. And I'm glad that I was. We've met a lot of great people and have made a lot of new friends through these stories. I hope you have enjoyed our adventures and have had a smile or a laugh or maybe a tear from them. We had lots of laughs and tears over the years, and we have made memories that will last us a lifetime.

I'm glad I got to know all of you, and I hope each and every one of you finds someone special to share your time with that will bring you such fun and enjoyment as we had. Till we meet again… I'll just say thanks.

Thunderfoot.

About the Author

Dan Bomkamp is an avid outdoor enthusiast. He grew up along the Wisconsin River and has made his home there since his college days at UW-LaCrosse. He has been involved in the sporting goods industry for many years and began his writing career by writing short stories for outdoor magazines in the early 1980s. He has hosted 30 foreign exchange students from 11 countries and has traveled to Europe to visit many of them.

He is the author of four previous books, *The Adventures of Thunderfoot, More Adventures of Thunderfoot, The Gosey* and *Voyageur.* He lives in Muscoda, Wisconsin with his Boston Terrier, Buster, and his cat, Tigger. You can contact the author at: *danbomkamp@live.com,*

or visit his website, *www.danbomkamp.com.*